Thanks fo[r]
I hope you enjoy the book.

Shattered Lives

Brad Bloemer

1663 LIBERTY DRIVE, SUITE 200
BLOOMINGTON, INDIANA 47403
(800) 839-8640
WWW.AUTHORHOUSE.COM

© 2005 Brad Bloemer. All Rights Reserved.

No part of this book may be reproduced, stored in a retrieval system, or transmitted by any means without the written permission of the author.

First published by AuthorHouse 08/19/05

ISBN: 1-4208-7407-1 (sc)

Printed in the United States of America
Bloomington, Indiana

This book is printed on acid-free paper.

Prologue
The Birth of Evil

Proverbs 22:6 "Train up a child in the ways he should go, and when he is old he will not depart from it."

Western, Kentucky, May 17, 1968

Using the eloquence and social skills that she had acquired throughout her privileged upbringing, twenty-nine-year-old Patricia Wells gracefully worked the crowd. As she excused herself from the company of the congressman and his wife, she suddenly felt lightheaded. The six or seven martinis she had consumed were beginning to take full effect. She took a few steps and grabbed the top of the bar to steady herself.

She giggled under her breath, and then immediately chastised herself for her undignified actions. It was inappropriate behavior for the club. She had come here to have a good time, and she certainly had not been disappointed.

From the bar, she scanned the room and felt a great sense of satisfaction. Although she had been coming here for years, this was the first time she felt she truly belonged on her own merits, instead of riding the coattails of her influential father.

The room contained Bedford County's finest. More exclusive than the country club, the membership reflected wealth, power, and prestige. The organization had no charter, bylaws, or governing board. In fact, it was void of any formal structure. Membership was extremely selective, and was obtained by invitation only.

Following a time-honored tradition as old as the county itself, the members gathered together the third Friday of each month. Although the meetings were mostly social in nature, they managed to conduct enough business to influence the outcome of each political election and to control most important decisions made in the county. Nothing of significance could be accomplished in the region without the blessing of the membership. They controlled the banks, local government, and most of the land in the county. They had the power to make or break any business, and they could ruin the career of any public official, who didn't see things their way.

They also protected each other's interests. Any new, untapped profit opportunity was sure to be steered toward one of the members. They liked to pad each other's pockets. They also made sure the courts looked favorably upon each other. No member had ever lost a court case, civil or criminal, in Bedford County. There were many perks for the privileged few that were lucky enough to be selected for membership.

They met in a lodge, located off a narrow, winding, blacktop road; twelve miles outside the town of Tyler, Kentucky. Sitting on a bluff overlooking Kentucky Lake, the obscure location offered one of the best views in the county. Inside, the lodge had one large room and three lavishly decorated conference rooms. The main room had a fireplace on one end and a well stocked, heavily used bar on the other. Floor to ceiling, tinted glass windows afforded the members a perfect view of the sun setting on the lake.

With darkness now looming outside, most of the twenty-five or so members began to make their exit through the front door. As she fumbled around in her purse for her car keys, Patricia shot a quick glance at Mike Williams and smiled. Fueled by the alcohol she had consumed, she could feel the desire build up inside her. The rendezvous at her cabin would be the perfect ending to one of the best days of her life.

With the keys in her hand, she stumbled through the door into the crisp, night air. She knew Mike would be following soon enough. They had agreed that he would wait five minutes, so there would be no suspicion.

The affair with Mike had been going on now for three months. This night, however, would be special. They had something to celebrate. Just five hours earlier, the verdict had been announced. The jury had voted in favor of her client, Good Hope Hospital. As the lead attorney for the defense, she had saved the hospital from a potential multi-million dollar judgment.

It hadn't taken long for the good news to spread. As the evening had worn on, she became the center of attention inside the lodge, and she relished every minute of it. She deserved to feel good about herself. After all, she was successful, attractive, and admired by the most powerful men in the county. Despite her young age, she had risen to heights that few women in this area had ever reached. She had graduated in the top five percent of her class in law school. Just five short years later, she had managed to make partner and secure the most lucrative clients in her firm. Not only was she the attorney for the local hospital, she was also lead counsel for the city and county government, and the largest bank in Tyler. She was a member of the school board, library board, and she was the first female to serve as head of the local chapter of the Kentucky Bar Association. It was obvious, to everyone who knew her, that she had inherited her father's intelligence, self-confidence, and ambition. It was equally as obvious to them that she had also inherited his obsession with power and his arrogance.

She was aware of the talk around town that she wouldn't have made it this far without her father's influence. She didn't care. To her these people were low achievers, who were simply jealous of her success. She had gotten to where she was by dedication. She was smart, had worked hard, and as a result, had earned her status in life. In addition, she would stop at nothing to obtain what she wanted; whether it was the best clients, most coveted possessions, or even the most desirable men.

Although she hadn't planned on being with Mike tonight, she was thrilled when the opportunity presented itself earlier in the evening. She had begun to tire of her husband. Unlike Mike, he was boring and mundane. He was ten years her senior, and was so busy with his internal medicine practice that he could not provide her with the attention she needed. On this particular night, he was on call for the hospital. An hour earlier, his beeper had gone off, notifying him that he was needed to report to the hospital immediately. The condition of one of his ICU patients had apparently worsened. Reluctantly, he had pecked her on the cheek, and headed out the door.

Within minutes after her husband's departure, she had found Mike and discreetly asked him to meet her at the cabin. Mike then casually slipped a pill into her hand. After glancing around the room to make sure no one was watching, she slid it into her mouth, and washed it down with the martini. Mike referred to the pill as a black beauty. She had no idea as to its street name, or how he had obtained it. She only knew it made her feel real good, and it added to the effects of the alcohol. It also made her time with him even more enjoyable.

Now, as she made her way toward her car, she began feeling dizzier. Her vision became cloudy, and she suddenly had difficulty controlling her movements. As she staggered through the parking lot, she lost her balance. Fortunately, she was able to avoid a fall by leaning against the hood of one of the parked cars. She quickly looked around to see if anyone had noticed.

She cursed under her breath when she saw her good friend and former law partner, Regina Phillips. Regina had witnessed the near mishap. Although Regina had left her firm two years ago to be the county prosecutor, the two had remained good friends. Both were accomplished litigators, even though neither had yet reached the age of thirty.

Regina approached her with a worried look.

"Are you okay, Patricia? Looks like you had a real good time tonight. Maybe you shouldn't drive home."

"I'm fine, Regina."

As she spoke, Patricia's tongue felt heavy, and her words came out slurred.

Regina then placed her hand on her friend's shoulder. "I don't know. I think I should drive you home. You're in no condition to drive."

The fuzziness in Patricia's head cleared momentarily, and she realized Regina's offer to drive her home would interfere with her plans to be with Mike. She could not allow that to happen. She quickly responded.

"Don't worry about me, Regina. If that fool for a sheriff tries to arrest me for a DWI, Daddy will make sure he never wins another election in the state of Kentucky. He'll be out of a job by sundown tomorrow. Besides, even if he were that stupid, I could probably count on a certain prosecutor to dismiss the charges, couldn't I?"

Both women laughed. Patricia then climbed into her front seat and started her car.

At exactly fifteen minutes after five, seven-year old Ricky Henry grabbed a baseball and two gloves, and sat on his front porch steps to wait for his dad to arrive home from work. Every Friday evening, he and his dad would play pitch and catch until dark. It was something Ricky looked forward to each week.

His dad, Tom Henry, was a deliveryman for Turner Dairy. Ricky knew he finished his last delivery around four-thirty, and it took him forty-five minutes to turn in his sales tickets at the warehouse and drive home. As he pulled into the driveway and climbed out of the dairy truck, Ricky tossed one of the gloves to him.

"Sorry, Son. I'm afraid something's come up, and we won't be able to play ball tonight."

Dejected, Ricky put his head down. "That's okay, Daddy."

Tom's response was accompanied with a broad smile. "Don't you want to know what we'll be doing, Ricky?"

"I guess," Ricky whispered softly, still disappointed.

"You and I need to get busy loading the truck. We're going camping. I suggest you hurry and pack your clothes, so you can help me bring the camping supplies down from the attic."

"Wow, I can't believe it!" exclaimed Ricky. He ran over and jumped into his dad's arms. "Thanks, Daddy." He then ran to his mom and gave her a hug.

Ricky's mom, Kathy, replied in typical, motherly fashion. "Don't forget your jacket, Ricky. It's supposed to be chilly tonight. You'll be pleased to know, young man, that I baked your favorite cookies for the trip: oatmeal raisin."

Ricky flashed a brilliant smile. "Thanks, Mom. I'll eat them around the campfire tonight."

Kathy smiled nervously as she watched Ricky and Tom pack. She was worried because Ricky had been having problems at school. Ricky's teacher told her he had been displaying antisocial behavior. Kathy knew he tended to be introverted, and he often preferred to play alone. Before now, however, she had never seriously considered the fact that he might need counseling. She thought a weekend away with Tom would be good for him. Tom had always held a special bond with him. He was Ricky's idol, and he was also the only person whom he would open up to.

As Ricky climbed in the front seat of his dad's 1964 Ford pickup, he could hardly contain his excitement. He and his dad were headed to his favorite campground on Kentucky Lake. They had the whole weekend ahead, just the two of them. His mind raced as he anticipated all of the things they would do. During the day they would fish, swim, and play ball. At night they would sit around the campfire telling stories. They would talk about baseball, fishing, and various other topics that dads and seven- year old boys like to discuss. It would be perfect.

As Tom guided the truck on the blacktop road toward the lake and campground, Ricky played with the radio dial to find a good station. He stopped when he heard a Beatle's song. He knew his dad liked the Beatles. He would do anything to please his dad.

Tom looked over at Ricky, smiled, and began singing the tune to *A Hard Days Night.*

Darkness was setting in as they drove along the narrow, winding road through the rolling hills of Western Kentucky. As he looked out the window, Ricky could see the dark outlines of the densely populated trees. Occasionally, there would be a small break in the woods, and he would see a tobacco barn just off the road. He knew that was where they dried tobacco leaves to make cigarettes.

The windows in the truck were rolled down, and the cool air whistling through the cab made Ricky shiver. "Its cold Daddy. Can you get my jacket?"

"Sure, Son. Aren't you glad your mom reminded you to pack it?" Tom pulled over to the side of the road and climbed out of the truck. Walking to the back, he reached over the tailgate and found Ricky's duffel bag. He then knelt down behind the tailgate and unzipped the bag. As he searched for the jacket, he failed to see the headlights of the approaching car.

While waiting in the truck, Ricky noticed the headlights. They were approaching very quickly. There was something unusual about them. They appeared to be heading directly towards the truck. As the lights came closer, he realized the car was in the wrong lane and was going to hit them head on. "Watch out Daddy!" he screamed.

Ricky's face exploded into the windshield. He then saw only darkness.

Several hours later, he awoke in a fog. He could hear voices, but found it difficult to open his eyes. When he was finally able to open them, he was looking directly into a bright, blinding light. He tried to move his head, but found he couldn't. Something was holding it in place. Two men then appeared in front of the light. They were wearing green masks, and were leaning over him.

One of the men began talking: "We are going to put you to sleep now, Ricky. We have to fix that arm of yours and remove the piece of glass from your neck. Don't worry, you won't feel a thing. It will all be over in a little while."

Suddenly, he began to remember what had happened. He started to panic. "Where's Daddy?" he cried.

The two doctors could only look at each other and shake their heads. One of them placed a mask over Ricky's head, and he fell asleep.

Nine years later: September 23, 1977

As he pulled off Interstate 24 onto the first Paducah exit, Ricky Henry felt his pulse race. He had been waiting years for this moment. His whole life it seemed had been spent in anticipation. His hands became sweaty as he anxiously thought of what lie ahead. Reaching across the car seat, he checked for what seemed like the hundredth time. No, he had not forgotten the latex gloves. He then glanced down at the seat and saw the hunting knife his stepfather had given him for Christmas. He was set.

Ricky's emotions quickly shifted to anger as he thought of her. Patricia Wells, the high and mighty socialite, who had single-handedly destroyed his family's life. Painful memories flooded through his mind as he reflected on that horrible night nine years ago. In his mind, he could still see the headlights. He could hear the awful sound of her car colliding with his dad's truck. It was as if it were happening all over again. Tonight, he would have his revenge.

His thoughts switched to his dad and of how much he missed him and needed him. His father had been his whole life. After his death, his mother had been unable to support Ricky and his younger sister. His mom desperately needed someone to pay the bills. Unfortunately, she turned to Frank Kroetz. Oh, how he hated Frank. He thought of all the times, when he had been younger, that Frank had beaten him. For nothing. He could still feel the pain as he was pummeled over and over again. Sometimes, it was Frank's fists; other times a leather strap.

He would cry out to his mother, but she was too afraid of Frank to help him. With tears in her eyes, she would only turn away and take another drink.

No one was there for him. Once, when he was nine, he managed the courage to ask for help. While a patient in the emergency room one night, he confided to the nurses that Frank had caused his arm to be broken. Instead of believing him, they bought Frank's lie that he had simply fallen down the basement stairs. Once they arrived back home, Frank locked him in a dark basement closet for a week to teach him a lesson. It worked. He never again told anyone about Frank.

Bitterly, he thought of the pathetic drunk his mother became after she married Frank. He thought of the way Frank treated his little sister, Carla. He became angrier. Carla had to be protected, and he knew he was the only one who could save her. He wished he could kill Frank tonight, along with Patricia Wells. A package deal. Two for the price of one. Frank's time would come, though. He smiled at the thought of watching Frank die.

He slammed his fist against the dashboard as his mind wondered to the prosecuting attorney, Regina Phillips. The only reason Regina wasn't dying tonight was that it would look too suspicious. Her time would come. *That much I promise*, he thought. She would pay for placing friendship above her duty. He hated her almost as much as Patricia Wells.

He thought of Patricia Well's lab results the night of the accident. She had a blood alcohol content of .20, twice the legal limit. Swept under the rug by Regina Phillips and the hospital. He took a deep breath, and tried to keep his eyes on the road.

The hospital emergency room had saved the drunk and allowed his father to die. The doctors said there was nothing they could do for his dad. They claimed he was in such bad condition they could not save him when he arrived at the emergency room. Ricky knew better. He knew the only doctor in the emergency room that night had abandoned his dad in an effort to save Patricia Wells. After all, Patricia's husband was a doctor on staff at the hospital. He had also learned that Patricia was the hospital's attorney. It was obvious that the hospital had protected its' own. They let his father die, and then concealed the evidence of Patricia's lab results. To these people, his father's life was worthless. To them, Tom Henry was only a blue-collar deliveryman. Patricia Wells, on the other hand, was a well-respected lawyer, who was married to a doctor. Her family had money. She was important.

The worst part about this had been the wait. Shortly after the accident, Patricia moved from Tyler to Paducah. Since Ricky's home in Tyler was sixty miles away from Paducah, there had been no easy way for him to get to Patricia. He had been forced to wait nine long years until he obtained his drivers license. Even after he received his license he had to wait. Frank would seldom give him permission to drive the Chevy Nova, the piece of junk that Frank referred to as the family car. Ricky finally solved his problem by reverting to theft.

The perfect time came earlier in the day when Mrs. Wooden, who lived a block away from him, left town to visit her daughter. It had been easy to climb through her bedroom window and find her car keys. Since she lived on the corner with a vacant, wooded lot next to her, he was able to back the car out of the garage and down the driveway without being seen.

Ricky had memorized the directions to Patricia's house. It turned out that it was easy to find her street. As he turned onto Brentwood Boulevard, he drove slowly until he found the address: 823 Brentwood. The house, as he expected, was a large one. Like all the houses around it, it was a brick two story. *Quite impressive*, he smirked.

He knew she would not be home yet. He had read in the papers that this was the night for the hospital benefit ball. He knew she would not dare miss the social event. This was what her type lived for. He would probably have to wait a few hours for her to return home. These fancy fundraisers tended to run late into the night. That was okay with him. He had waited nine years for this. He could certainly handle another two or three hours.

His only real fear was that she would not come home alone. He knew she was no longer married. Her husband left her shortly after the accident. Patricia had managed to avoid a criminal conviction and she had even retained her law license, but in the end she and her husband could not withstand the constant gossip that surrounded them in Tyler. Despite the best effort of the prosecutor and the hospital officials to cover it up, word leaked out that Patricia had been drinking heavily the night of the accident. The public humiliation had forced her to leave Tyler and move to Paducah. In an effort to save his medical practice, her husband had divorced her.

Ricky did not know for sure if she had a boyfriend or not. She was still subject to speculation in Tyler; surely he would have heard if she had one. It was unlikely that she would bring a gentleman friend home with her, but it was possible. He was prepared to do whatever needed to be done.

After locating the house, he drove two blocks to a grocery store. He parked Mrs. Wooden's car, slid the knife behind his shirt, stuffed the gloves in his pocket, and casually walked down the street to her house.

It was easy breaking into the house. She had left a bathroom window unlocked. He climbed through the window, and then found a hall closet to hide in. All he had to do now was wait.

At approximately twelve-thirty a.m., he heard the garage door open. His back tensed. His heart began racing. This was it. The time had finally arrived. The door leading from the garage into the kitchen opened. As he peeked through the closet door, he was relieved. She was alone.

Patricia Wells walked over to the kitchen table, and set her purse down. She then went to the sink for a glass of water. As she turned from the sink, she gasped. The glass of water shattered on the floor.

"At last we meet again," Ricky said. "Do you remember me?"

Patricia trembled as she stared at the knife. In a shaky voice, she replied. "No. Who are you? What do you want?"

Ricky pulled out a photograph and flicked it to her. He then motioned for her to pick it up. She bent down, but her hands were shaking so much she could barely hold the small picture. She was confused as she glanced at the picture. In it, she saw a little boy, with dark hair and dark eyes, sitting on his father's knee. The boy was holding a baseball glove. She immediately recognized the two.

"Oh, no!" she exclaimed.

"It's been nine long years. I am here to seek justice."

Tears formed in Patricia Well's eyes as she realized she was going to die. "You're the boy that was in the truck, aren't you?"

She never had time to plead for her life. Before she could utter another word, the knife pierced her chest and she fell to the floor. Releasing the fury that had grown inside him over the past nine years, Ricky then stabbed her twenty additional times.

Part 1:
Injustice

Chapter 1

Sikeston, Missouri: June 18, 1978

"Hey Robbie. Are you there?"

I immediately recognized the boy behind the whisper. I turned the volume down on my radio and eased over to the screen covering my open bedroom window. As I pressed my face against the screen, I could see my best friend, Steve, crouched down below.

"Yeah, I'm here," I replied in a low voice.

"Come on, he's there right now."

It didn't take long for the adrenaline to begin pumping through my veins. Within seconds, I had removed the screen, and climbed through the window. After replacing the screen, Steve and I both crouched down low as we made our way along the side of the house to my backyard. We dared not make a sound for fear of getting caught. My father, George Gibson, was a strict disciplinarian. He wouldn't be at all pleased to find his twelve-year-old son, sneaking around the neighborhood at eleven thirty at night. I had a strict nine-thirty curfew. No exceptions.

Our plan had its risks; there was no doubt about it. Not only were we violating our parent's curfew, we had also borrowed my grandfather's camera without his permission, and we were about to garner the wrath of the high school football team's starting right tackle.

The supplies we needed (the borrowed camera, flashlight, Vaseline, and firecrackers) were hidden in the tool shed in my backyard. The immediate problem we faced was that the tool shed was located just outside my parent's open bedroom window, in plain sight.

Very quietly, we eased around the perimeter of the yard, making sure we stayed out of sight from the windows. Once we were safely in back of the tool shed, we formulated our plan. We decided it would be better if I went into the tool shed alone. Besides, I didn't know if I could trust Steve to keep quiet.

I had to somehow remove the lock and open the door, without making a sound. If either Mom or Dad heard me or happened to look out their window, I would be caught. One thing I had in my favor, however, was the sound of the radio coming from the bedroom. The Cardinals were playing the Dodgers on the West Coast, so the game was still going on at this late hour. Jack Buck's booming voice, calling the play by play, was sweet music to my ears. It would provide a barrier to the noise I would no doubt make as I gathered the supplies. I was somewhat surprised that Dad would be listening to the game this late at night. The Cardinals were having a terrible season, so the games weren't very interesting. I, for one, was disgusted with them. After the game two nights ago, when Tom Seaver threw the no-hitter against them, I vowed not to listen to any more games the rest of the season. Apparently, Dad was a more loyal fan.

Keeping one eye on the bedroom window, I slowly eased to the front of the tool shed. Carefully, I removed the lock. I cringed at the sound of the door, as it swung open. I immediately regretted not having thought to spray it with WD-40. I realized then that hiding our supplies in the tool shed had been a stupid idea. At the time we made our plans, Steve and I weren't thinking about how difficult it would be to retrieve them. I'm not sure we could have found a better place, anyway. My mother was a clean freak, and she most likely would have found our stuff if we had hidden it in the house.

I took two steps inside the doorway and slowly closed the door behind me, praying that Dad wouldn't hear the creaking of the rusted hinges. The inside of the shed was completely dark, and smelled of gasoline and molded grass. Unable to see, I had to use my hands to feel my way to the back, while trying not to trip over the lawn mower, tools, and other junk I knew were in my path. Dad had been trying to get me to clean the shed. I wished now that I would have obliged him.

Finally, I made it to the back corner of the shed. I felt around for the box, which contained our stash. As I lifted the lid off the box and placed my hands inside, I thought of the very strong possibility that there could be a brown recluse spider in the box, just waiting for the opportunity to nab me. I carefully moved some oil rags and car wax to the side, and pushed my hand deeper into the box until I felt the camera. I then removed the camera, flashlight, Vaseline, and firecrackers. So far, so good.

The firecrackers and can of Vaseline were stuffed into my jeans pocket. I was holding the camera and flashlight in my right hand, and I used my left hand to feel my way back to the door. The end of a built-in counter top served as my guide in the darkness. As I reached the wall, however, I failed to notice the stepladder, standing in the corner. My foot hit the ladder, and I instinctively grabbed the top of the counter for balance. As I did, I felt something run across the top of my hand and up my arm. My heart suddenly stopped. Before I could react, the mouse had crawled up onto my shoulder. Shocked, I staggered backwards, tripping over the lawn mower. The back of my head crashed into a shelf that held a number of different tools. The impact sent the tools, a rake, and a shovel to the concrete floor. The sound of the metal hitting the concrete made a sound loud enough to wake up half the neighborhood. In addition, my Grandfather's brand new, Polaroid One-Step camera had fallen to the floor, probably broken.

I knew the pounding in my head that I now felt was nothing compared to the whipping I would receive when Dad arrived. I was cooked; done. I slowly climbed to my feet, and reluctantly opened the door a crack, expecting to see Dad charging around the corner of the house. As I looked, I saw nothing and heard nothing, other than the sound of Jack Buck's voice on the radio. *Could it be that he hadn't heard?*

I then heard a knock on the side of the shed. Next, I heard Steve's voice. "What happened in there?"

"Shut up, you idiot. Do you want us to get caught?" I replied in an angry whisper.

I felt around the floor until I found the camera and flashlight. Reluctantly, I slowly opened the door and made my way out of the shed. As I crawled around the side of the shed to Steve, I still half expected Dad to come around the corner. He didn't. I let out a big breath of air. Apparently, we had dodged a bullet. Without saying a word, we then ran through my backyard and down the alley.

It wasn't until we reached the end of the alley that I stopped shaking. Steve then looked at me as if I were crazy.

"What happened in there? It sounded like you were being attacked."

"Well, if you thought I was being attacked, then why didn't you come in and help me?"

"I figured you could take whatever it was. So tell me, what was it? Did that stray dog we've been seeing around here somehow get in the shed?"

"It was a mouse."

"A mouse?" Steve replied, as he chuckled.

"It was a big mouse. I thought at first it was a snake."

Steve began laughing so hard he could barely control himself. "So, you got whooped by a mouse? And here I am counting on you to help watch my back while we defend my brother's honor."

"Let's go!" I replied, eager to change the subject.

"First, you'd better try that camera. I'll bet you broke it."

I pointed the camera at Steve, pressed the button, and was relieved when the film shot out from the front of the camera. Luck was on my side tonight.

Although I was embarrassed by the mouse attack, I was also relieved. As far as I was concerned, the most difficult part was now behind us. I had feared getting caught by my father much more than I feared the high school bully we were about to face.

We quickly ran through several yards, until we were behind a large, oak tree in back of the abandoned house.

Our neighborhood consisted of average sized homes in an older section of Sikeston. The yards were small, and the houses were close together. This intimacy made neighbors seem like family. All the yards were very well maintained. The residents took pride in their homes and yards. That was the reason the vacant, Harwell house angered so many. It was an eyesore, but despite pressure from the neighborhood residents, the city had done nothing about it.

The Harwell house was just two blocks from my house. It was at the end of a dead end street, set deep in the back of a large wooded lot. Because of the large, untrimmed trees and overgrown brush, the house could barely be seen from the street. Old man Harwell was a recluse, and had lived alone in the house for forty years, until his death three years ago. He had no heirs, so the house sat vacant after his death. The house was never properly maintained, and it looked as though it could fall down at any minute.

Unlike the other residents, Steve and I had grown to love that old house. We had used it as our own personal hideaway. Recently, some high school teens had begun using it at night as a hangout. The isolated location gave them a place where they could hide from parents and local law enforcement. They could make out, drink beer, smoke dope, and commit other sins; without fear of getting caught.

Often, in the evenings Steve and I would sneak up to the house and observe them. In doing so, we had learned a great deal more than we ever learned in our biology class. It was even better than watching an R-rated movie. So far, we had avoided being seen.

One frequent visitor to the house was a high school senior, named Ron Posey. Ron was the starting right tackle for the Sikeston high school football team. He was big, strong, and cocky. He enjoyed harassing teachers and picking on fellow classmates. One of these classmates was Steve's older brother, Gary. Ron lived two houses down from Gary, and had been abusing him for years. Gary was considered a bookworm; was not very athletic, and made an easy target. Recently, Steve had witnessed Ron ridiculing his brother in the presence of a group of girls. I guess, for some pitiful reason, it made Ron feel important. This was more than Steve could take. If Gary couldn't defend himself, Steve was determined that we would do it for him. Tonight would be pay back time.

When Steve solicited my help, I did not hesitate. Gary had always been nice to me, and I really liked him. He often volunteered to drive Steve and I around town. I figured I owed it to him. Besides, I had seen

Ron Posey a few times, and I thought he was a jerk. I would enjoy the opportunity to make his life a little miserable.

Steve had formulated our plan a couple of weeks ago. We had simply been waiting for the right time. When Steve saw Ron earlier in the evening with a date, he knew tonight would be the night. Ron's date was not his girlfriend. He never took his girlfriend to the Harwell house. She was too classy for that. But, he loved to take other, looser girls there. As soon as Steve confirmed that Ron's truck was parked behind the house, he came and knocked on my window.

If we had really thought about what we were doing, we would have realized it was stupid. But then again, no one had ever described either one of us as being a brilliant thinker. We were two, scrawny, twelve-year-old kids, trying to antagonize a six foot two, two hundred fifty pound gorilla made of pure muscle. Of the fourteen thousand people living in Sikeston, we could not have picked a bigger, meaner, bully than Ron Posey. If he caught us, we would suffer an unimaginable fate. If everything went according to plan, however, we would do our thing and be long gone before he made it out of the house.

The first order of business was to place Vaseline under the door handles of his truck. That was done to simply make him angry. Then, Steve took a pen and slowly let the air out of one of the tires. The purpose of that was to prevent him from circling the neighborhood, looking for us after the attack. Once this was successfully done, we eased our way to the back porch. Using the flashlight, we crawled through the hole in the porch screen. We stopped briefly to place stocking hats on our heads. The hats completely covered our faces, with holes for both eyes. In case we were spotted, Ron would not be able to recognize us.

As I followed Steve into the area that used to be the kitchen, I began having second thoughts. Steve had nerves of steel, but not me. I began sweating profusely as we crawled to the opening of the living room. At this point, there was no way Steve was going to let me back out, so I tried to build my courage up.

The kitchen was next to the living room, where we knew Ron would be. We peeked around the corner of the wall, just enough to see into the living room. As expected, we could see a portion of a sleeping bag and a cooler. Next to the cooler was an open bottle of wine. A radio nearby was playing a Carpenter's song. I was surprised. Ron didn't seem to be the Karen Carpenter type.

"What a romantic!" Steve whispered. "The wine and music go so well with the musty smell and filthy carpet in this house"

I was too nervous to laugh. As scared as I was, I still managed to allow my curiosity to get the better of me. I pulled up next to Steve, and leaned further into the opening to get a better look. I caught a quick glimpse of the girl's face. She appeared to be very pretty. I wondered how an idiot like Ron Posey could get so many good -looking girls.

While the two weren't completely naked, they were close enough. When I moved my head a little further, I could tell that they both had their shirts off. I noticed they both still had their pants on. Too bad for Ron. They were wrapped around each other like the two pythons I had recently seen at the St. Louis zoo.

Steve motioned for me to get the camera ready, while he pulled out the cigarette lighter and the firecrackers. The plan was to scare them with the firecrackers, snap a quick picture of them as they scrambled for cover; and then run like heck. We would later mail the picture to Ron's girlfriend. She deserved to know what kind of garbage she had been dating.

I had the camera poised as Steve lit the firecrackers. We both stepped out from behind the wall. The firecrackers landed about three feet from where they were laying. As the firecrackers exploded, we heard loud, piercing shrieks. As he let out a yell, Ron jumped several feet into the air. Steve was laughing. I was not. I quickly focused the camera and pressed my finger down on the shutter. Then I ran.

As the screen door slammed behind me, I quickly looked back. Steve was right on my tail. My heart then skipped a beat. Barreling out of the house, was a half-naked, extremely agitated, madman, in full sprint.

"Run Steve, run!" I yelled.

I couldn't help but look behind me. I could see him gaining ground. We hadn't expected him to run after us. Even if he did, we thought he would be slow. We had obviously miscalculated his running speed. For a big man, he could run. He had no shoes on, but the graveled driveway didn't seem to be slowing him down. Our only chance was to make it to my house.

As we turned onto the alley, I could see my house in the distance. Before we could get there, however, I heard Steve yelp. Ron had caught him by his shirt collar. As I turned back to look, I saw a figure move in from behind the shadows of the nearby trees. The next thing I saw was Ron lying face down in the alley. He was knocked out cold.

I had the presence of mind to shine my flashlight on the shadowy figure. What I saw could have come straight out of a horror movie. As the light hit his face, I saw a hideous scar running down the side of his neck. In the dark, he looked almost inhuman. As I lowered the beam of the flashlight, I could see blood dripping from his knuckles. His face was expressionless, and he said nothing. Steve began backing away from him.

"Let's get out of here!" Steve yelled.

We didn't remove our sock caps until we reached the safety of my bedroom. As our heart rates began to drop back down to normal, we wondered whom the mysterious person was who had just saved us. As much as we disliked him, we hoped Ron was okay. We also tried to convince each other that, with our faces covered, there was no way he could have recognized us. As we sat on my bedroom floor, we both vowed never to try anything like that again.

As I started my lawn mower, I was still trying to recover from the previous night's terrifying experience. I felt a little better, knowing that Ron Posey was alive and well. The first thing this morning, I ran down the alley to the spot where we left him. I was relieved when I didn't see his body. I later rode my bike past his house. I saw him in his carport, lifting weights. He had a large bandage over his nose.

Although I had just started my mower, I was already sweating. It was only ten o'clock, but the temperature was already approaching ninety-five degrees. Sikeston was located in the Missouri Bootheel, exactly halfway between St. Louis and Memphis. It was known for its hot, humid summers.

Although I didn't exactly enjoy mowing yards in this intolerable heat, it still beat the air-conditioned classrooms that I had to suffer though for nine months out of the year. I smiled as I thought about the additional ten weeks I would enjoy before going back to the monotonous routine of the classroom. There would be plenty of lazy days ahead, with nothing to do but play ball and swim at the public pool, which was located just six blocks from my house.

I mowed several neighborhood yards. The yards and the part time job at my uncle's grocery store enabled me to earn some spending money. I lived only ten blocks from Sikeston's downtown, so I never had to wait very long for a chance to spend my earnings.

I sucked in a deep breath of that hot, humid, Southeast Missouri air and tried to put Ron Posey and last night's experience behind me. The house I was mowing was owned by Mrs. Taylor. She had recently been placed in a nursing home. Her son, an attorney in Memphis, had hired me to mow her yard for the summer.

As I pushed the mower, I began daydreaming. I often pictured myself playing second base for the St. Louis Cardinals, or of being Roger Staubach, the quarterback of the Dallas Cowboys. I knew I would never be good enough to play pro baseball or football. In reality, I was only an average baseball player, and an even worse football player. It never hurt to dream, though.

As I swung the mower around and faced the front of the house, I saw a curtain moving in one of Mrs. Taylor's second floor bedroom windows. I was surprised because the house had been vacant ever since Mrs. Taylor moved into the nursing home over a year ago. There shouldn't have been anyone in the house. I rubbed my eyes; looked again, and saw nothing.

Mr. Taylor had informed me, when he hired me, that he intended to honor his mother's wishes and leave the house vacant. There was a chance her health would improve, and she would be able to return to her house. It was unlikely that Mr. Taylor would have changed his mind and rented the house. Besides, I would have noticed if someone had moved in.

Since he had hired me to look after her yard, I considered it my duty to make sure no one was in the house that shouldn't be. I let the mower idle, and walked toward one of the first floor windows to have a look inside. Before I reached the house, my knees suddenly buckled. I saw a man's face behind a different window.

As my mind began to process the situation from a logical perspective, I convinced myself that no one was in the house. I had simply been out in the sun too long. Maybe I had heat stroke and didn't realize it. I didn't feel sick, but what did I know about heat stroke? I was probably experiencing hallucinations. I decided it was time for a break.

Mrs. Taylor's backyard butted up against my backyard, with only an alley separating the two. I turned off the mower, and started to walk through her backyard to my house for a cold Pepsi. As I reached the alley, I heard a noise that sounded like a door opening. As I turned around to look, my heart suddenly stopped. Outside Mrs. Taylor's screened, porch door stood a girl wearing nothing but a red bikini. She was beautiful. Better yet, she was smiling at me. She then waved for me to come over.

I couldn't believe my eyes. This gorgeous, perfectly tanned girl wanted to talk to me. As I walked toward her, I became oblivious to my surroundings. It was like a dream; a fantasy.

The fantasy was short-lived, however. Before I could reach her, I felt a painful jab in my right knee. I then realized that I was losing my balance because I had walked right into the water meter. I fell over the meter headfirst, and my chin slammed hard into a large rock. At first, I was dazed. When I was finally able to crawl to my feet, I felt blood pouring down my neck.

I had never been so embarrassed in my life. Heat seemed to rise from my legs up through my face. I wanted to run and duck behind the hedge in the alley. But, I quickly overcame my embarrassment when she ran over to me, and put her hands against my cheeks.

"Are you all right? That was quite a fall."

I wanted to speak, but the words would not come out. Finally, I regained my composure. "Yeah, I'm alright," I lied. It hurt like the devil, but I wasn't about to let her know it. Boys are supposed to act tough when they are around girls, right? "The only thing hurt is my pride."

She grinned and then laughed in a soft, sympathetic way. Her face was now only inches away. She was so pretty, and she smelled good. I realized her smell was from the sun tan lotion she was wearing. The aroma brought back a pleasant recollection of the vacation my family had taken two years ago in Florida.

Suddenly, I became self-conscious. I knew I probably looked and smelled awful.

I tried to look down at her body, but I stopped because I was too embarrassed. She must have known what I was thinking, because she smiled a seductive smile. I had only seen a smile like that in movies.

I was relieved when she began talking. "My name is Carla Henry. What's yours?"

"Robbie Gipson."

"That cut looks pretty bad, Robbie. I'll go get a washrag and a bandaid."

Before I could stop her, she was jogging towards the back porch. I was disappointed when she emerged a couple of minutes later wearing a T-shirt over her swimsuit.

As she wiped my chin with the washcloth, I felt my pulse race. "Do you live here?" I asked.

"Yes, we just moved here from Kentucky. My step-dad, Frank, just got a job transfer to Sikeston. He's going to work at the wire factory. He's some kind of foreman."

"Ever been to Sikeston before?"

"No. Is there a lot to do here?"

"I guess. The swimming pool's not too far, and you can ride your bike to the movie theater. They have matinees on Wednesdays. You can get in with a can of food. When did you move in? I haven't seen anyone moving."

"We moved in two nights ago, using a rented U-Haul truck. We had to drive it back to Kentucky last night and pick up our car. We were late getting back. Mom and Frank are still asleep. Who knows what my brother, Ricky, is doing. I was bored, so I thought I would lay out and get a tan."

That's fine with me. Lay out all you want, I thought. I looked down at her legs and suddenly hoped that sunbathing turned out to be a favorite hobby of hers. "Are you related to Mrs. Taylor?"

"No. Frank's boss knows Mrs. Taylor's son. He arranged for us to rent the house."

"How old are you?"

"Fourteen. How old are you?"

"Twelve."

Suddenly, I heard a man screaming from inside the house. "I am going to kill that damn kid for waking me up with that lawn mower". Then, after a few seconds pause, he began yelling again. "That's not right Ricky. Can't you do anything right! You've got the hot and cold water hoses hooked up backwards."

Carla must have seen the frightened look on my face because she patted me on the shoulder. "Don't worry Robbie. That's just Frank. He's always yelling. That's the way he is."

Apparently, Frank had been sleeping, and he didn't appreciate the fact that my mower woke him up. He was also displeased with the way Ricky had hooked up the washing machine.

I did not hear Ricky's response to Frank, but judging by what happened next Frank did not take it too well.

"Get out!" Frank screamed.

Suddenly the screen door opened and Ricky appeared, with a smirk on his face. I was startled when I saw him. I now knew the identity of the mystery man, who had saved us. The scar didn't look quite as intimidating in the daylight, as it had last night.

"I'm sick of that old man. One day he will be sorry," Ricky muttered as he stomped down the porch steps. As I watched Ricky, I noticed he was quite a bit older than Carla. He had on black jeans and a black T-shirt. I also noticed an angry, defiant expression on his face. He had two nasty scars: the large one that I recognized from last night, on the right side of his neck; and a smaller one to the left of his nose. The scars stood out so much that it was difficult to look at him.

Even though I knew he hadn't seen my face last night, I wondered if he thought I was one of the boys he had saved in the alley. He gave no indication that he did. I knew the right thing to do would be to thank him. Somehow, though, I couldn't bring myself to do it.

Ricky then walked up to me. He must not have noticed that I was staring at his scars because his expression quickly changed into a flashing smile. "Don't worry", he said. "Frank's bark is worse than his bite."

He then pounded me on the back. "I guess I owe you one. I am indebted to anyone who raises Frank's blood pressure." The smile then vanished, and was replaced by an icy stare that made me shutter. Hey, you weren't fooling around with my sister were you?" he asked.

"Uh, uh no," I stammered.

Again, he flashed a grin. "Okay, I believe you. Just remember, no one messes with Carla and gets by with it," he said.

"Ricky, leave Robbie alone", yelled Carla. "He's not bothering anybody. Mind your own business."

Ricky's gaze then focused on my chin. "Hey, what happened? Did you get into a fight?"

"Not quite. I kind of had an accident." I was relieved when he didn't press the issue for more details. I didn't feel like explaining how I had tripped over a water meter. I had already suffered enough embarrassment for one day.

He then walked toward the carport. A couple of minutes later he backed out of the driveway in the family's dated, blue Chevy Nova.

Despite the fact that he saved my neck last night, I had a strange feeling about him. Something wasn't right. Maybe it was his eyes. They appeared angry and cold. His scars made him appear tough and reckless. I didn't care much for his voice either. It sounded raspy, like someone does when they have a sore throat. I thought he sounded like Marlon Brando did in the movie, *The Godfather*. My first impression of Ricky Henry was that he could be very dangerous.

Chapter 2

June 28, 1978

Over the past ten days, I saw Carla three times. I made it a habit to be outside whenever she was outside. She was by far the prettiest girl I had ever been around. On top of that, she was very nice.

Last night, I almost worked up the nerve to ask her to my little league baseball game. After considerable thought, I decided that would not be a good idea. We were facing Kiwanis, and they had a hard throwing pitcher named Kevin Watson. I was afraid I might strike out against Kevin, and I certainly didn't want Carla to see me fail. It turns out that I made the right decision. Kevin struck me out not once, but twice. To make matters worse, I made an error that led to two runs, and we lost the game six to two. I would have been humiliated if Carla had seen that performance.

At two o'clock in the afternoon, I was still sulking from the previous night's baseball debacle. I had already finished my mowing for the day, and had the rest of the afternoon to do as I pleased. Since I did not have a game that night, I thought I might grab Steve and head to the pool. I had my swimming trunks and T-shirt on, and I was ready to hop on my bike when Carla approached. All of a sudden the prospects for the rest of the day became much brighter. Steve would have to make do without me today.

"Hey, do you want to go to the pool with me?" I asked with my fingers crossed. When Carla did not answer, I knew something was wrong. As she walked closer, I discovered what it was. Carla had a large bruise on her right arm. Her lips were also swollen.

I guess Carla needed someone to talk to that afternoon. We went inside my house to the TV room, and that afternoon I heard Carla's sad life's story. I learned that Ricky was now seventeen. He received the two nasty scars ten years ago when he was seven. He and his real father had been on their way to a campground. They were pulled off the side of the road when a woman swerved off the road and hit them head on. The accident killed Carla's father, left Ricky hospitalized for over six weeks, and caused irreparable damage to Ricky's vocal chords. Carla was only four at the time of the accident.

The woman driver had been drinking heavily. She was a successful attorney, and due to her social connections she had avoided a conviction. In fact, she did not spend one single night in jail. According to Carla, the woman eventually got what was coming to her, however. She was found murdered in her home in Paducah, Kentucky last year. Carla said that the murder case was still unsolved and there have been no suspects.

Carla's mother married Frank Kroetz within one year of the accident. From the beginning, Frank had been abusive to Kathy Henry. Kathy soon found that gin and tonics helped take the edge off, and helped her to cope with Frank's frequent mood swings. She was seldom seen without a drink in her hand.

Frank resented having Carla and Ricky around. For the first few years, Frank beat Ricky mercilessly. Several times Ricky was beaten so badly he had to miss school. As Ricky became older, Frank left him alone. Carla believed Frank became afraid of Ricky.

Frank had rarely touched Carla, but last night had been the exception. Frank had been out drinking with the new friends he met at work. When he returned home from the night out with the boys, he discovered that Carla had lost the TV remote control. As was his custom when things weren't in perfect order, he flew into a rage. He grabbed Carla by the arm, threw her to the floor, and slapped her across the face.

The only bright spot in Carla's life was Ricky. It was apparent that Ricky adored her. He was also her protector. Last night, after Frank hit her, he grabbed a baseball bat and knocked Frank to the floor. He then stood over Frank, raised the bat, and started to swing. Carla thought he would have killed Frank, if her mother hadn't interfered.

Tears welled up in my eyes as she finished. As she stood up to leave, she thanked me for listening, and she kissed me. I guess everyone remembers their first kiss. My first kiss, however, was not as I expected it to be. There was no joy, only sadness. As Carla left my house that afternoon, I realized for the first time that life was truly unfair. I felt guilty. I had a wonderful and loving mother and father. My greatest worry, at that point in my life, was how well I was going to play at my next baseball game. Carla, on the other hand, had already lost her father. She had a drunk for a mother, who just went through the motions of life. She had to live with a stepfather, who resented her, and a brother, who I thought was crazy. I realized that Carla had no chance whatsoever in this life.

I suddenly felt the urge to find my mother. I ran into the kitchen and gave her a hug. Mom's reaction was one of skepticism; and rightfully so. Usually, the only time I hugged her was when I had done something wrong. I reasoned that the preemptive hug might soften the inevitable punishment I would later receive. It usually worked with Mom; never with Dad.

"What's this all about?" Mom asked.

I was somewhat embarrassed as I released my grasp on her.

Mom knew something was wrong. "Tell me what's going on Robbie. What did you do this time? Please tell me you and Steve didn't break Mrs. Winters window again with your baseball."

I was relieved to be able to tell Mom about Carla. She almost started crying as I told her about Carla's past. She then promised me that we would do everything we could to help her.

The rest of the evening I lay in my bed thinking of Carla. No matter how hard I tried, I could not get her off my mind.

Four months later: October 17, 1978

Over the remainder of the summer of 1978, I tried my best to be a friend to Carla. Mom did her part as well. Mom invited her to eat dinner with us at least one night a week. She insisted that Carla attend church with us, and she even bought her two dresses so that she would look nice for church. She also invited Ricky, but he had refused.

Sundays that summer took on a special meaning for me. Before, it had often been a pain to get dressed and go to church. I would have much rather played ball with the neighborhood kids or gone to the pool, instead of sitting on those hard pews at the First Street Baptist Church. That summer, however, I actually looked forward to attending church. I was proud as I walked through the front doors with Carla. I was the envy of all my friends in Sunday school. I even studied my Sunday school lesson so that I could impress her with my knowledge.

Those long, boring sermons that seemed to go on forever didn't even seem that long during the summer of 1978.

The best part of Sunday was that Carla usually spent the afternoon with us. After church, we would eat my mother's roast beef, carrots, and potatoes. This was the same food we had every Sunday. Mom said it was easy because she could let it cook in the crock pot while we were at church. Anyway, I was sick of it, but Carla seemed to like it. I guess she didn't get many home cooked meals.

After lunch on Sundays, Carla and I would either ride our bikes to the matinee at the Malone Theater, or we would head to the public pool. Steve tried to join us every chance he could. I tried to discourage him, usually without success, because I wanted Carla all to myself. I didn't want to admit it to myself, but I was jealous.

Carla even went to a couple of my ball games that summer. I was always nervous during the games that she attended. I wanted so much to do well and impress her. She once told me she liked my uniform. After that I began to wear my uniform several hours before my games in hopes that she would take notice.

On days when I didn't have lawns to mow or didn't have to work at the store, Carla and I would ride our bikes to either Boston's Dairy Queen or downtown. Downtown Sikeston had Sterling's dime store and several other stores in which a kid could blow through yard money or an allowance. Downtown also had two drugstores with soda fountains. The best part of downtown, however, was Kirbys. I took great pleasure in introducing Carla to a Kirbyburger. In my opinion, Kirby's had the best hamburgers in the world.

Nothing unusual occurred in the Frank Kroetz household during the remainder of the summer. Thanks to Ricky, Frank never again laid a hand on Carla. I always made it a point to make sure Frank's car was gone before I went over to Carla's house. I had no desire to be around Frank.

As that summer wore on, I began to believe that my first impression of Ricky may have been wrong. Maybe he wasn't so bad. Carla sure seemed to adore him. He apparently liked me, or at least tolerated me. The first few times I came over to visit Carla, he had given me the first degree. Over time, though, he accepted me. Occasionally, when I would see him outside I would ask him to play ball. At first I was surprised when he agreed to play. After all, he was five years older than me. I was also surprised because he turned out to be very good. It was obvious that Ricky had played before. He even taught me how to throw a knuckle ball.

I began to feel sorry for Ricky. In addition to the horrible accident and the abuse he had suffered during his childhood, he appeared lonely. He apparently had no friends. I never saw him hang around anyone close to his age. Carla told me he had never made friends easily. My mom said it had to be difficult for him because he was beginning his senior year in a new school. Mom knew one of Ricky's teachers at the high school, who told her the other kids thought Ricky was strange. She said some of the kids were even afraid of him. I was sure the big scar on his neck and his raspy voice did not help other's impression of him.

Dad and I would often play ball in the backyard. During the summer, he would hit one ground ball after another to me to improve my fielding. Several times when Dad and I were playing, I noticed Ricky watching us from his back porch steps. I often wondered if he was reflecting on a time long ago when his dad had played ball with him. I thought of how difficult it would be not having a father to play ball with.

Dad also took me to two or three Cardinal games in St. Louis each summer. His job as a purchasing manager for an electrical distributor enabled him, occasionally, to obtain free tickets. The seats were excellent, usually field box. I knew Ricky liked baseball, and I wondered if he had ever seen a major league game. Once again, I realized that compared to most kids I lived a very privileged life.

As summer ended and school started, I began to see a change in Carla. Unlike Ricky, Carla made friends easily. She quickly adapted to Sikeston Junior High. In a very short time, she became very popular. Her good looks did not go unnoticed by the eighth grade boys in her class. Since she now had friends her own age, she relied less on me. I began to realize that a two-year age gap is significant to a fourteen-year old girl.

Occasionally, I still saw Carla out in the yard. We continued to have our talks, although they were less frequent. It was definitely not the same as it had been in the summer. Mom continued to invite her to dinner and church, but she seldom took her up on the offer.

As the weeks passed, I almost came to the conclusion that Ricky was harmless. Almost. Then on Monday, October 17, 1978, something happened that would forever convince me that my first impression of Ricky was correct. I realized for certain that Ricky was very dangerous.

Early that afternoon, Ricky and I were throwing the football around in my backyard. As I dropped back to pass, pretending to be Roger Staubach, Ricky ran across the yard as if he were going out for a pass play. I put a little too much air under the ball and it sailed over his head. He quickly turned around and, in an effort to catch up to the ball, he ran right through Mrs. Wright's flowers.

Mrs. Wright was our elderly, next-door neighbor. She was very particular about her yard, especially her flowers. It just so happened that she was looking out her kitchen window at precisely the same time that Ricky trampled through her tulips. She flew out her back door and proceeded to let Ricky know, in no uncertain terms, that she did not appreciate the fact that he had damaged the flower garden that she was so proud of. She pointed her finger at Ricky and let him have it.

Mrs. Wright had been widowed for about ten years. She lived alone with her cocker spaniel, Bridget. The only two things in life that mattered to Mrs. Wright were her yard and Bridget. I learned a couple of years ago, the hard way, to avoid her flowers. That time, Steve and I were the guilty parties. For compensation for the ruined flowers, Dad made us clean her garage.

I felt terrible about the incident. It was my fault but Ricky was taking all the blame. If I hadn't overthrown the pass, the flowers would still be intact. I walked over and apologized to Mrs. Wright. My apology didn't seem to lessen her anger, but it made me feel a little better.

When Mrs. Wright began her tirade on Ricky, I was afraid of what Ricky might do. He never said a word, however. I was shocked that it didn't seem to bother him. I expected him to be angry and to smart off at Mrs. Wright. Instead, he stood there motionless. He would later laugh about it as we continued playing.

That night, about nine o'clock, I was in my bedroom listening to the new Eagles album I purchased with my lawn mowing money. It was a cool fall night, so I had my bedroom window open. I suddenly jumped when I heard a loud shriek, followed by gut-wrenching sobbing. Dad and I arrived at the back door about the same time. We saw Mrs. Wright holding her dog, who was covered in blood.

"Bridget is dead!" she cried.

Out of the corner of my eye, I saw movement. I turned my head and caught a glimpse of Ricky ducking behind the hedge that separated

Mrs. Wright's yard from the alley. He had been crouched down in the alley watching Mrs. Wright. I knew then that Ricky was responsible for killing the dog.

My dad walked over to Mrs. Wright, and gently pulled the dog away from her.

"Who could have done this?" sobbed Mrs. Wright. "Bridget is such a good dog. She is all I have."

"Whoever did this is sick," said my father. "If I ever find out who is responsible, I promise you they will answer to me."

I knew he meant it too. Dad had a temper, and you didn't want to be the one responsible for causing him to lose it. I knew all too well that he followed through with his promises.

Dad and I drove to my grandfather's farm and buried Bridgett. It made me sick to look at the poor dog. According to Dad, the dog's throat had been slashed with a knife. As I held the shovel, I thought about Ricky. Goosebumps popped up on my arms, and I began to shiver. I was afraid of Ricky, and I didn't know what to do about it.

I was the only one who knew who had killed Mrs. Wright's dog. At first I thought about telling Dad about Ricky, but I was afraid of what Ricky might do to me if he found out I told. I decided I would keep it to myself.

After we arrived back home, I went into my room, closed the door and lay on my bed worrying. I knew it wasn't right to keep this from Dad. I also knew Ricky shouldn't get by with it. The truth was, however, that I was afraid and I hated myself for it.

Later that night, I pulled the trash can toward the alley to drop off the garbage. As I reached the alley, I heard a rustling from the nearby trees. Before I had a chance to react, I was grabbed and yanked behind a bush. I was then lifted up where I was forced to look directly into

Ricky's face. Terrified to the point where I could not catch my breath, I looked into his cold, dark eyes.

In a soft, raspy voice he said, "If you ever tell anyone, you will be very, very sorry." He then smiled. "I never liked that dog anyway, did you Robbie?"

As he dropped me to the ground and let go of my arm, I tried to run. At first my legs refused to move. I guess I was in shock. When I was finally able to gain control of my faculties I ran as hard as I could to the safety of my bedroom.

Ten minutes later I was drenched with sweat, and I was still shaking. For the first time in my life, I had experienced true fear. From that day forward, I tried to avoid Ricky.

Chapter 3

November 21, 1978

    I didn't see Ricky much after he killed Mrs. Wright's dog. He found a job working as a mechanic at a car repair shop just south of town. He enrolled in the vocational program at the high school, which allowed him to go to school during the mornings and work at the shop in the afternoons.

    Ricky must have done well at his new job. Shortly after he started working, he bought a 1976 blue Chevy pickup truck. Based on what I knew of Frank, I was sure Ricky, not Frank, was responsible for making the payments on the truck.

    Ricky was apparently enjoying his new freedom. Ever since he had purchased the truck, he was seldom home. I had no idea what he did every night, but I was glad he was not around.

    I also rarely, if ever, saw Carla anymore. She had her friends and activities at the Junior High School. Meanwhile, I was still stuck at Middle School, with my same circle of friends. My lawn mowing was over for the year, but I still managed to stay busy. I played little league football, and I also worked two evenings a week and every Saturday afternoon in my uncle's grocery store.

I guess I recovered from my first crush. At first I really missed Carla, but as the weeks passed I thought about her less often. There was one thing that I couldn't get out of my mind, though. I wondered how Ricky and Carla had turned out so different. They both grew up in the same environment, yet Carla seemed perfectly normal while Ricky had numerous problems. Was it because Carla had been too young to remember her father? Maybe she didn't have the memories that Ricky had, and she did not realize what she had lost. Maybe the trauma of the accident had caused Ricky to be so bitter, or maybe Frank had treated Carla better than Ricky. Whatever the reason, Ricky was definitely messed up, while Carla appeared to be normal.

It was a Friday night, and I was excited as I sat down at the dinner table. Steve and I had plans to go to the movies. The movie *Halloween* began playing in Sikeston the previous week. Steve's older brother, Gary, told him about the movie. According to Gary, it was the scariest movie ever made. *Halloween* was one of three movies playing at the Malco Trio Cinema. The problem was the movie was rated R, and Steve and I were too young to buy a ticket. We had a plan, however. We would buy a ticket to the PG rated show playing that night. After the movie started, we would sneak over to *Halloween* when no one was looking. It had worked before, and I saw no reason why it wouldn't work again. I hated to think of what Dad would do to me if we got caught. If the movie was as good as everyone said it was, I figured it would be worth the risk.

Mom had prepared my favorite dinner: fried chicken, mashed potatoes, and corn on the cob. As I ate, I listened to Mom and Dad discuss the tragedy that had occurred three days ago. They were saying that nine hundred Americans had committed suicide in Guyana, a small country in South America. A cult preacher named Jim Jones had convinced them to drink Koolaid, laced with cyanide. Mom said she felt sorry for the people because they had been misled. Dad said they were idiots. It was hard for me to believe that one person could convince that many people to take their own lives.

After dinner I sat in the TV room with my parents, while I waited for Steve's mom to pick me up for the movie. They were watching the news. President Carter was talking about controlling inflation by setting price standards and deregulating industries. I had no idea what he was talking about and really didn't care. I was more interested in the gruesome murders I would get to see later on the big screen. I had heard Mom say that Jimmy Carter was a fine person, that you could trust him. Dad said that he was in over his head. Earlier in the year in my social studies class, we were required to read an entire newspaper front to back. I remember one of the articles referring to President Carter as "the peace loving president." That sounded pretty good to me. I made up my mind then that I liked Jimmy Carter.

Mom was telling Dad that she couldn't wait for nine o'clock. Her favorite show, *Dallas*, would be on. Mom said she liked Bobby; said he was good looking. I could tell from Dad's reaction that it made him angry. Sometimes, when they were having an argument, mom would call dad JR. I never watched *Dallas*, but I assumed from mom's reaction that JR was a villain in the show.

I was relieved when Steve's mom pulled into our driveway and honked the horn. Dad asked me again which movie we were watching. "That's not a bad show you're going to watch, is it Robbie?"

"No Dad, of course not," I lied.

Steve and I paid for our ticket, and reluctantly walked into cinema number two. The movie we paid for was about a dog named Benji. How embarrassing. We checked to make sure no one was there that we knew. Thank goodness no one saw us watching *Benji*. We then waited until the movie started, and sneaked out through the swinging doors into the hallway. The owner, a short, fat man who liked to patrol the aisles, was nowhere to be found. The timing was perfect. We ran down the hall and through the doors into cinema number one. Fortunately, there were two empty seats in the back row. That was perfect because the owner could not see the back row when he peered through the doors.

As my eyes began adjusting to the darkness in the theatre, I noticed Ricky seated to our right. He was in the second to the last row, next to the wall curtain. He was alone. Knowing Ricky was there made the movie that much more terrifying. I couldn't help but associate Ricky with the psychopathic killer in the movie.

I was scared to death as I watched the masked killer, Michael Myers, stab teenager after teenager. When the bloodbath was finally over, I felt drained.

After the movie ended, we waited in our seats a few minutes to make sure we didn't run into Ricky. When it was safe, we walked out into the lobby of the theater and discussed the movie as though we were two experienced movie critics.

"What a great show," Steve said.

"Yeah," I replied. "I sure thought he would get his sister. The movie would have been better if Michael had not killed the babysitter. She sure was pretty."

"Yeah, and she sure looked good with her top off," marveled Steve.

As we climbed into the car, Steve's mom asked us how we liked *Benji*. "Oh, it was great," said Steve. "That Benji sure leads an exciting life." It was all we could do to keep from laughing out loud in the back seat of Mrs. Parker's car.

* * *

As Ricky watched the movie, he became entranced with Michael Myers. As the killer plunged the knife into each of his victims, Ricky was reminded of his encounter the previous year with Patricia Wells. The euphoric feeling and the rush he received as he watched Patricia die was unlike anything he had ever experienced. He suddenly desired that feeling again.

The power he had felt as he watched Patricia draw her last breath was intoxicating. Afterward, during the ride from Patricia's house back to Tyler that night, he felt as though he was floating in air. The best part of the whole experience came when he watched the news coverage on television the next night. That's when he realized the significance of his actions. He had finally managed to capture the attention of those who thought they were better than him. He was in control now; not them.

The anchorman began the broadcast that night with the top story: "Prominent local attorney found murdered in her home." A field reporter standing directly in front of Patricia's house presented the story. The camera focused on Patricia's covered body as it was being removed from the house on a gurney. The reporter then interviewed several of Patricia's closest associates: attorneys, judges, and doctors. They commented on how they could not imagine anyone hurting Patricia. After all, she was a pillar of the community. They spoke of the cases she had won; the not-for-profit boards she had served on; the fundraisers she had chaired. They all failed to mention the fact that a few years back she had killed a young father and badly injured a seven-year old boy, after having a few too many cocktails. The story took up ten minutes of the thirty-minute news broadcast that night. Knowing that he dominated the news made Ricky feel very powerful.

As the movie wore on, Ricky suddenly felt an uncontrollable urge to kill again. His preferred target was the prosecutor, Regina Phillips.

As badly as he wanted to kill her, he knew the timing was not right. It was too soon after Patricia's death. The police might get lucky and make a connection between Regina's murder and Patricia's murder. This was a risk he could not afford to take. Unfortunately, Regina would be allowed to live a little longer. Someone would have to take her place.

He had been keeping up with Regina in the papers. She was no longer a prosecuting attorney. She had moved from Tyler, and was now working in a large law firm in downtown St. Louis. He had also learned that her husband was an investment banker, and she now had two kids. She seemed to have the perfect life. *So did I*, he thought, *until they messed it up.* He knew that he would be making a road trip to St. Louis in the not too distant future.

As Ricky drove home from the movie, he began feeling very restless. Thinking of Regina always brought back the anger. It was becoming harder and harder to control it. His hands began sweating as he thought of Patricia and Regina: the two women he blamed for ruining his life. Pressure started building up inside him. It had to be released before it choked him.

He felt as though his chest would explode as he thought of all the girls in the past who had laughed and made fun of him. It was that awful scar on his neck. He had never been with a girl; never even been on a date. He also knew that he never would. They all thought they were better than him, smarter than him. A new resolve swept over him. He had to prove them wrong. He must teach them a lesson.

He pulled his truck into his driveway and slammed the door shut. Still feeling restless, he opened the back door and walked into the kitchen. Directly in front of him, he could see his mother asleep on the couch. No doubt passed out. As usual, Frank was seated in his favorite recliner, his eyes glued to the television, drinking a beer. With his face unshaven, beer gut hanging over his waist, and wearing only a pair of boxers and a sleeveless T-shirt, he looked every bit the loser Ricky knew him to be. The sight of his stepfather served to further fan the flames of his anger and hatred.

Ricky then walked down the hall to Carla's room to check on her. She was asleep. To him, she looked like a princess. She deserved a better life. As he stared at his precious sister, his thoughts drifted back to the time so long ago when they were a real family. They used to be so happy. He knew his father had counted on him to protect Carla and his mother. He had failed. He had let his father down.

As he walked back to the kitchen, he glared at Frank. He hated Frank, and he hated what his mother had become. He knew things would have turned out differently, if only Regina Phillips had done her job and not interfered with the investigation. If Patricia Wells had been held accountable for the accident, his mother would have received a monetary settlement. She would not have felt compelled to marry Frank, and their lives would have been totally different. He despised Regina Phillips and all women like her. They had no regard for common, ordinary people like him. Just like Patricia Wells, they must pay. Justice must be carried out.

As he walked to the refrigerator for a soda, the newspaper lying on the counter caught his attention. The front page of the *Sikeston Daily Standard* had an article featuring Dr. Lora Smith, the town's first female emergency room physician. Ricky stared at her picture. She was smiling, no doubt laughing at him. He had never met her, but that didn't matter. She was one of them. To her, he was just plain white trash. Ricky smiled. He knew who his next victim would be.

Dr. Lora Smith refilled her coffee cup and sat down on the couch in the doctor's lounge. She was relieved. It had been a particularly busy

Friday night in the emergency room. She had already encountered a patient in full cardiac arrest, a drug overdose, and a stabbing victim. This was in addition to the thirty or so patients who had presented with routine problems, such as sore throats, cuts, high fevers, and broken bones. Finally, she had caught a break. She had discharged the last patient and everything was quiet for the time being. With only one hour to go on her shift, she was looking forward to a hot bath when she went home. As she sipped her coffee, she reviewed the chart of the patient who had coded. She had intubated him, and he was now in stable condition in the ICU.

Lora had been working at the Sikeston Community Hospital now for six months. She was proud of the fact that she was the first female physician ever to be on staff in the hospital's emergency room. In 1978, medicine was a male dominated profession, but she had somehow managed to break through the barriers.

Lora had grown up in Sikeston. She had graduated as valedictorian from Sikeston High School in 1967. She attended medical school at St. Louis' Washington University, and completed her residency at prestigious Barnes Hospital in St. Louis. She decided to practice medicine in her hometown, so that she could make a difference. She also enjoyed the many challenges she faced in the Sikeston emergency room. When she practiced in St. Louis, she was required to obtain a resident consult for most serious problems. Sikeston had few medical specialists, so she was forced to handle most problems by herself.

It had definitely been a difficult journey for Lora to get to this point in her career. It had been much harder for her than her male counterparts in medical school. She was one of only two females in her class at Washington University. Her looks also made it difficult for her to be taken seriously as a potential physician. She was very attractive:

big blue eyes, blond hair, thin lips, nice smile. She had even been encouraged to go into modeling when she had been a teenager.

The worst part of medical school had been the clinical rotation in surgery. Several of the staff surgeons at Barnes had made moves on her, but the chief of cardiac surgery had been relentless. She had found the great Robert Burns, III, M.D. to be disgusting. In his esteemed opinion, he was God's gift to women. His arrogance and mood swings were legendary at the hospital. One minute he would be screaming at the nurses and residents in the operating room suite, and the next minute he would be telling jokes, expecting everyone to laugh. Once, after she had dodged one of his sexual advances, he attempted to blackmail her by threatening to write a negative recommendation to the dean of the medical school. Somehow, Lora had managed to graduate despite the efforts of Dr. Robert Burns, III. He was, however, the main reason she had chosen emergency medicine over surgery.

Lora had made it though. Her life now appeared to be headed in the right direction. She had a great career, and she was engaged to a Sikeston attorney. They were so much in love. She had it all. She had fulfilled her career ambitions and would soon have the family she always dreamed about.

At precisely eleven p.m., Lora completed her dictation and turned the ER over to the physician covering the night shift. She was relieved to be able to leave on time. Usually on Friday nights, the ER was so backed up that she had to stay an extra hour or so to assist the new physician coming on duty. Lora waved goodbye to the charge nurse and headed to her car. She was exhausted as she climbed into her brand new Mercedes. She turned on the radio and cranked up the volume to the disco group, KC and the Sunshine Band.

As she pulled into her carport on North Ranney Street, she noticed there were no lights on in the house. That was strange. She always left the lamp on in the living room. *Oh well, the bulb must have burned out*, she thought. She opened the back door that led into her kitchen. After turning on the kitchen light, she headed directly to the phone to call her fiancée, Mike. After three rings, Mike answered.

"Hey beautiful, can I come over tonight? I have a bottle of your favorite white wine," he replied in response to her greeting.

"No, not tonight Mike, I'm beat. Let's get together tomorrow night. I promise I'll make it up to you. You remember the negligee you bought me last Christmas? Maybe I'll wear it tomorrow night."

"All right. That is definitely worth waiting for. I'll be dreaming of red lace tonight."

Lora smiled as she hung up the phone. She went to the bathroom and turned the water on in the tub. While the tub was filling, she walked back to the kitchen and poured herself a glass of white wine. She smiled as she reflected on how happy and content she was at this point in her life. Little did she know it, but in a matter of seconds her fairy tale life would come to an abrupt halt.

As she walked back toward the bathroom, she was suddenly grabbed from behind. Sheer terror consumed her. As she was dragged into the bedroom, she was unable to catch her breath. When she was finally able to focus, the first thing she noticed about her attacker was the large scar on the side of his neck.

The last ten minutes of Lora's life were total hell. Unlike Patricia Wells, her death was not quick or painless. Ricky's needs were escalating.

After having released the rage that had been building up inside him, Ricky left Lora's house and walked across the street to where his truck was parked. He calmly opened the toolbox in the back of his pickup, tossed his knife in, and closed it. As he opened the door of his truck, he noticed an elderly lady in the house across the street, peeking through her curtains. He had been careless, and he had allowed himself to be seen. He thought about eliminating the elderly witness, but decided against the idea when the woman's next-door neighbor suddenly pulled into his driveway. It would be too risky. Angry with himself, he started his truck and drove away.

.

Chapter 4

November 22, 1978

    I first knew something bad had occurred when I heard the siren. It was early Saturday afternoon. Steve and I were throwing a football around in my front yard when we heard the familiar sound of an ambulance. It appeared as though it was coming directly toward us. Whatever it was that had happened, we knew it was close. Out of curiosity, we both hopped on our bikes and followed the sound. The commotion was coming from North Ranney Street, three blocks from my house. When we arrived, we saw three police cars and an ambulance parked in the driveway and along the street in front of the house. There was also a large crowd gathered in the front yard.

    Steve and I noticed Mrs. Pinkston, our science teacher, standing among the crowd, and we quickly approached her. "What happened, Mrs. Pinkston?" I asked.

    "That young doctor, Lora Smith, was found murdered. They said her boyfriend found her body about thirty minutes ago. That's him over there."

Mrs. Pinkston was pointing to the front porch. I looked and saw a man sobbing uncontrollably. He was surrounded by several people, one of whom had her arms around him. I didn't know the man, but I sure felt sorry for him.

Steve and I had witnessed all we cared to see. The whole scene made us sick to our stomachs. We jumped on our bikes, and headed back to my house.

Later that afternoon, Steve and I rode downtown. We stopped at James Drug Store for a milkshake and a hamburger. We sat on two stools at the counter next to two elderly gentlemen. We recognized the two men. They were regular patrons of the old-fashioned soda fountain. We couldn't help but overhear their conversation. They were discussing the murder. Word travels fast in a small town.

"First murder in Sikeston in over ten years," said one of the men as he took a puff from his pipe.

The other man shook his head. "I heard she was stabbed several times. The bed was covered with her blood. They say it was not a pretty sight."

Steve and I looked at each other. This is not what we needed to hear the day after watching *Halloween*. We were both still reeling from the horrors of the movie. Now, it appeared we had a real Michael Myers on the loose in our own neighborhood. The milkshake went down good, but neither of us could finish our hamburger. We were no longer hungry.

That night I watched the news with Mom and Dad. A reporter was stationed in front of Dr. Smith's house, interviewing Sikeston's chief of police, Ted Nelson. I knew Mr. Nelson from our church. I remembered playing softball with him at the church picnic. I hoped he was better at solving crimes than he was at playing third base.

"Never before in my twenty years of police work have I witnessed a crime scene like this," he told the reporter. "This is the work of an animal. Rest assured, however, that the perpetrator will be caught."

"Ted Nelson's a fine man," said Dad, "but he's not much of a detective. I'll bet we never catch the creep."

That night, Dad checked all the doors and windows twice before he went to bed. Mom came into my room and checked on me before she went to bed. For the first time in years, I wanted to crawl in bed with Mom and Dad. I knew that I couldn't, however.

Later that night, I woke up in a cold sweat. I had dreamed that Michael Myers was standing over my bed, holding a knife.

January 8, 1979

Up until November 1978 the town of Sikeston had been a relatively uneventful place. The biggest story that I could ever remember occurred a couple of years ago when one of the local bankers was arrested for embezzlement. That particular incident kept everyone talking for months. At the time Dad had said that the banker was trying to be a big shot. He and his wife had been living beyond their means, and he had been forced to steal to keep up their lifestyle. In Dad's opinion, he got off easy. He was in one of those country club prisons where they played golf and lifted weights. Dad said he was in the same prison the criminals from Watergate were sent. If that was the punishment, I wondered why more bank employees didn't steal from their employers.

Apparently, the banker's wife suffered a worse fate than the banker. Dad said she wasted no time cutting ties with her husband. Within a month after her husband's conviction, she divorced him. Dad said he actually felt sorry for the poor man. Most of the money he stole was to support her spending habits. She claimed she was unaware that her husband was stealing, but everyone knew better.

After the conviction, she was effectively banned from the Sikeston social scene. No more benefit balls to chair and no more fundraising luncheons. The invitations for the afternoon teas stopped arriving in the mail. Her best friends suddenly stopped calling. This was more than she could bear. Disgraced, she ended up moving back to her hometown in Tennessee.

The banking scandal, juicy as it was, paled in comparison to the recent murder of Lora Smith. The murder was by far the biggest story in Sikeston during my lifetime. Six weeks after the murder, everyone was still talking about it. Would the killer strike again? Did he live in Sikeston or was he just passing through? The rumors were nonstop. The police had no suspects, and it was beginning to appear as though the killer would escape justice.

Just when things started to simmer down, another tragedy hit Sikeston. This time it had a direct impact on me.

January 8, 1979 was a bitterly cold night in Sikeston, with the temperature dipping into the single digits. The town was recovering from a six-inch snow the previous day. I was excited as I went to bed because school had already been cancelled for the next day. I was looking forward to the snow day.

Shortly after I had gone to bed, I was awakened. For the second time in two months the sound of sirens was heard in our neighborhood. I jumped out of bed, put my jeans and shoes on, grabbed my coat, and raced out the back door. Dad was already outside. We saw flashing red and blue lights from the direction of our back yard.

I couldn't believe it. They were coming from Carla's house. My first thought was that Frank must have hurt Carla or her mother. As Dad and I ran through our back yard to Carla's house, I prayed it wasn't Carla. As we reached her front yard, I saw several policemen and paramedics. I was relieved to see Carla standing in the front yard. When she saw us, she ran up to me and put her arms around me. Before I could ask her what had happened, I saw a police officer leading Ricky out the front door and into the police car. Ricky was handcuffed.

With tears streaming down her cheeks, Carla informed me that Ricky had killed Frank.

One of the paramedics was rolling a stretcher toward us. I looked up and saw that it was Carla's mother on the stretcher. Her face appeared swollen and was covered in blood. Carla ran to her and held her hand. As her mother was loaded into the back of the ambulance, Carla started to climb in.

The paramedic grabbed her arm. "I'm sorry, dear, you can't ride in the ambulance with your mother. It's against policy."

"I have to go with Mom!" yelled Carla.

Dad then told Carla that we would take her to the hospital.

"I'll see you at the hospital, Mom," yelled Carla.

As we started trudging through the snow to get our car, we saw a second stretcher being wheeled from the house. The body was covered by a sheet. It was Frank.

Mom joined us as we drove Carla to the hospital to see her mother. When we arrived, we learned that Kathy Henry was being admitted directly from the emergency room to the ICU. The three of us sat in the ICU waiting room for over an hour while Carla sat at her mother's bedside. When we saw Kathy's doctor, Dr. Rice, Dad asked him for an update on Kathy's condition. He gave us the encouraging news that he thought she would be okay. Fortunately, all she had was a broken nose and a concussion. They were going to keep her in the hospital for a couple of days to monitor her and run some additional tests.

Carla came out of the ICU, and told us we could go in to see her mother. As we walked into the ICU, I became sick to my stomach. I had never been in an ICU before. There were no doors, so we were able to see all the patients. Each patient had numerous tubes sticking out of their arms, mouth, and nose. *What a depressing place,* I thought.

Kathy assured us that she looked a whole lot worse than she felt. She had a swollen nose, busted lip, and a deep cut under her right eye. It was obvious that she had also been crying. She told us she was not sorry that Frank was dead. She was, however, worried about what would happen to Ricky.

Dad told Kathy that Carla was welcome to stay with us while she was in the hospital. He also said that he would check on Ricky at the jail, and he would find out what charges they were going to file against him. Kathy was extremely grateful.

Just as we were leaving the hospital, two policemen showed up. They asked Carla if she felt well enough to talk. She agreed. As we sat in the ICU waiting room, Carla described the events that night.

After work, Frank had gone to a bar with some of his friends. He arrived home around nine o'clock. As was his custom after an evening on the town, he was in a foul mood. What set him off this time was that his dinner was cold. The fact that the food was cold because he was three hours late apparently didn't seem to register with him.

Frank began screaming at Kathy. He then knocked Kathy's drink out of her hand, calling her a useless drunk. Next, he hit her with all the force he could muster. She fell hard. Her head hit the corner of a coffee table.

Ricky had been upstairs at the time. After hearing the noise, he ran down the stairs to confront Frank. When he saw his mother lying on the floor covered in blood, he lost control.

According to Carla, Ricky then viciously attacked Frank, hitting him several times. Frank fell to the kitchen floor. Ricky then grabbed a steak knife from the kitchen counter and stabbed Frank repeatedly. In a panic, Carla called 911. Frank was already dead when the ambulance arrived.

"What's going to happen to Ricky?" asked Carla.

One of the officers indicated that he didn't know for sure, but it didn't look good because it did not appear to be self-defense. He said Ricky would be assigned an attorney, and the attorney could provide us with more information.

After we arrived home from the hospital, we sat in the living room and talked with Carla. Like Kathy, it was obvious that Carla felt no sympathy for Frank. She was very concerned about Ricky, however. Tears welled in her eyes as she talked about him.

"Ricky shouldn't have to go to prison. Frank deserved this for the way he treated us. Ricky had it the worst. Frank is paying for the way he used to beat Ricky and run him down. He constantly told Ricky that he was no good and would never amount to anything. I guess Ricky finally had enough. He finally snapped. Frank got just what he deserved."

I was glad Carla was at our house. Mom had a knack for comforting people after they experienced a tragedy. Just after midnight, Mom took Carla into our guest bedroom, which would serve as her room for the next few nights. Since the guestroom is next to my bedroom, I could hear them talking. They were still talking when I fell asleep around two o'clock that night.

As I lay in bed that night, I started feeling guilty. I was glad that Frank was dead. I knew it was wrong to think that way, but I just couldn't help it. As much as I tried, I could not make myself feel sorry for Frank. I hated him for what he had done to Carla, and I knew he would never be able to hurt her again. I planned on asking Mom in the morning if it was a sin to have the feelings I was experiencing. Just to be safe, I thought I would say a prayer asking God to forgive me.

The next morning we took Carla to the city jail to visit Ricky. I had never been in a jail before, so I had hoped that we would be able to walk past some of the cells so I could see what a jail cell looked like. I was disappointed when the clerk led us directly into a small conference room.

Ricky and his court appointed attorney were already in the conference room when we arrived. The attorney's name was Sam Wilson. In my opinion, Sam didn't inspire a great deal of confidence. He was seriously overweight, and he wore a tie that fell a good six inches short of his belt. His white shirt was untucked and had a yellow stain just underneath the collar. His hair looked as if a comb had never touched it. He reminded me of Jackie Gleason on the *Honeymooners*.

Sam introduced himself to us. He told us the prosecutor's office was closed for the day due to the snow. He had, however, been able to reach the prosecutor by phone. The news was not good. The prosecutor was planning to seek second-degree murder charges against Ricky. Sam also said they were going to try Ricky as an adult. He said Ricky really did not appear to have much of a defense because Frank was not threatening him at the time of the stabbing. The fact that Ricky stabbed him numerous times also did not help his case. He went on to say that due to extenuating circumstances, he believed the prosecutor might be persuaded to accept a plea of voluntary manslaughter. If so, Ricky would probably receive a twenty-year sentence. He could be out on parole in fifteen years. If the prosecutor would not accept a reduced plea, he would probably be facing life in prison.

Sam promised us that he would do everything in his power to convince the prosecutor to reduce the charges. "At least if we can plea down to manslaughter, Ricky can still have a life," he said.

Ricky sat motionless during the entire conversation. He was polite, and he answered all of Sam's questions. He asked about his mother, and thanked us for taking care of Carla.

Chapter 5

February 1, 1979

    Chief of police Ted Nelson smiled as he walked out the front door of the crime lab in St. Louis. The fingerprints were a perfect match. He finally had the break he was looking for in the case and now had a legitimate suspect. He felt relieved. This had been the biggest case he had worked in his twenty-year career. He knew he was under the public microscope, and he did not want to blow it.

    Up until a week ago, the motive for Dr. Lora Smith's murder had been a mystery. Ted had ruled out robbery because nothing of value had been taken. He had also ruled out a lovers quarrel as a possible motive. Both the fiancé and former boyfriend were eliminated as potential suspects. He also knew it was not a sex crime because Lora had not been raped.

    As he interviewed Lora's coworkers, he discovered a possible motive. Several of the nurses told him that it was not uncommon for patients to come to the emergency room to feed their drug habit. These patients were quite clever in coming up with symptoms necessary for a narcotics prescription. They were after Demerol, Morphine, Percodan, Codein; anything that would give them the buzz they craved. They would often fake migraine headaches, back pain, muscle pulls, anything to obtain the prescription. Some of the more desperate patients would even resort to intentionally hurting themselves. These patients often became very agitated and aggressive if the doctor refused to write the prescription.

One particular patient stood out from the others. His name was Darrell Rogers. According to the hospital staff, Darrell came into the emergency room two nights before Dr. Smith was murdered. He was complaining of severe back pain and asked for Demerol or Percodan. Dr. Smith suspected he was a drug seeker and refused to write the prescription. Darrell became very abusive, and he had to be controlled by hospital security. As the two security guards escorted him out the front doors of the emergency room, he threatened Dr. Smith, warning her that she would regret having him thrown out..

Ted received a lucky break when he found that the State had Darrell's fingerprints on file. Darrell had a previous arrest for domestic abuse. A set of fingerprints found in Lora Smith's apartment matched the set the State had on file of him. This placed Darrell Rogers at the crime scene.

Ted quickly walked to the nearest pay phone and called his assistant. "Don, we found a match. I believe we now have sufficient evidence to justify a search warrant. See if you can obtain a warrant from Judge Davis to search Roger's apartment this afternoon. I think we have something here. I'll see you tonight."

* * *

February 2, 1979

For the first time in months, Darrell Rogers felt free. Just a few minutes ago, he had been discharged from the Hope Recovery Center. Now, as he walked out the front door of the center, he felt proud of himself. He had made it, beaten the habit. The program had been tough, but he had stuck with it. The cravings were gone.

Darrell thought of the mess he had made of his life. Just one short year ago, he had a beautiful wife, Lisa, and a two-year old daughter, Sara. He also had plenty of friends. He earned a good living as a warehouse supervisor for the area's largest farm chemical distributor. He had the perfect life, but he threw it all away. He lost his family, his job, everything that was important to him.

His problems started innocently enough. About ten months ago Darrell had an operation after he broke his arm. The surgery involved inserting plates and pins in his right arm. Upon his discharge following the surgery, the surgeon wrote a prescription for Percodan, with two refills. At first he followed the instructions on the bottle, taking the prescribed one pill every four hours. Once, he mistakenly took two pills within one hour, and found that he enjoyed the euphoric feeling the drug provided. Next, he tried three and it provided an even better feeling. He continued taking Percodans even after he no longer felt the pain from his surgery. He began to rationalize the use in his own mind: he would convince himself that he had a headache, backache, whatever. Darrell soon found the Percodans helped him to deal with the everyday stresses in life.

At first the drug seemed to help. Darrell enjoyed the effects of the drug: the good feeling, the carefree attitude. Initially, he could control when he took the drug. He would take it after work only; never allowing it to interfere with his job.

By the time he obtained his second refill, his tolerance for the drug had increased to the point where he no longer received the same euphoric feeling. It would take four or five pills to create the buzz he craved. After awhile, he began to need the drug just to function. When the drug wasn't in his system, he felt awful. Nothing seemed to satisfy him. He no longer enjoyed the things he used to enjoy unless he was under the influence of four or five Percodans.

The first real problem occurred when his prescription ran out. As he was down to his last four or five pills, he became desperate. He convinced his surgeon to give him an additional refill. After that, he learned different tricks to obtain new prescriptions. He purchased the *Physicians Desk Reference*, a detailed reference book on drugs. He would memorize the symptoms necessary to obtain the prescription. He made visits to different doctor's offices or the hospital emergency room to obtain his fix. The drug he received depended on the doctor and on how good a performance he played in faking his pain. It could be Percodan, Percocet, Codeine, or Demerol. It didn't matter. They would all do.

As his dependency increased, his mood swings became more pronounced. He began taking the drugs at work. As a result, his job performance began to deteriorate rapidly. Darrell once was a very conscientious worker, who had not missed a day of work in over five years. He became unreliable and uncaring. He called in sick frequently and had sporadic arguments with his supervisor. His performance and attitude eventually cost him his job.

Just two days before he was fired from his job, he came home from work and found a note saying that Lisa and Sara were leaving him.. His wife said he was a different person. She could no longer take his frequent mood swings. The note said they had moved in with her mother.

The low point came when he confronted Lisa at her mother's house. They had an argument. He then did something for which he never thought he was capable. He hit Lisa. His mother-in-law called the police, and he had the humiliating experience of being handcuffed and carted off to jail.

Finally, on Wednesday November 19, 1979 he became so desperate that he knew he needed to seek treatment. He had run out of pills. The doctors in town were now on to him and were refusing to see him. He was feeling the familiar effects of withdrawal. Early that evening, he went to the Sikeston emergency room, confident that he could convince the physician on duty to write a prescription. The emergency room doctors were usually so busy that they tended to be easier to con. At the triage desk, Darrell complained of severe back pain. He was examined that night by a doctor he had never seen before. The doctor's name was Lora Smith. Unlike most of the other ER doctors, she realized he was faking. She refused to write the prescription. As Darrell desperately pleaded with her, she called security. He was escorted out of the building by two security guards. He couldn't remember exactly what he had said to the doctor, but he remembered the security guard warning him that if he said anything like that again to her, he would pay for it.

Darrell left the emergency room and, as he had done several times before when he was suffering from withdrawals, found a source on the west end of town. The source was a well-known drug dealer. He purchased 30 Demerol, at a price of ten dollars per pill.

Darrell had no idea why he did it, but later that night he drove his truck to Dr. Smith's house. By this time he was high as a kite. He had no idea what he would do when he saw her. Luckily for him she was not home. After knocking on the front door and receiving no response, he then tried opening the front and back doors. Both were locked.

Next, he checked the windows and found one of the bedroom windows unlocked. Without considering the consequences, he climbed through the window into the house. As he walked through Dr. Smith's house, he saw a blank prescription pad lying on a desk. He became excited as he realized he could use this to forge prescriptions.

He then searched through the desk drawers until he located her checkbook. Using the signature he found on a carbon copy check, he then did a pretty good job of forging her signature on the prescription pad. He wrote himself a prescription for Demerol.

Two days later, when he ran out of the illegally obtained bottle of Demerol, he filled the forged prescription at a Super D drugstore.

When he woke up the next morning, he realized just how desperate his life had become. He had hit rock bottom. He knew he desperately needed help. One week later he found himself checking into the Hope Recovery Center, determined to get his life back.

Now, after successfully completing two months of therapy, he felt like a new person. He, not the pills, controlled his life. As he drove his blue Chevy pickup truck, the sky looked bluer, the clean air felt crisper. He was committed to doing whatever it would take to win his family back. During the two months in therapy, he had not spoken to his wife or daughter. The staff had discouraged it. He did write them several letters. Lisa replied to one of his letters, and her response was encouraging. Maybe she would give him a chance to make it up to her. He was nervous as he thought of what he would say to them. Simple words would not make up for the pain he had caused them. All he could do now was apologize, plead for forgiveness, and promise to be a better husband and father. He hoped that would be enough. If given a second chance, he wouldn't blow it this time.

Darrell knew they would not be at the apartment. They were probably still living with Lisa's mother. He planned on dropping off his bags at the apartment and heading straight over to his mother-in-law's house.

As he entered the parking lot to his apartment complex, he saw two police cars parked directly in front of the entrance to the building. *I wonder what's going on here*, he thought.

As he walked up the stairs to his apartment, he noticed that two uniformed officers and a man wearing a long sleeved shirt and tie were in his apartment. He immediately recognized the man with the tie as police chief Ted Nelson. A nervous knot began forming in the pit of his stomach. His first thought was that they were investigating the drug dealer who had sold him the Demerol.

As Darrell tentatively stepped through the door opening, Chief Nelson looked up. A broad grin suddenly appeared on the chief's face as he recognized Darrell. The knot in Darrell's stomach suddenly felt as large as a watermelon.

"How nice of you to join us, Darrell. It's my pleasure to notify you that we are placing you under arrest for the murder of Lora Smith. You have the right to remain silent. Anything you say can be used against you . . ."

Darrell was taken to the station, and was interrogated by Chief Nelson and detective Rod Knight. It was then he learned that Dr. Smith had been murdered just two nights after he had been in her house. They informed him they had fingerprints placing him at the scene. They also found Lora Smith's prescription pad in his apartment. Darrell realized then that he was in serious trouble.

Chapter 6

February 16, 1979

Despite his uninspiring appearance, Sam Wilson turned out to be a pretty good attorney. He managed to convince the county prosecutor to agree to reduce the charges down to voluntary manslaughter in exchange for a guilty plea from Ricky. After hearing of Frank's abuse and Ricky's tragic life, the prosecutor became somewhat sympathetic towards Ricky. As a result, Sam was also able to persuade him to ask the judge for some leniency at sentencing.

Judge Davis sentenced Ricky to fifteen years. Sam felt that, with good behavior, Ricky could be out in ten years. If that occurred, Ricky would only be twenty-seven when he was released. Sam told us Ricky was fortunate considering voluntary manslaughter usually carried a sentence of at least twenty years. I still thought it was harsh considering what Frank had done to Kathy Henry that night. In my opinion, Ricky should not have to go to prison. I felt he was only protecting Carla and Mrs. Henry.

Dad told me he worried about what might happen to Ricky in prison. He said it was very dangerous for young inmates like him. The prisoners liked to give new inmates a hard time, especially those as young as Ricky.

Immediately after sentencing, Dad and I went to the jail one last time to see Ricky. He was to be transported the next day to the state maximum-security prison in Jefferson City. When asked if he was afraid of prison, Ricky laughed and said he could take care of himself. I believed him.

Ricky seemed particularly interested in the Lora Smith case. He said he met Darrell Rogers in jail, and they had become friends. He asked Dad what he thought Darrell's chances were at trial. Dad indicated that he didn't know, although everyone in Sikeston seemed to have an opinion one way or another as to his guilt or innocence. I thought it was strange that Ricky was so concerned about Darrell Rogers.

Kathy and Carla appeared to be doing very well. Kathy finally recovered from the beating she took from Frank, although she ended up spending a full ten days in the hospital. She didn't seem to progress as quickly as the doctors thought she would. I felt she would have recovered much faster if a little gin had been placed in her IV.

One of the few positive things that Frank ever did his life was to purchase a life insurance policy in the amount of one hundred thousand dollars. The life insurance had a double indemnity clause, which paid twice the death benefit if the death was ruled an accident. As a result, Kathy and Carla ended up with two hundred thousand dollars.

With nothing tying them to Sikeston, they decided to move back to Kentucky to be near Kathy's relatives. The life insurance money would enable Kathy to buy a new house and car, and it would afford her the opportunity to attend junior college. Kathy said she eventually wanted to find a decent job, so she could become self-sufficient. She vowed never to marry again.

Two days after Ricky's sentencing, Dad and I helped Kathy and Carla load their possessions into a U-haul truck. I had mixed feelings as I watched them back out of the driveway for the last time. I would miss Carla, but at the same time, I was happy for her because she would be starting a new life. Without Frank around, Kathy seemed to have a purpose in life once again. Maybe she would finally be the mother Carla needed and deserved. I wondered if I would ever see Carla again.

After Kathy and Carla left Sikeston, my life seemed to settle back down to normal. From the time I first met Carla back in the summer, everything in my life seemed to turn chaotic. During the past eight months my neighbor's dog had been killed; a doctor, living three blocks from my house, had been murdered; and my friend's brother had murdered his step-dad. I was ready for things to be back to normal. I missed the old Sikeston, where everyone was safe and nothing really ever happened.

I was also ready for spring. 1979 had been Sikeston's harshest winter in decades. We had several large snows. One snow in late January caused school to be cancelled for an entire week. The snowstorm paralyzed the whole town. Unlike northern towns, we weren't used to heavy snows, and we didn't know quite how to react when we had one.

For me, the timing of the snowstorm could not have come at a better time. It began snowing on January 21, just hours after the completion of Super Bowl XIII. Although I lived only one hundred fifty miles south of St. Louis and I was a huge Cardinal baseball fan, I was not loyal to the St. Louis Cardinal's football team. I was a Dallas Cowboys fan. I had not been bashful in predicting that Dallas would whip Pittsburgh in the Super Bowl. Dallas ended up losing the game thirty-five to thirty one, and my favorite player, Roger Staubach, had been outgunned by Terry Bradshaw. I knew my friends would razz me mercilessly at school. I was relieved because the snowstorm provided an extra week before I had to face them.

Despite enjoying the time off from school during the snow days, I was ready for winter to be over. I was tired of the cold weather, and I was ready to get my baseball glove out of the closet. In a way, I was also glad the Frank Kroetz family was out of our lives.

Chapter 7

Three months later: May 27, 1979

While the trial of Bruno Hauptmann for the Lindbergh baby kidnapping and murder is recognized as the nation's trial of the century, Sikeston Missouri had its own trial of the century. The trial of Darrell Rogers for the murder of Dr. Lora Smith captivated the town. As the trial date neared, it was the topic of conversation at the coffee pot, barbershop, cafe, grocery store, church; everywhere. It seemed everyone had a prediction for the outcome.

There were two reasons the trial was so interesting. One reason was that Darrell Rogers was an unlikely murder suspect. He did not fit the profile of a murderer. Most women found Darrell's looks appealing. He had that innocent, John Boy Walton look. He had a beautiful family, and up until a year ago had been a good family man. He was bright, educated, and had a good job in management. He was described by his family and friends as a good-natured, mild-mannered person. The people who knew him claimed he was incapable of cold-blooded murder.

In the minds of many experts, the State had a flimsy case. The only evidence they had was circumstantial: the verbal threat Darrell made in the emergency room; Darrell's fingerprints in Lora's house; Lora's prescription pad found in Darrell's apartment; and the forged prescription obtained by Darrell on the night of the murder. There was no evidence directly linking him to the crime. There were no witnesses to the murder, and the police could not find a murder weapon. In addition, the police could not find any physical evidence, such as Darrell's blood, skin, clothing fibers, etc. near Lora's body.

The prosecution did have, however, a very shaky eyewitness that placed Darrell at Lora's house the night of the murder. Mrs. Ethel Hammonds lived across the street from Lora. Mrs. Hammonds was eighty-five years old and in poor health. She was willing to testify that she saw Darrell leaving Lora's house on Friday night, November 21; the night of the murder. The problem with Mrs. Hammond's testimony was that she was known to have memory lapses.

Darrell admitted to the police that he had broken into Lora's house. He was adamant, however, that it was Wednesday, November 19, two nights before the murder. Unfortunately for him, he waited until Friday night to fill the forged prescription. If he would have filled the prescription immediately after he stole the prescription pad, he could have proven the break-in occurred on Wednesday, not Friday.

The second reason the upcoming trial was so interesting had to do with the cast of characters participating in the trial. Darrell's family had scraped up enough money to hire Sikeston's best known and most successful attorney, J.D. Blackman. Twenty five years and one hundred pounds ago, when J.D. was a young attorney, he won a large lawsuit against a manufacturer of baby cribs. With J.D. as their lawyer, a Charleston, Missouri family successfully sued the manufacturer for negligence in the death of their six-month old daughter. J.D. pocketed thirty percent of the settlement, becoming rich overnight. After that case, J.D. was in demand. He won several large cases over the years, both civil and criminal. Now in his late fifties, he was the most recognized lawyer in Southeast Missouri.

J.D. was proud of his success, and he liked to flaunt it. He had the biggest house in Sikeston, and he owned no fewer than two Mercedes and three Cadillac's. Now on his third wife, he liked to shower her (and also his mistress) with expensive jewelry. Never wanting to be outdone, he always hosted the biggest parties in Sikeston. He was on the board of directors of the largest bank in town and almost every major charity in town.

Some residents of the county were comparing the two trial combatants to David verses Goliath. To the average person, J.D. was the superstar of lawyers. He was Goliath. If you were really in trouble, you had to hire J.D. His successes in the courtroom were legendary. He could work miracles.

Many local members of the Missouri bar, however, had started to question J.D.'s abilities. They felt he was no longer as formidable an opponent as he once was. His reputation now far surpassed his skills. As is the case with many successful lawyers, their abilities cannot keep up with their egos. They tend to spend less time preparing for cases. It was the common feeling in the legal community that J.D. had too much confidence in his own abilities. As a result, he was gaining a reputation for appearing in court unprepared.

It was also no secret that J.D. had become quite partial to scotch over the years. Most evenings after work, he could be found sitting in the lounge at the Sikeston Country Club, holding court, telling anyone who would listen about his legal heroics. J.D. would usually knock down six or seven scotch and waters per night. Some were beginning to wonder if the alcohol was having an impact on his performance.

David, in this case, turned out to be Scott County prosecutor, Jim Bryant. What Jim lacked in reputation and experience, he more than made up for with ambition. He was the twenty-nine-year-old son of Sikeston's wealthiest man, George Bryant. His family owned a bank, a farm equipment dealership, an insurance agency, over ten thousand acres of prime farmland, and some of the best commercial real estate property in Sikeston.

From his birth, George Bryant groomed Jim for big things. Jim wasn't going to settle for simply running the family businesses. He had a burning desire to be a major player in politics. After graduating from Harvard law school, he worked for a large, prestigious Washington law firm for two years. He then decided to move back home, where he felt his imminent rise to political power would be much faster if he took advantage of his father's significant influence. The Scott County prosecutor's office was just the first step of many in his bright future. His first major goal was to be elected to Congress. After that, who knew where he would end up. The sky was the limit for Jim Bryant.

Jim was definitely his father's son. When he was just a small boy, his father knew he was something special. He was extremely intelligent, just like George. Unlike his older brother, Mike, Jim had real potential. Mike was too much like his mother. He had no ambition, no desire. Mike had principles that he would not violate at any cost. Jim was not weak like Mike. Like his father, Jim would let nothing stand in the way of achieving his goals

Up to this point in his life, Jim had done all the right things necessary for name recognition. He had been the president of both the Sikeston Jaycees and the Sikeston Rotary Club. He had been active in the local Republican Party. He served on the Sikeston City Council. He was elected as the Scott County Prosecutor. He stood side by side with his father as they hosted political fundraisers for all the major Republican candidates. He had also learned and perfected all the proper social skills of a refined gentleman. All this was designed to help him one day be elected to the United States Congress.

Jim was so confident in his future that he had already strategically positioned himself for his time in Congress. While he was living in Washington, he met and married Taylor Carter, the daughter of the powerful congressman from Tennessee, Jack Carter. Jack Carter was a conservative republican and was Chairman of the House Appropriations Committee. Jim had it all planned out. He would use his father's money and influence to be elected. He would then use the influence of his father-in-law to rise to the top ranks within Congress.

Jim knew that it was necessary to make sacrifices to be successful in politics. He had made the ultimate sacrifice. He ditched the girl he loved to marry Taylor. Jim still thought of Cheryl every day. Oh, how he missed her. He knew it would have never worked out, though. They were just too different. When he first began dating Cheryl, his father told him it was okay to date her, but he could not have a long-term future with her. He knew his father was right, but it was still hard to let go. "She is not our type, Jim," his father had warned. "Your backgrounds are so different. Cheryl will only hinder your career." Jim knew that Cheryl was not the country club type. She came from a middle class family. She was a free spirit and wasn't impressed with money and social status.

The day Jim ended their relationship had been the worst day of his life. With tears in her eyes, she wished him the best and told him she hoped his career was worth it. It had been worth it. The exposure from the wedding to Taylor was invaluable. Several congressmen had attended the wedding, as well as ambassadors, and former cabinet members. So what if he didn't love Taylor? That was a small price to pay for the dividends she would pay in advancing his career. After all, he would be too busy to spend much time with her anyway.

The stage was set. All Jim needed now was a jump-start. The Darrell Rogers case was a dream come true. This was his break, a chance to make a name for himself. It would be a high profile case. The timing couldn't be better either. Crime was in the forefront of people's minds. The 70's was the decade of drugs, sex, and rock & roll. It was also the decade in which the term "serial killer" was born. The nation was shocked at the crimes committed by monsters such as Bundy, Gacy, and Berkowitz. Residents in small town, conservative communities such as Sikeston were worried sick that drugs and crime would penetrate their area.

Jim Bryant was going to put those fears to rest. He would send a clear message that crime would not be tolerated in his county. He would prove to the world that he was tough as nails when it came to fighting crime. He would emphasize this point by seeking the death penalty against Darrell.

As a bonus, he would defeat the great J.D. Blackman in the process. He would convict Darrell Rogers, and humiliate the county's best-known attorney by obtaining a death sentence. This case was the break of a lifetime. It would attract media attention from the entire region. He was sure that winning this case would put him on the fast track to congress.

Jim knew that it would be risky, however. If he lost the case, the damage to his political career may be insurmountable. This was a risk he was willing to take. He was worried more about the lack of evidence he had to work with than the quality of his opponent. In his mind, J.D. Blackman was just an egomaniac. Jim's father had taught him to be refined, graceful, and eloquent. J.D. did not possess any of these personal traits. He had no use for the likes of J.D. Blackman. J.D.

was a boisterous, obnoxious, pompous bag-of-wind, who at one time knew how to work a jury. Jim despised him. He also knew, with the preparation he would put into this case, that J.D. would be no match for him in court.

The lack of evidence really bothered Jim. He would have felt much better with a reliable eyewitness, a blood match, or a murder weapon. He would just have to be that much better.

The real decision was whether or not he would place Mrs. Hammonds on the witness stand. He was not even sure himself if he believed everything she told him. He was fairly sure, however, that she actually saw Darrell leaving the house. After all, she did pick him out of a police lineup. He didn't believe she would make a good witness, though. Her memory was bad, and her statements were at times inconsistent.

Once, when he questioned her she mentioned she had been watching the show *Hawaii Five O* just before she saw Darrell leave Lora's house that night. Jim knew that *Hawaii Five O* aired on Wednesdays, not Fridays. At first, he was stunned. This coincided with Darrell's claim that the break-in occurred on Wednesday night, not Friday night. His whole case centered on the fact that Darrell was in Lora's house the night of the murder. Jim then asked Mrs. Hammonds if she was sure it was *Hawaii Five O* she had been watching that night. She then backed off, saying it could have been one of the other detective shows. She claimed she watched them all. She liked those good-looking detectives. She admitted it could have been *The Rockford Files, McCloud,* or Mannox, instead of *Hawaii Five O.* Mrs. Hammonds was insistent, however, that no matter which show it was, she remembered very clearly that it was a Friday night that she saw Darrell; the night before they found Lora's body.

Jim knew if he decided to put her on the stand, he would have to prep her before her testimony. It was unethical to coach a witness, but with so much on the line, he may have to bend the rules a little. After all, he was almost certain that Darrell was guilty. Who else could have committed the murder?

A personal dilemma for Jim was whether or not to seek the death penalty. Under normal circumstances, he wouldn't have even considered the death penalty in a case such as this. This was no ordinary case, though. This was the case that could jump start his political career. He knew that by securing a death sentence, he would gain a reputation as being tough on crime. He was determined not to let his conscious get in his way.

The biggest trial in the history of Scott County started on Monday May 27, 1979. The trial was held in the Scott County Courthouse in Benton Missouri. The courthouse was an imposing structure, and had served as the site for criminal trials in Scott County since 1913. Benton was a small town, with less than one-thousand residents. Located in the geographic center of the county, it was approximately fifteen miles north of Sikeston.

All pretrial motions had been decided and the jury had been selected. It was now show time. Many were shocked that J.D. did not request a change of venue. Most lawyers thought it was a mistake for the defense to try the case in Scott County. Everyone in the county was familiar with the case, and Dr. Lora Smith made a very sympathetic victim. She was a local girl, who had made something of her life. She had the potential to make a difference in a lot of lives, until that was taken away from her. Local citizens would demand that someone pay for taking a life filled with so much promise.

Most people speculated that ego was the only reason J.D. did not seek a change of venue. In his mind he could win any case, anywhere, at any time, with any jury.

The judge on the case was Tony Davis. Judge Davis had a reputation for being a prosecutor's judge. This was another reason many felt J.D. should have attempted to move the trial. J.D. would probably not catch many breaks during the trial. Most rulings from Judge Davis would favor the prosecution.

The atmosphere around the Benton courthouse was carnival-like. Some people arrived at the courthouse two hours early to assure themselves of a seat. There were reporters and camera crews from all three local news affiliates. There were also reporters from every newspaper within a fifty-mile radius of Benton. Everywhere you looked, reporters could be seen interviewing spectators outside the courtroom, asking them if they thought Darrell was guilty or innocent, and if they thought the State should seek the death penalty. People weren't hesitant to share their opinions. Most felt strongly one way or the other.

The trial was scheduled to start at 9:00 a.m. At five minutes before nine, Darrell was escorted into the circuit courtroom by a deputy sheriff. Darrell looked around the crowded courtroom and suddenly felt very nauseas. He began to perspire. It was really happening.

Up until now, he never thought they would proceed with a trial. This was the United States of America, and innocent people do not stand trial for capital murder. For the past three and one-half months, as he sat in his jail cell he had expected any minute that the sheriff would appear and tell him they had caught the real killer; that he was free to go. They would admit to making a horrible mistake. It was now painfully obvious that would not happen. He knew he deserved to be punished for breaking into Lora Smith's house and for forging a prescription, but he certainly didn't deserve this. He kept wondering how all this could have happened.

As Darrell was seated next to J.D. at the defense table, he turned around and saw Lisa seated in the front row, directly behind him. He smiled at her. The only positive thing that had occurred since this nightmare began was that Lisa had forgiven him. She had visited him every day since he had been in the county jail. She was special, and he would never again take her for granted. He wouldn't have made it this far without her love and support.

Darrell looked over at J.D. and began feeling a little better. After all, he was innocent and he also had the best attorney in the area defending him. He just wanted the whole thing to be over; to be declared innocent; and to move as far away from Sikeston as possible. He, Lisa, and Sarah would then start a new life.

Darrell remembered how confident J.D. was when he assured him and Lisa that the prosecutor would never secure a conviction with the evidence they had in the case. The one thing that bothered Darrell was that he didn't know for sure if J.D. really believed he was innocent. If J.D. thought he was guilty, how passionate would he be in his defense?

Jim Bryant looked around the packed courtroom. In front of him, behind the judge's bench, stood the Missouri and United States flags. The Missouri State Seal hung on the wall between the two flags. To him, these were symbols of power; the kind of power that he would have in the near future.

This was his big moment. He was prepared and confident. He was receiving the media attention he coveted; now all he had to do was win the case. The three interviews this morning had been priceless. He thought of the number of voters who would be watching the interviews on the evening news. They would see a man committed to fighting crime; a man who supported victim's rights; a man unafraid to seek the most severe of all punishments. In his mind, he could already count the votes.

The opening arguments demonstrated the contrast in styles of the two attorneys. J.D. was animated, loud, and wordy. His opening statement went on for more than thirty minutes. Jim was soft-spoken, polite, and to the point. He wrapped his opening statement up in less than ten minutes.

The prosecution's case was simple: 1.Darrell had an uncontrollable addiction to prescription drugs. Jim presented, as evidence, pharmacy records showing the staggering number of prescriptions that had been filled in Darrell's name over the ten-month period. 2. Jim demonstrated to the jury that Darrell had a propensity for violence. Jim called the two police officers, who had arrested Darrell for domestic disturbance, to the witness stand. They testified that Darrell had been arrested for hitting his wife. They also described the abusive behavior he demonstrated as they arrested him. 3. Jim then presented the motive to the jury. The motive for the murder was that Darrell was angry because Dr. Smith refused to write him a narcotics prescription. Jim introduced into evidence Darrell's medical record for the emergency room visit. Dr. Smith's notes indicated that Darrell became abusive when he was denied the prescription. 4. Two nurses and a security guard testified that Darrell threatened Dr. Smith on his way out of the emergency room, just two nights before the murder. 5. A technician at the State Crime Lab testified that the fingerprints found at Dr. Smith's house were a match. 6. Chief Nelson testified that he found Dr. Smith's prescription pad in Darrell's apartment. 7. The Super D pharmacist testified that Darrell forged Dr. Smith's signature on a prescription pad, using it to fill a prescription for Demerol the night of the murder. 8. Jim called a psychologist to the stand, who testified that heavy use of painkillers over a long period of time can alter a person's personality, making them violent. He told the jury he had seen other cases where drugs caused a normally non-violent person to commit murder while under the influence. 9. Jim had Chief Nelson testify to the brutal nature of the murder. For added effect, Jim showed the jury the photographs from the crime scene. By the expressions on the juror's faces, it was obvious this had the desired impact.

As Jim presented the State's case, the jury hung on every word. He was masterful as he pieced together the circumstantial evidence, leaving little room for doubt.

The most damaging testimony came from Mrs. Ethyl Hammonds. Jim made the difficult decision the previous night to allow her to testify. He risked everything, including his law license, by putting her on the stand. He knew that if her testimony went well and the jury believed her, it would seal the conviction. Despite all the circumstantial evidence he had presented to the jury, he still could not refute Darrell's claim that the break-in occurred on Wednesday; not Friday night. If he could not disprove Darrell, the jury may find reasonable doubt. Mrs. Hammond's testimony would refute Darrell's story that the break-in occurred two nights prior to the murder, and would place him in Lora's house the same night the murder occurred.

At court recess, just minutes before she was to be called to the stand, Mrs. Hammonds dropped a bombshell on Jim. She informed him that before she saw Darrell drive away that night, she saw him place an object in a toolbox that was attached to his truck bed. Jim was shocked. He had spoken with Mrs. Hammonds on three previous occasions, and she had never before mentioned anything about a toolbox. Worse yet, Jim knew that Darrell did not have a built-in toolbox in the back of his truck.

The thought that Darrell may, in fact, be innocent began to enter his mind. He quickly brushed the thought aside. *Darrell has to be the one; it all fits*, he reasoned. *She probably saw something that looked like a toolbox. After all, her vision is poor.*

Jim knew that he had gone too far to turn back. He had to do whatever was necessary to secure a conviction. The jury and the defense must never hear about the toolbox. So what if he violated a few ethics along the way? Everyone does from time to time. After all, the ends would justify the means. The killer would be brought to justice.

Jim now had to find a way to deal with Mrs. Hammonds. Any mention of the toolbox would provide the defense the break they needed. Her testimony could destroy their whole case.

He wanted to yell at her. Tell her she was about to ruin his career. But, in as kind a manner as possible, he informed Mrs. Hammonds that it could not have been a toolbox she saw that night because Darrell did not have a built-in toolbox on his truck. Jim then told her that if she mentioned this, the jury would more than likely find Darrell not guilty. "You don't want Lora's killer to go free, do you?" he said.

"Heavens no! Well, maybe it wasn't a toolbox I saw. It sure looked like one, though," she replied. "I guess it was kind of dark that night."

As Jim began coaching Mrs. Hammond's testimony, he started regretting his decision to put her on the stand. It was too risky. What if she became confused? There was no way to predict what she would say. J.D. would probably eat her alive. He knew now, though, that if he did not call her, J.D. would know something was wrong, and he would probably talk to her. He had to go through with it. He had no choice.

Jim' stomach was churning when he called Mrs. Hammonds to the stand. The frail eighty-one year old surprised everyone, including Jim Bryant, when she took the stand. As her name was called, she tossed aside her walking cane, held her head high, and walked briskly to the witness stand. Her normally weak voice suddenly became strong. Jim was stunned as she described in great detail, watching Darrell leave from Lora's house that night. She never mentioned the toolbox.

Mrs. Hammonds also held up well under cross-examination. No matter how hard he tried, J.D. could not get her to admit that it may not have been Darrell she saw that night. "I never forget a face," she said. She explained that the street where the truck was parked was only thirty feet from her living room window, and the streetlight directly in front of her house provided plenty of light. She described the blue Chevy truck she saw (which matched the description of Darrell's truck). Jim was very relieved when she omitted the part about the toolbox.

J.D. also pressed her as to the date. "How can you be sure, Mrs. Hammonds, that it was Friday night and not Wednesday night that you saw the defendant leaving the house?"

Her reply was the fatal blow to Darrell's case. "Look you young whippersnapper, I may look old and decrepit, but I am sharp as a tack. Don't you think I would remember the exact time I saw someone leave my neighbor's house the night she was murdered?" The courtroom burst into laughter.

Despite J.D.'s objections, Mrs. Hammond went on to describe the many favors Lora had done for her: took her to the grocery store, picked up her medications from the pharmacy, looked in on her when she was sick. After Mrs. Hammond's testimony, the jury was ready to lynch Darrell.

Jim Bryant was surprised that J.D. didn't attempt to present evidence supporting Mrs. Hammond's poor memory and poor eyesight.

He reasoned that J.D was probably afraid to test Mrs. Hammonds again. Jim was also surprised he didn't question Sheriff Nelson more aggressively regarding the lack of physical evidence tying Darrell to the crime scene.

As the trial progressed, Darrell began having second thoughts regarding his selection of an attorney. He didn't think J.D. was aggressive enough. He kept waiting for the big punch that J.D. was known for; the knockout blow that would mesmerize the jury. It never came.

J.D. felt, however, that he did his best in presenting a defense. He knew it was hopeless. He hated losing, but he knew that sometimes clients just didn't give you much to work with. "Some clients are so guilty even the best attorney can't get them off," he would later tell others. "Well, at least Darrell had the best defense possible."

J.D. called several character witnesses to the stand. Each of them stated that Darrell was incapable of murder. From the looks on the juror's faces, Darrell knew they weren't buying it.

Darrell was the last to testify at the trial. Despite pleading to the jury that he did not murder Lora Smith, he knew they did not believe him. They saw him as a deranged, drug-crazed lunatic bent on revenge that night. The jury deliberated less than three hours. The deciding factor in their decision to render a guilty verdict was the testimony of Mrs. Hammonds. They believed her testimony that she saw Darrell at the house the night of the murder.

As the judge read the verdict, Darrell's mind went blank. This was it. His life was over. Lisa began screaming at the jury: "You've made a terrible mistake. Darrell did not do this. You have convicted an innocent man." As Darrell was led away, he could not bear to look at Lisa.

* * *

The sentencing phase of the trial began the next week. J.D. placed Lisa on the stand to plead for her husband's life. With tears pouring down her cheeks, she begged the jury to spare his life, pleading with them not to take Sara's daddy away from her. J.D. then called Darrell's mother and several of his closest friends. They spoke of all the good that Darrell had done for them over the years.

J.D. felt he had done a good job convincing the jury that Darrell's life was worth saving. He had one major problem, however. He could not convince Darrell to testify on his own behalf. He felt the jury needed Darrell to exhibit some remorse, and they needed to hear him say he could contribute something to society if he were spared the death sentence. This did not occur.

After the conviction, Darrell had become very depressed and angry. He was mad at the system: the police, the prosecutor, the judge, the jury. He had finally gotten his life straightened out, and then they took it away from him. He wasn't about to give the court the satisfaction of seeing him beg for his life. He refused to show remorse for something he didn't do. During the sentencing hearing, Darrell appeared defiant. He seldom looked at the jury, and when he did, he glared at them. To the jury, he looked like a cold-blooded killer.

Jim played on the jury's sympathy for the victim. One by one, Jim's witnesses described what a wonderful and caring person Lora Smith was. Her colleagues talked about the dozens of lives she had saved in the emergency room. Her mother informed the jury that while growing up all Lora wanted was to become a doctor. She was genuine and truly wanted to help others. She made tremendous sacrifices to achieve her dream: four years of college, four years of medical school, a three year residency, and a board certification examination. Just when she had realized her dream, it had been taken away from her. It was so senseless.

Just when he had the jury on the verge of tears, Jim reminded them of the suffering and pain Lora went through on that awful night. It was no surprise when the jury came back with a recommendation for a death sentence.

After the death sentence was pronounced, Jim immediately set up a news conference on the front steps of the courthouse. This was the moment he had been waiting for. As he basked in his glory, he reminded the drug dealers, the rapists, the murderers, the embezzlers, that they were not welcome in his county. He would not tolerate crime, and if you dared to try, look what would happen to you. Everyone applauded as he discussed the need for politicians to do more to make our streets safer and to protect our children. He was setting the stage.

As he climbed into his brand new BMW and lit his victory cigar, he briefly thought of Darrell Rogers and the testimony of Mrs. Hammonds. He wondered if she really did see a toolbox in the back of the pickup truck that night, and could it possibly have been someone else leaving Lora's house. He shook his head. He knew he had to remove those thoughts from his mind. Darrell was guilty, and he needed to celebrate his victory and enjoy the moment. He knew nothing could stop him now. Soon he would have the power he had dreamed of his whole life.

Jim cranked up the radio and floored the accelerator as he listened to *The Dancing Queen*, by the rock group Abba. He looked forward to the party his father would throw in his honor later in the evening. But first, he needed to unwind. As he drove south down Highway 61 toward Sikeston, he thought of his assistant, Denise. He would pick her up from the office and have a little rendezvous in her apartment. His wife could wait.

Chapter 8

He was in the back yard with his mother, father, and sister. It was a nice, cool, summer evening. The grass was freshly mowed, and he could hear the birds chirping in the background. His mother and sister were sitting in lawn chairs, watching him play ball. His dad squatted behind the makeshift home plate, holding out his catcher's mitt.

"Come on Son, fire the ball in here. Give it all you've got. Alright, it's a perfect strike. Just like Bob Gipson. You keep throwing like that, you're gonna tear up little league next year."

Carla yelled "Way to go Ricky!" He smiled and wound up for another pitch.

Suddenly, he was no longer in the backyard. Something was wrong. He was looking at a light in the distance. The light became brighter and it was coming closer and closer. Panic swept over him. He then heard the awful sound of metal against metal and saw the glass explode into his face. He could see his father drifting above his head, being taken farther and farther; away from him forever.

Next, he could feel the worn leather strap, as it tore into his bare skin, over and over again. He could feel the pain and see the blood sliding down his leg. He cried out "Mommy help me!" His mom turned her face away from him. With tears in his eyes, he felt the sting of the strap again, and he watched his mother walk away.

The light was now out. It was dark, damp, and musty in the basement closet. All he could see was the sliver of light coming from underneath the locked door. He was shivering from the cold, but there was no way to become warm because he had no blanket and all he was wearing was a pair of underwear. His mouth was dry; he was so thirsty. How long had it been since he had a drink of water? How many days had passed since Frank locked him in here? He wouldn't cry, however. He had stopped crying long ago. It would do no good. It never did.

Ricky sat up in a cold sweat. It took him a moment to collect his bearings. Then he remembered the dream. It was the same terrible dream he had been having periodically the past eleven years. It never changed. It still seemed so real; like he was still that small boy.

He looked around the small cell, then climbed off his narrow bunk, took two steps to the sink, and drank a cup of water. It was nearly one in the morning. No noise could be heard. The hours from midnight to seven a.m. were the only time this place was quiet. At any other time of the day, he would hear constant yelling. Every day, all day; constant noise.

He had been confined in the Missouri State Penitentiary at Jefferson City for almost six months now. The prison first opened in 1836, and it was the oldest penitentiary west of the Mississippi River. The prison had an ominous appearance, with its tall limestone walls and fifteen guard towers. The housing unit, where Ricky's cell was located, was built in 1868 and had housed some of America's most notorious prisoners. The prison was extremely dangerous.

Ricky was not concerned with the danger, though. He had successfully taken care of that. He knew no one would dare mess with him now. The worst part of prison for him was the lack of privacy. He enjoyed solitude and quiet. This place was so noisy he couldn't think. Other than that, it really wasn't so bad.

In many ways, Ricky preferred prison to the free world. In prison, there is no social hierarchy that is predetermined at birth. In prison, an individual's social status is earned. Everyone has an equal shot. Status is gained by earning respect.

Unlike the real world, in prison Ricky was at the top of the social ladder. He was looked up to by the other prisoners. This was a right he had earned; it had not been given to him. He found that he enjoyed the attention and the respect he received from other inmates.

It wasn't always that way. When Ricky first arrived at the prison, he was seen as prey. He was viewed as an eighteen-year old kid, who would be an easy target.

He quickly learned that the guards did not control the prison. The prison was controlled by gangs. There were six major gangs. Two of the gangs were black gangs that were offshoots of the original street gangs from Kansas City and St. Louis. There was also a black, Muslim gang; the most feared in the prison. There was one Hispanic gang, and two white gangs. One of the white gangs was a racist group, who hated all minorities. They were called "the White Aryans" and many of their members were ex KKK. The other white gang was called "the Sorority" by other inmates because of their predominantly homosexual tendencies.

It was in the best interest of new inmates to join one of the gangs for protection. Most ordinary, young inmates could not survive without protection. Ricky was no ordinary inmate, though.

Ricky was recruited by both the "White Aryans" and "the Sorority." After hearing that the initiation involved becoming one of the members personal "slaves," Ricky politely declined their offer. He was neither a racist nor a homosexual, and he didn't intend to convert to either doctrine.

By declining protection, he knew he would immediately become a target. He viewed the threat of harm as a nuisance that should be dealt with head on. He first needed a weapon. Since he was a non-smoker, he traded a months worth of cigarette rations for a shank.

The first job assigned to him was in the prison laundry. He knew this was where the attack would most likely occur because of the laundry's relative isolation from the rest of the prison. He hid the shank behind a cabinet in the laundry. When he first entered the laundry each day to work his shift, he would place the shank in one of his socks.

On the fourth day of his confinement, three members of "the Sorority" attacked. As he was removing sheets from the five hundred pound washer, the three "sisters" approached him. They spread around him in a circle. One "sister" had a metal pipe and another had a crowbar.

Ricky had no idea if their purpose was to beat him or rape him. He never gave them the chance to explain. Striking like a rattlesnake, he whipped out his shank and, before they could respond, he slit the throats of two of the attackers. He then grabbed the crowbar from one of the dying victims, and chased the remaining "sister" to the back of the laundry. As the "sister" pleaded for his life, Ricky smashed in his skull.

Ricky calmly removed his bloody uniform, threw it into the washer, and replaced it with a clean uniform, just washed. He then turned the washer on, rinsed his face and hands, and calmly walked back to his cell.

The three killings were never pinned to Ricky. The guards either assumed it was a gang related slaying or they just didn't care. The guards detested the "Sorority" members; therefore they did not expend a great deal of energy on the investigation.

The inmates, on the other hand, were all very aware of what had occurred. Ricky's fame spread quickly, and he soon became a celebrity within the prison walls. He was now feared and respected. From that day on, no one dared to bother him.

Ricky kept to himself most of the time. He passed the days and nights by working in the laundry and reading books. He also fantasized about the things he would do when he was released. Oftentimes, he would think of Regina Phillips. They had some unfinished business, and he knew he would be paying her a visit shortly after he was released. It would be at least nine more years, but he could wait. He had waited once before.

As school let out for the summer, life was back to normal in Sikeston. The Darrell Roger's trial had concluded, and the media frenzy that surrounded the Sikeston area began to subside. Even though the trial was over, the topic still dominated the conversation at the coffee shops. Most people seemed to agree with the verdict, but some felt the death sentence was too harsh for the crime.

I was mesmerized by the story, wondering what it would be like to be on death row, just waiting for your day to arrive. In 1979, Missouri's form of execution was the gas chamber. I remembered from reading a book on crime and punishment that the condemned man was strapped to a chair in an airtight chamber. Then, cyanide pellets were dropped into water, and the Inmate would sometimes struggled up to ten minutes before dying.

Missouri had not yet performed an execution since the Supreme Court had reinstated capital punishment. I asked Mom and Dad what the chances were that the State would really execute Darrell. Mom replied that she didn't know for sure, but that she felt it was barbaric. Dad, on the other hand, believed in an eye for an eye. He said that society was becoming sick of these senseless crimes, and he predicted that executions would someday be a regular occurrence, just as they were before the Supreme Court abolished the death penalty in 1972. He said it may take a few years, but they would execute Darrell.

I really didn't know for sure how I felt about Darrell's punishment. I did know, however, that I felt sorry for his wife and daughter. After the trial, they moved out of Sikeston to escape the uncomfortable looks and constant stares that seemed to follow them wherever they went. I had heard that his wife obtained a job as a waitress in Jefferson City. I thought she probably did that to be closer to Darrell.

One person, who emerged from the trial a big winner, was Jim Bryant. Everyone was talking about how he defeated J.D. Blackman, making him look bad. Before the trial, people thought of him only as George Bryant's son; a boy who grew up with a silver spoon in his mouth, whose father's money got him elected as the county prosecutor. But now, they recognized him as the common sense man, who would not let big city problems move into the small towns in Southeast Missouri.

Many believed he would run for congress next term against Sam Eldridge. Old Sam had already served twelve straight terms, and people were beginning to wonder if he ever did anything. He seldom left Washington, and he rarely interacted with his constituents. An article in the St. Louis Post Dispatch listed the attendance records of all the members of the US House of Representatives. Sam Eldridge topped the list, holding the distinction of having the worst attendance record in the House. Many felt Old Sam had lost touch, and he had allowed his ego to get the better of him. He was more interested in what he could do for the lobbyists, who showered him with campaign contributions and perks, than he was in helping the people who elected him. Old Sam was primed to be beaten, and many felt Jim Bryant was the man to do it.

As I settled into my summer routine of playing baseball, mowing yards, and working at the store, I often thought of Darrell and how a seemingly normal person could have committed such a gruesome murder. I also thought of Ricky and wondered how he was getting along in prison. I tried not to think too much about Carla, but I couldn't help myself. I hoped she and her mother finally had the life they deserved.

Chapter 9

Twelve years later: October 5, 1991

Darrell knew it wouldn't be much longer now. The warden was scheduled to arrive at his cell in fifteen minutes. He was okay now and could handle what lie in front of him. God was with him. He felt a peace unlike anything he had ever felt before. It had taken him a long time, but he had finally accepted his fate. The bitterness was gone. He now knew that everything happened for a reason. Maybe something good would finally come of this.

The worse part was over. An hour earlier, he had said his final good byes to Lisa and Sara. The hardest thing he had ever done in his life was finally letting go of Sara, his precious daughter. She refused to release her grasp around his neck when he told her she had to go. It was all he could do to keep from crying, but he knew he had to be strong for her. As he fought back the tears, he reminded Sara that this was not the end. He would see her again some day in heaven. With his voice choking, he told her he would always be with her in her heart.

As they had left the holding area and the door closed behind them, his knees gave out and he slumped to the floor. He broke down and began sobbing uncontrollably. His heart ached, for he knew he would never see Sara again. Within a couple of minutes, however, the familiar feeling of God's presence overpowered him. He had the sudden reassurance that God would take care of Lisa and Sara.

As he sat on the bunk to wait the final fifteen minutes, he reflected on his life in prison. When he first arrived at the Missouri State Penitentiary in Jefferson City, he was in a severe depression. He was wallowing in self-pity. He had lost his family, his reputation, everything. His life consisted of living in a nine foot by six-foot cage. There was no window. His only view was of a drab green hallway and wall, directly in front of his cell, that he could look at through bars that extended from the floor to the top of his cell. He had absolutely no privacy. At any time of the day, a group of individuals could be touring the prison and there was no place to hide within his cage. He felt like an animal in a zoo. The worse part was knowing that he was living among society's worst. Everyone on the death row unit was a convicted murderer. He wasn't worried about his safety, though. He would have welcomed being stabbed to death by one of the other inmates in the unit.

About a year after his arrival on death row, he finally decided he had to do something other than sleep and watch soap operas. After his conviction, J.D. Blackman had visited him only once. Since it appeared to him that J.D. was not too interested in his appeals, he fired him and decided to work on the appeals himself. He took advantage of the law books in the prison library. With the assistance of a young attorney who specialized in death penalty cases, he drafted his own motions and pleadings. He became so knowledgeable that he also began assisting other death row inmates with their appeals. Soon, the legal work kept him busy every day.

Darrell had more success with other inmates appeals than he did with his own. He could never escape the influence of Congressman Jim Bryant. Jim Bryant wielded his significant power at every turn in the appeals process. Jim knew many of the judges on the appeals court, and he did not hesitate to wine and dine them. He also influenced public opinion by constantly harping on the need for tougher sentences and the need to hold people accountable for their actions. He often used Darrell's case as an example in his speeches. It appeared he was on a personal crusade to have Darrell executed. Darrell often wondered why he had it in for him so much.

Darrell also passed the time by reading the Bible that was provided to him by the Gideons. Before this nightmare, he and Lisa had occasionally attended the Presbyterian Church in Sikeston, although neither had been overly religious. But as he read the Bible in prison, he found a personal relationship with God that he had never known before. He no longer suffered from depression, and he actually started feeling good about himself once again.

In February 1989, Missouri opened a new penitentiary in Potosi, Missouri, located approximately fifty miles southwest of St. Louis. The State made the decision to perform all executions at the new prison, so all death row inmates were moved from Jefferson City to Potosi. Missouri also changed the method of execution from the gas chamber to the more humane method of lethal injection.

Darrell found the environment to be much better at Potosi. Just as he had in Jefferson City, he made friends with the guards, and he would spend hours each day talking to them. The guards often solicited advice from Darrell regarding spiritual matters, marriage difficulties, problems with their children, whatever. Darrell sometimes felt more like a counselor than an inmate. Most of the guards were convinced that Darrell was innocent, so they began having a difficult time dealing with the situation as the fateful day approached.

Darrell's mind was jarred back to the present when he heard a door slam. His eyes slowly turned to the clock that hung on the wall just outside his cell. It was ten minutes until midnight. The warden and two guards, whom Darrell knew very well, appeared in front of his cell. "Darrell, it's time," the warden announced.

Darrell said a short prayer, asking God to give him the courage to face the situation with dignity. As they entered his cell, he stood up to allow the guards to place the handcuffs and leg chains on him. One of the guards, Herb Johnson, was fighting back tears as he clasped the cuffs together.

"Don't be sad, Herb. I am going to a much better place. Trust me, everything is going to be alright."

Darrell then turned to the warden and the other guard, and thanked them for everything they had done for him.

The warden looked into Darrell's eyes. He had never felt this way about an execution. This was the first time he was unsure about a condemned man's guilt. Many inmates in the past claimed innocence, but in the end they usually showed remorse and were afraid of dying. This one, however, seemed totally at peace. He showed no fear.

As Darrell shuffled along the hall toward the execution chamber, several other death row inmates wished him well. One was crying. Darrell smiled at them, and said he would miss them. He looked at Herb and told him to take care, and to never take his wife and children for granted. At the chamber door, he stopped and shook hands with the warden and two guards. He then stepped inside the death chamber.

The death chamber had two windows, both covered with curtains. Behind one window sat the witnesses for the State and the condemned.

Behind the other curtain sat the witnesses for the victim, Lora Smith. As Darrell was strapped to the gurney, and the hospital doctor started the IV, he felt total peace, total relaxation.

As the windows opened, he looked at Lisa and smiled. The warden then read the death warrant, and asked Darrell if he had any last words.

"Yes, thank you warden." Darrell then took a deep breath as he spoke the words he had been preparing for weeks.

He turned and looked at Lora Smith's parents. "I am truly sorry for your loss. I cannot imagine what you have gone through. I hope someday your daughter's real killer is found, and you will have peace."

He then told Lisa and his mother that he loved them, and would see them again some day. "I'll be waiting for you," he said.

As he nodded to the warden, the lethal combination of sodium thiopental, Pavulon, and potassium chloride was fed into the IV.

Behind the glass sat Lora Smith's father. In his mind his world ended that Saturday afternoon twelve years ago, when he received the phone call that his only child had been murdered. Since that time, the only thing that kept him going was the need to see Darrell pay for what he had done; to see him suffer. He somehow thought the execution would make him feel better; bring some sort of closure. As he looked into Darrell's eyes, he suddenly felt very uneasy. Something wasn't right. It was the peaceful look on his face, unlike anything he had ever seen. The feeling of hatred he had harbored for the man was melting away. A horrible feeling rushed over him as Darrell took his last breath.

"We have just executed an innocent man!" he exclaimed.

Chapter 10

Congressman Jim Bryant sat in the library of his seven-thousand square foot home in Washington D.C. He glanced at his watch and smiled. He lifted the glass of bourbon as if to propose a toast. He drained the glass and smacked his lips, as he relished the warm feel of the bourbon sliding down his throat. It was 12:05 a.m., and he knew the execution was underway. His greatest fear was now behind him.

Jim walked across the room and looked at the picture of his father hanging on the wall. *We survived the scare, Dad*, he said to himself. Of course, his father knew nothing of the danger that, up until a few minutes ago, had threatened his political career. His father would never find out either. Jim would do whatever was necessary to make sure of that.

Jim was now completing his fifth term as a United States Representative, and he was in the process of running for the United States Senate. Twelve years ago, he had taken advantage of the notoriety he had gained from the Darrell Roger's trial. As a result of his newfound popularity, he handily defeated his democratic opponent, Roy Eldridge, in the 1980 congressional election.

At the time of the 1980 election, the public demanded punishment for criminals, not rehabilitation. People wanted to feel safe again, to be able to walk the streets without the fear of being robbed. They wanted criminals kept locked up, not paroled where they could repeat their crimes. Jim Bryant's tough stand on crime was exactly what the public wanted.

Once in Congress, Jim's popularity continued to climb. He wasted no time utilizing the influence of his powerful father-in-law, Jack Carter. He was soon placed on important House committees, and within a couple of years, he became known as a major force in Washington politics.

Due to the Bryant Crime Bill that was passed one year ago, Jim was now recognized across the country. Jim was the sponsor of the bill baring his name, and due to the bill he would be forever known for his tough and aggressive stance against crime. The bill was one of the most significant pieces of legislation to affect domestic policy since the Civil Rights Act was passed in 1964. The crime bill required the Federal Government to allocate $100 billion per year to local and state governments to be used to increase the number of police officers and to build new prisons. The bill required the states to impose stricter sentences for certain crimes and for repeat offenders. The bill also limited the appeals of death row inmates, expediting executions. The legislation had the support of eighty percent of Americans, and it made Jim Bryant a household name. The only major segment of the population opposed to the bill was the extreme left wing liberals. Jim knew he wouldn't receive their votes anyway. As a result of his popularity and his aggressive stance on crime, he was poised to win the Senate seat in a landslide.

Congressman Bryant had become the people's voice for numerous causes: victim's rights; the fight against drugs, and mandatory sentences. As a result, he had been basking in the public spotlight. Many political insiders believed that due to his enormous popularity, he would someday make a strong presidential candidate. In the past three months, all this had been jeopardized, however.

Jim thought of the senatorial election, just thirteen months away. He knew now that he was back on track. The threat was almost over. He could once again look forward to being a United States Senator. As he took another sip of bourbon, he could taste the success, feel the power. He realized how close he had come to losing it; how lucky he had been. "Was it luck or was it divine destiny?" he wondered.

He then lit a cigar and reflected on the events that had occurred during the past few months. He thought of how invincible he had been just three months earlier. Just ninety short days ago, it seemed nothing could stand in the way of him becoming the next United States senator from Missouri. Then everything unraveled. Jim clenched his teeth as he reflected on that horrible day when the former Sikeston detective, Eric Lowe, appeared at his front door.

When Jim answered the door that day and saw Eric Lowe, he immediately recognized him from his days as the Scott County prosecuting attorney. He had worked several cases with Detective Lowe. He remembered Lowe as being the sharpest detective on Sikeston's Police Force. He also recalled hearing that Eric Lowe had been fired a couple of years ago for official misconduct.

Eric Lowe informed Jim that he was now a private investigator, and he had been hired by the Darrell Roger's defense team to prove Darrell's innocence in Lora Smith's murder. At first Jim had been amused, thinking the detective was there as a last ditch effort to convince him to speak to the Governor on Darrell's behalf. His amusement soon turned to shock as Eric Lowe informed him he now had convincing proof of Darrell's innocence.

As Eric Lowe methodically walked him through the new evidence he had turned up, he tried his best to conceal his desperation. He wanted to scream; to put his fist right through the man. This man was telling him the very conviction that won him recognition, jump-started his political career, and propelled him to the United States House of Representatives, had been a big mistake. He knew that if this became public it would destroy his whole career; everything he had worked for the past twelve years.

As Jim poured himself another bourbon, he angrily recalled Lowe's reaction that night. Lowe had thoroughly enjoyed watching him squirm as Lowe described in detail how he had encouraged Mrs. Hammonds to omit from her testimony the fact that she saw the toolbox in the back of the murderer's truck that night.

Jim's father had always taught him to be cool headed, to never panic, and to think things through. As the former detective, turned private investigator, finished his story that night, Jim began going over in his mind the current situation. He knew his whole political career would be finished once the news leaked out that he had convicted an innocent man of capital murder. Worse yet, since the conviction was based largely on a tainted testimony that he, himself, had encouraged, he could face even more serious problems.

Jim had been the leading congressional spokesman in support of the death penalty. The opponents of the death penalty's main argument was that since we could never be sure that an innocent person is never executed, the death penalty should be abolished. Jim had countered their argument, stating that they could not provide proof of a single incident where an innocent man had ever been executed in this country. He knew that he would be made to look like a fool when the media found out that his own, high profile capital conviction was of an innocent man. At first, he thought the situation was hopeless.

Suddenly, he realized that something didn't make sense. Why was Lowe here telling him this? It would not be Lowe's responsibility to notify him, and he could think of no logical reason for him to do so. Then it dawned on him that the former detective was here to blackmail him. At that point, he knew he had a chance to wiggle out of this after all.

Jim then asked the million-dollar question, "Who else knows about this information?"

"Not a soul, except you and me," he had replied. "And, there is no reason for anyone to find out either, as long as you and I understand each other."

Jim soon learned that the mutual understanding that Lowe had been referring to would wind up costing him five million. It really had been an easy decision. He had the money, and he knew he could never allow the truth to come out. Knowing he had no choice, he had agreed to pay the five million. After paying the blackmail, it became a simple matter of nervously awaiting the execution date.

Now that Darrell was officially executed, he could relax. The attention given to the case would die down, and there would be less chance of someone else finding out the truth. Jim also knew it was now too late to turn back and make it right. He had committed a criminal act. He would have to do whatever was necessary to keep anyone from finding out.

Jim took another puff from the cigar, as he thought about the sleazy P.I. and how he had taken advantage of him. It angered him that he was forced to succumb to a blackmail threat from a lowlife like Eric Lowe. *Nobody does that to me and gets away with it, he thought.* He was used to being the one calling the shots, and he did not like being threatened.

Even though he had paid the blackmail, he knew he wasn't off the hook yet. He had dealt with the likes of Eric Lowe before. He knew it was just a matter of time before Lowe squandered the $5 million, then he would be back at Jim's doorstep demanding more. What if, after having too much to drink one night, Lowe told someone about the blackmail? Jim knew he couldn't take that chance. Eric Lowe was the only person who knew what he had done to Darrell Rogers. Eric Lowe was too much of a threat, and as long as he was alive, Jim's political future would be in jeopardy. He could never have peace. He knew he would have to deal with Lowe, and the sooner the better. Eric Lowe was just another threat he would have to eliminate. Like other similar problems he had dealt with in the past, Jim knew it could be handled with just a simple phone call. He dreaded the thought of involving Roy Weston, but Lowe had given him no choice.

Jim smiled as he thought of Eric Lowe's future fate. *It serves him right*, he thought. *He blackmailed the wrong person.* Jim would have his revenge.

Jim looked out the window and thought of how miserable he had been during the past three months. He had been a nervous wreck; worried that Darrell's defense team would uncover the truth. The opponents of the death penalty had made Darrell Rogers their poster child. Darrell had apparently been a model prisoner. He had helped inmates with their appeals, provided counseling, and even led the Sunday worship for the death row inmates. Darrell was a favorite of the guards at Potosi, and two retired guards actually came forward, stating they believed Darrell was innocent of the crime for which he had been convicted.

The organization aptly named the British Against the Death Penalty (BADP) came to Darrell's aid in a big manner. The BADP was organized to oppose civilized countries that still allowed capital punishment. Their primary focus in recent years had been to promote their agenda in the United States. To the BADP, Darrell Rogers was a dream come true. The positive influence he had on other inmates in prison, plus the shaky evidence which led to his conviction, gave them a sympathetic victim to rally around. The BADP had significant resources and they did not hesitate to use them on Darrell's behalf. Just two months prior to the execution, they had aired a television documentary featuring Darrell. The BADP also provided the funding for Darrell's appeals, and they were responsible for the hiring of Eric Lowe. Jim had known that until Darrell was dead, they would not stop trying to prove his innocence. If Eric Lowe was able to prove that Ricky Henry was the real killer, so could someone else. Now that Darrell was dead, the BADP would no longer be a threat.

Even though the BADP was out of his hair (and so would Eric Lowe soon enough), Jim had another problem to worry about. He now had to worry about Ricky Henry. He had learned from Eric Lowe that Ricky Henry was Lora Smith's probable killer. He knew that Ricky was also, more than likely, responsible for the murder of Patricia Wells twenty years earlier. A former prison guard from Jefferson City had also informed Lowe, off the record, that Ricky had been responsible for three prison stabbings twelve years ago.

It was apparent to Jim that Ricky was a psychopath. He also knew that Ricky was scheduled for parole in just two months. What if that lunatic went on a killing spree, got caught, and then confessed to Lora Smith's murder? He knew that the motive for many killers was publicity, and being captured and recognized for their crimes was just part of their fantasy. He could not take a chance on Ricky being arrested. Ricky would have to be monitored.

At first Jim felt a twinge of guilt that he was responsible for an innocent man losing his life. There was too much at stake, however, for him to be too concerned. Besides, he knew the ends justified the means. The country needed his leadership, and after all, Darrell Rogers was a nobody. Even before the murder, Darrell had made no significant contribution to the world. He was just a supervisor in a run of the mill warehouse. The world would never miss him. Congressman Jim Bryant, on the other hand, would make a difference in people's lives. If Darrell Rogers had to be sacrificed for the cause, then so be it.

Jim knew politics was often dirty, and he knew he would have to become accustomed to making tough decisions. He wasn't weak like his brother. His brother could never have stood by and allowed an innocent man to be executed to save his own career. Jim was strong, however; just like his father. Jim knew that all great men had to make difficult decisions and had to live through adversity. He knew he was special, a cut above the rest. He had been destined for greatness. His father had been telling him that since he was a little boy, and he knew he could never let his father down. His biggest threat was now behind him. All he had to do now was to eliminate Eric Lowe and then nothing could stop him. The senate, then the presidency.

His thoughts were interrupted by the knock on the library door. He looked up and saw his wife slowly open the library door. "Jim, a reporter from CNN is here. He wants to know if you would like to make a statement."

Eagerly, Jim walked into the living room to greet the reporter. In his opinion, a candidate can never have too much publicity. As a result, he decided he would never turn down an interview. During the live interview, he did not hesitate to once again reiterate the brutality of the murder. He talked about how we should remember the victim, Lora Smith, and not the killer who had just been executed. He spoke of how the execution will bring closure to the Smith family, and how it will be a deterrent for other potential murderers.

When the reporter asked him if there was any way the BADP was correct and Darrell had, in fact, been innocent, he replied: "Absolutely not. If I thought there was even a remote possibility of his innocence, I would have personally stopped this execution from taking place."

Immediately after the interview, he went back into his library and called Roy Weston.

Chapter 11

One month later: November 10, 1991

His newly found wealth brought Eric Lowe opportunities he had never before dreamed possible. As soon as the five million dollar wire transfer was secure in the offshore accounts he had set up, Eric went on a two-week gambling spree in Las Vegas. He followed this up with a week in New Orleans; drinking hurricanes, Dixie beer, and watching strippers. After throwing a couple of thousand dollars her way, he convinced a knockout stripper named Ginger, who worked for one of the upscale clubs on Bourbon Street, to have dinner with him.

Compared to the other women Eric had dated over the years, Ginger was a goddess. Most women considered Eric average looking, at best. He was certainly not considered a ladies man, and he had never even been close to having a relationship with a woman as beautiful as Ginger. He enjoyed the important feeling he had when he was with her. In addition, he relished the fact that other guys looked at him with envy.

He decided he would treat himself and keep Ginger around for a while. Although he was not much on fancy clothes and fancy restaurants, he knew Ginger had acquired expensive tastes since moving to New Orleans. He decided to impress her by buying her jewelry on Royal Street and clothes at the Riverwalk. He also took her to four-star restaurants, such as Emeril's and Commanders Palace.

It took about twenty-thousand dollars worth of gifts, clothes, and fancy meals, but Eric finally convinced Ginger to accompany him to Myrtle Beach. While still in New Orleans, he and Ginger found a new Audi convertible that they just could not resist. Behind the wheel of the new Audi, Eric and Ginger drove from New Orleans to the East coast where Eric plunked down six-hundred thousand for a condominium in North Myrtle Beach. Within just one month, Eric had already blown through one million dollars of his fortune.

After spending the past two weeks admiring Ginger's near perfect body, Eric decided his own body could use a little conditioning. For the first time in his life, he began exercising. He joined a fitness club just one mile from his condo, determined to rid himself of the beer gut he had worked to develop over the past twenty years. At age forty-two, Eric Lowe had a new lease on life.

Since joining the Sikeston police force twenty years earlier, Eric had always looked for ways to make a fast buck. He enjoyed gambling and women, and he had found over the years that these two hobbies required more money than his detective's salary could provide. As a result, he needed to find a means to supplement his income. Twice, he had accepted bribes from drug dealers he had caught on the west-end of Sikeston.

Eric had always dreamed of the big score. He had fantasized about what he would do if he had a million bucks. He came close a few years back when he attempted to pull off a blackmail attempt against one of

Sikeston's most prominent citizens, Davis Rutledge. During a routine robbery investigation at the Rutledge house, Eric uncovered evidence that Davis was having an affair. Since the Rutledge's inherited wealth came from his wife's side of the family, Eric thought Davis would be willing to pay a large sum to keep his indiscretions a secret. His gamble backfired. Davis' wife already knew of the affair and she was, in fact, having an affair of her own. When Davis found out about Eric's plan, he became furious and saw to it that Eric was fired from the Sikeston police force.

After the blackmail attempt failed, Eric had almost given up on his dream of the good life. He had become fairly content with his comfortable life as a private investigator. Due to his investigative skills and excellent reputation, he had stayed fairly busy and actually earned a decent living.

At the time he received the visit from the two representatives of the BADP, Eric had been a private detective for five years. During that time period, he had successfully proven the innocence of several citizens, who had been wrongfully accused. At first, this job appeared to be very similar to these other jobs. The BADP hired him to find new evidence they could use to stop Darrell Roger's execution. The BADP willingly agreed to pay him his standard fee of one hundred dollars per hour plus expenses. What appeared to be a fairly routine engagement at first, turned out to be the break of a lifetime.

Eric began his investigation by reading the court transcript to familiarize himself with the case. He then made a list of the witnesses to interview in hopes that he could uncover something that may have been missed by Darrell's attorney, J.D. Blackman.

The first witness he interviewed was Mrs. Ethyl Hammonds, now ninety-four years old. Although feeble in appearance, Eric was surprised at how sharp her mind was for her age. She seemed to recall every detail of the events the night of the murder thirteen years ago. As Mrs. Hammonds recounted her story, suddenly Eric's attention raised a notch when she described Darrell's pickup truck. She said the truck was a blue Ford with a built-in toolbox in the front of the truck bed, just below the sliding glass window.

As she was talking, Eric quickly skimmed the transcript again. Having found the section he wanted, he looked up at Mrs. Hammonds.

"There is no mention in the court transcript of the toolbox, Mrs. Hammonds. Are you sure?"

"What do you mean, am I sure?" she yelled. "I know what I saw. The reason it is not in the transcript is that I didn't mention it when I testified. That cocky prosecutor told me not to. He said if I mentioned it I would be responsible for letting that sweet girl's killer get off scott free."

Eric struggled to contain his emotions. He knew he was on to something. *What was it about a blue truck and a toolbox?* he thought. There was something familiar about it. He was pretty sure it was a case he had worked on while he was still a detective with the police force. He just couldn't recall it.

He left Mrs. Hammond's house and immediately drove back to his apartment. Fortunately, he had kept his old notebooks, containing the notes he had taken on cases he worked while employed by the Sikeston police force.

As he skimmed through the notebooks, he came across the Frank Kroetz murder that occurred just six weeks after the Lora Smith murder. *That's it*, he thought. *That teenage boy, Ricky Henry, drove a blue, Ford pickup truck, and it had a built-in toolbox in the back.* As Eric's mind wandered back to that cold night thirteen years ago, he remembered that Ricky Henry had brutally stabbed his stepfather after his stepfather had beaten Ricky's mother. Eric recalled the cold eyes and lack of remorse that Ricky displayed. He became excited as he realized that Ricky Henry could very well be Lora Smith's real killer.

Eric's investigation soon led him to Tyler, Kentucky and the drunk driving accident that killed Ricky's father and left Ricky severely injured. He then discovered that the drunk driver, Patricia Wells, was murdered nine years later in Paducah, Kentucky and the case had never been solved. The instincts he had developed over the years told him this was too much of a coincidence.

Next, Eric interviewed several of Ricky's former teachers and neighbors and found that Ricky's life changed drastically after the accident. Ricky's mother remarried, and Ricky was severely abused by his stepfather and was neglected by his mother. While interviewing the former psychologist that treated Ricky for two years after the accident, Eric learned that Ricky harbored deep seeded hatred for the driver who had killed his father. The counselor suspected that Ricky might be a sociopath.

As Eric reviewed the police case file on the Patricia Wells murder, he noted similarities between her murder and Lora Smith's murder. In both cases, the killer broke in through the bathroom window. In both cases, the killer used latex gloves. It also appeared the murder weapon was the same type of knife. The forensic report indicated both killers were of the same height, and the stab wounds were very similar.

Eric was now convinced that Ricky Henry had killed both Patricia Wells and Lora Smith. Now, all he had to do was come up with definitive proof, and he would be set for life. He now knew that Darrell Rogers was innocent, and that Congressman Jim Bryant had encouraged a witness to withhold critical evidence at trial. It didn't get any better than this. If he could prove it, he knew that Jim Bryant would pay whatever he asked to keep this from becoming public.

Eric soon found the proof he needed. As he reviewed Darrell Roger's trial transcript, he noticed there was a spot of blood found in Lora Smith's bathroom that did not match either Lora or Darrell. Darrell's attorney, J.D. Blackman, has used this blood evidence as a key component in Darrell's defense. He knew that spot of blood could be the key to both proving Darrell's innocence and making himself a millionaire.

Having been employed by the Sikeston Public Safety Department previously, Eric knew the evidence room by heart. Fortunately, he had had the foresight to have a key made before he was terminated. His key to the evidence room had come in handy a few times before.

Using his key, he broke into the evidence room. His familiarity paid off, as he had no trouble locating the evidence bag containing the blood. Fortunately, DNA testing was now available, whereas it wasn't at the time of Lora Smith's murder in 1978. He then called in a favor and asked a technician at the State Crime Lab to perform a DNA test on the blood. In exchange for a small fee, the technician agreed to keep the results anonymous. The DNA was a perfect match to Ricky Henry. Apparently, Ricky had incurred a slight cut as he climbed though Lora's window that night.

Eric's investigation next led him to Jefferson City, where he interviewed several prisoners and current and former guards. Two former guards told him they suspected that Ricky was responsible for three murders shortly after he became an inmate. According to the guards and prisoners, Ricky was "a bad dude", and he was both feared and respected within the prison walls.

With proof in hand, it was then a simple matter of making the visit to Senator Jim Bryant. The end result was that he was now a multimillionaire. Now, thanks to Ricky Henry, Darrell Roger, and Jim Bryant, he was living the good life.

As he sat at the tiki bar with Ginger by his side, he realized he was living the American dream. He would never have to work again. He would enjoy Ginger until he tired of her; then he would find a new toy. As he looked at Ginger, he was amazed at the power of money. Before, he could have never had a woman like her. He had always had to settle for mediocrity; but now, with his newfound wealth, he was in the big leagues. He admired Ginger in her thong bikini, and he realized it may be quite a while before he tired of her.

For the next two weeks, he and Ginger spent their time lounging on the beach; drinking beer and margaritas; eating seafood at Barefoot Landing; and dancing to the music at the House of Blues. Eric could have done this forever, but he realized that Ginger was starting to become bored. It also appeared she was beginning to lose interest in him. Since he was not yet ready to turn her loose, he decided he needed to spice up the relationship.

While in New Orleans, Ginger made good money in the upscale gentlemen's club, sometimes clearing as much as two-thousand-dollars per night. As a result, she had developed expensive tastes. Although Eric was perfectly content to frequent pool halls and bar and grills, he knew that if he wanted companionship with a woman like Ginger, he would have to learn a little culture and become a little more refined.

Although Eric knew absolutely nothing about romance and culture, he felt confident he could learn. He was now in the big leagues, and he needed to play the part. He remembered reading in a brochure he found at Barefoot Landing that Charleston, South Carolina had the greatest collection of historical homes and elegant gardens in the United States. Although he had never been to Charleston, he had heard it referred to as the cultural center of the south. It sounded like a good place to begin his transformation and cure Ginger of her boredom..

Eric booked a room in an eighteenth century bed and breakfast in the historic district of Charleston. A weekend of carriage rides, fancy restaurants, and shopping along the historic streets should recharge Ginger's batteries.

Two days later, he and Ginger were driving south on Highway 17 toward Charleston. After a two and one-half hour drive, they checked into the bed and breakfast on Church Street. One hour later, he found himself accompanying Ginger as she roamed the fancy shops on King Street, armed with his Mastercard.

Chapter 12

November 15, 1991

From the street, Roy Weston could see Eric and Ginger walking into the bed and breakfast inn. Roy had followed Eric from Sikeston to Las Vegas, to New Orleans, to Myrtle Beach, and finally to Charleston, South Carolina. He was sick of waiting. He felt Jim Bryant was being too paranoid. Jim had instructed him to wait a few weeks after the execution so that the BADP would not be suspicious when Eric Lowe turned up missing. Last night, Jim called to give him the green light. Roy was finally set to go to work.

Roy, now forty-one, had worked for the Bryant family off and on ever since he left New York and the Balducci crime family in 1975. Prior to joining the mafia as a hit man, Roy had been a green beret in Vietnam, where he had earned both the Congressional medal of honor and a purple heart. His greatest attribute was his ability to follow orders without question. This extreme loyalty is what George Bryant (and later Jim Bryant) found so appealing.

He first began working for George Bryant in 1975 when one of George's friends recommended him to solve a certain problem George was having at the time. George Bryant realized the growth potential just south of Sikeston's city limits, and he tried to capitalize on this by developing the land for commercial use. George was able to purchase all the land from the southern border of the city limits south to Highway 60, except for one parcel. That parcel of land threatened to jeopardize his entire plan. Roy was engaged to help make the owner understand the importance of selling his land to George.

After a late night visit from Roy, the landowner suddenly saw the light and became very willing to sell the property to George Bryant. George paid Roy a small fortune for the job, and ever since, he used Roy from time to time to handle other sensitive issues. For these jobs, Roy was always compensated very well.

Jim Bryant first utilized Roy's services during the 1980 congressional campaign. Although Jim ended up winning the general election against the incumbent easily, the primary election had been very close. In fact, just one month prior to the primary, Jim was behind in the polls. His opponent's only known weakness was that he was rumored to have experimented with LSD in the sixties, a fact he adamantly denied. The press had made an issue out of his suspected drug use. Jim decided he should capitalize on this perceived weakness.

He hired Roy to plant cocaine in his opponent's car. Roy then placed an anonymous phone call to the police. When word of the arrest hit the media, the election was over, and Jim went on to defeat Roy Eldridge to become a United States Congressman.

He never told his father about the drug plant. Although George Bryant was not above intimidation and breaking the rules a little, Jim knew that he would never approve of such drastic means to win an election. Jim knew that Roy would never tell his father because Roy would go to his grave without ever violating the confidence of any of his clients. Roy was the only person he would trust to handle sensitive issues.

Roy Weston had been freelancing now for the past sixteen years. He had several clients in addition to the Bryants, and as a result, never seemed to go too long without work. His list of clients included wealthy American businessmen, drug lords, mafia bosses, and even foreign dictators. He was very discreet and non-judgmental. As long as the client paid his fee, he didn't particularly care what kind of job he was hired to do. The fact is, the more challenging the job the more he enjoyed it.

Over the years, Roy had killed over fifty people and had never even come close to being caught. The killings never really bothered him. He looked at them as just part of his job. He figured they had it coming to them or else his client would not be paying to have them killed. The military training he received as a green beret, and the three years he spent in the jungles of Vietnam had provided him with an intelligence and a sixth sense that enabled him to elude being captured.

Roy knew Eric Lowe was a very good private detective. For that reason, he knew he needed to be very careful. However, compared to the dangerous mafia hit men and drug dealers he had taken out in the past, the detective should be a piece of cake.

Since there was no easy way to get into Eric's and Ginger's room in the bed and breakfast without being detected, Roy planned to wait until they left the inn. He then planned to follow them until they were on a fairly isolated street and could not be seen by other tourists. He decided the best time for the hit would be after dark. He attached the silencer on the end of the pistol and placed it in his jacket pocket. Now all he had to do was wait for the right moment.

* * *

After spending three boring hours in the shops on King Street, Eric finally managed to convince Ginger to head back to their room. He was now three thousand dollars poorer, and as he struggled to carry the four sacks of clothes she had purchased, he began wondering if her body was really worth all this aggravation.

As though she were reading his mind, she suddenly informed him that all the shopping had stressed her out and that she wanted him to give her a back rub in the jacuzzi that came with their room. Eric smiled as he thought of spending the next few hours rubbing her luxurious body. All of a sudden, he didn't mind carrying the four sacks of clothes.

That night, after dinner on East Bay Street, Eric and Ginger browsed the City Market. Although Eric was not in the mood to shop, he much preferred the Market to the fancy shops on King Street. Hoping that Ginger had the shopping out of her system, he began to look forward to the next day. Tonight, they decided to head to an Irish pub for a quick drink before they turned in for the night.

As they left the crowded market and walked down Cumberland Street, they passed by the side of the magnificent St. Phillip's Episcopal Church, one of the oldest churches in the country. It was now after ten o'clock, and the streets were becoming deserted. They both wanted to take a closer look at the historic church, so they turned onto Church Street for a better view.

As they walked toward the front of the church arm in arm, Ginger suddenly felt Eric jerk, and then she felt something wet on her right arm. As she wiped her arm with her hand, she let out a scream when she realized it was Eric's blood. Before she had a chance to catch her breath, Eric released his grip on her arm, and he fell to the sidewalk. In terror, she looked down and saw his shirt covered in blood.

Roy Weston stood up from behind the row of shrubs across the street, slipped the pistol back into his jacket pocket, and casually cut through the back yards of the historic homes to Market Street, where he blended in with the tourists. Another job completed.

Part 2:
The Investigation

Chapter 13

Fourteen Years Later: April 5, 2003 - St. Louis, Missouri

It was seven a.m., and as I turned my worn out 1995 Ford Windstar off Memorial Drive onto Market Street in downtown St. Louis, I began to anticipate the day ahead of me. During the morning, I planned to review and sign off the Memorial County Hospital audit. Next, I had a luncheon meeting with our senior partner, Stan Henson. My mid-afternoon would be spent presenting the audit report to the Board of Directors of a local school for the blind. At six o'clock, I had to be at my son's baseball practice, and at seven-thirty my presence was required at my oldest daughter's choir concert. No one could accuse thirty-seven year old Rob Gibson of living a dull life.

As I turned into the parking garage at One Boatmens Plaza, I thought of how busy my life had become. For the most part, I enjoy participating in my kid's activities, but like most parents I think my wife and I have gone overboard. I often believe I play a small role in our society's ever-growing madness. My generation has become too busy to enjoy life. In my opinion, this may explain why our nation's prescription drug costs are increasing thirty percent a year. Everyone is so stressed out from demanding schedules they have to take a boatload of prescriptions just to cope: Prozac, Paxil, Zoloft, Valium, whatever.

Little league baseball used to last three months out of the year. Now, with the new "traveling leagues" the season can last as long as seven months. Instead of having the games played locally, we now have to travel up to three hours just to get to the ballpark. Soccer used to be a fall sport. Now, it is a fall and spring sport. The kids are also playing at much younger ages than they used to. Instead of starting little league baseball at age seven, like it used to be, they now begin playing T-ball at age four.

Three years ago my wife signed me up to coach my son's T-ball team. I had no idea what I was getting myself into. At the time, my son, Bobby, was only four years old. I have no idea why I thought four-year olds could be taught to play baseball, but I quickly learned that I was fighting a losing battle. Instead of coaching baseball that summer, I found myself spending two nights a week babysitting and trying to placate parents. By the end of the summer, the only thing I had accomplished was teaching the kids how to run to first base after they hit the ball off the tee. I often wondered who the nut was who reduced the starting age of little league from seven to four.

Despite my sometimes, hectic schedule, I am content with my life. Just three years shy of forty, I have now been married twelve years. My wife, Stacy, and I have been blessed with three wonderful, healthy kids: Christine (age eleven), Amanda (age eight) and Bobby (age seven). For the most part, I enjoy my job and I live in a great city that offers plenty of family friendly things to do. I also live within a two-hour drive from my parents, who still live in Sikeston.

One of the great benefits of being a parent is that you have the opportunity to relive your childhood through your children. My son,

Bobby, is now in Little League, and when I coach his games I feel like I am once again a small boy out on the ball field. I experience the same excitement and nervousness for him that I felt when I was his age.

Being a father also allows you to act like a kid again, without being embarrassed. I am able to ride roller coasters, go-carts, roller skate, and watch cartoons. I guess I really never completely grew up, and now I have a perfect excuse to act like a kid again.

I unlocked the front door to the offices of my employer, Roberts and Larkin, LLP. Since I was the first one in the office, I started the coffee. A couple of minutes later, with a fresh cup of coffee in my hand, I went to my office to read the morning paper, *The St. Louis Post Dispatch*.

My office is on the nineteenth floor in the Bank of America tower. I am a manager for the Roberts and Larkin CPA firm. Roberts and Larkin is a regional accounting firm, with offices in St. Louis, Kansas City, and Indianapolis. In the St. Louis office, the firm has one hundred twenty employees; seventy of whom are CPA's. Ten of the CPAs are partners.

I have been employed by Roberts and Larkin four years now, and this represents my second run at public accounting. After graduating college, I worked for a large national accounting firm in St. Louis. After five years, I left that firm to become the controller, and then the chief financial officer, of a small hospital in Southern Illinois. It took me three long years as CFO of the hospital to realize I wasn't cut out for the personnel and physician problems that had to be addressed in a hospital management position. I also realized I could never adapt to the numerous social commitments expected of an officer of a community hospital. As a result, I found myself back in public accounting and living once again in St. Louis.

As I opened the newspaper, I turned my chair around to my window facing the downtown skyline. My firm's building is directly across the street from Busch Stadium, the home of the St. Louis Cardinals, and my office has a perfect view of the stadium and the Gateway Arch directly behind it.

The lead story on the front page immediately caught my attention. The article described yet another murder. This time the murder occurred in South County, approximately one mile from my home.

According to the article, the FBI and the local authorities have now linked at least ten local murders to the same killer. The St. Louis area has a serial killer on the loose. The killer's first victim was murdered over ten years ago, in February 1992. Since that time he has killed nine more times, and the killings are coming closer and closer together. The entire St. Louis area is now paralyzed in fear.

St. Louis has had many infamous crimes and criminals during its two hundred thirty six year history, but none have captivated the public's fear and attention like this killer.

I heard a knock on my office door, and I looked up and saw my friend, Jeff Barnwell. Jeff and I have been friends since I joined the firm four years earlier. We both have a lot in common. We each have three kids, are managers in the firm, and we have common interests (mainly Cardinals baseball, Rams football, and Blues hockey). Jeff is one of those guys that can eat continuously and never gain a pound. He amazed me because he managed to stay fit, despite the fact that he never once worked out.

Our firm has three divisions: audit and consulting; tax; and strategic development. Jeff and I are both in the audit and consulting division. Within our division, we have eight different industry segments. I am the manager of the firm's healthcare practice, and Jeff is manager of the firm's banking practice. Jeff has been with the firm for seven years, and like me, he will probably never make partner.

When I left the hospital and came to the firm, I was somewhat burned out. As my former hospital's CFO, I worked a lot of hours and was required to be active in the community. I became tired of dealing with the personnel problems inherent with managing a large number of employees. When I was hired by Roberts and Larkin, I informed the partners that I had no intention of becoming a partner. Being a partner requires dealing with the personnel issues, and it also involves a significant time commitment. One of the primary functions of a partner is to beat the bushes and find new clients. It also involves wining and dining CEOs and CFOs in order to maintain their business. I realized a few years ago that socializing was not my cup of tea. One of the reasons I left the hospital was that I grew tired of all the parties and fund raisers that were required as part of my position. I have no desire to be a country clubber or to host parties every weekend. Instead, I am perfectly content being with my family and close friends. I am also grateful I do not have the responsibilities and worries shared by the partners. I enjoy only being responsible for the firm's small healthcare practice. I only have to supervise the six accountants and four assistants we have in the department. It is actually ten more than I would like to manage, but this is the least amount of responsibility I can have and still draw a paycheck satisfactory enough for our lifestyle.

"Rob, did you hear? He struck again last night," said Jeff.

"Yeah, I just read about it in the paper. This time he struck within a mile of my house," I replied.

"My wife is scared to death. I wonder when he'll hit again."

"I wish I knew, Jeff. According to today's article, his first three murders were about two years apart. Then the murders started occurring more frequently. The three most recent murders have come just one month apart. The psychologist they interviewed says the killer's need to kill is intensifying, and we can expect the attacks to become even more and more frequent. I don't think we need to worry too much about our families, though. The victims are not random; they are carefully selected, and he appears to be targeting only highly successful, professional women. Since both our wives only work part-time and are not in highly visible positions, I don't think they could be targets."

"I'm not willing to take that chance, Rob. There's no telling what goes through the mind of a psychopath."

"Well, you have a point there. Maybe I'll load my shotgun just in case. Hey, to change the subject, did you see the Cardinals last night?"

"Yeah, that Albert Puhols sure is something special. He's the next Musial. Well, I gotta run. I have to be in Clayton for a meeting at nine."

"See you this afternoon, Jeff."

After Jeff left my office, I settled in to complete the final review of the Memorial County Hospital audit work papers. Just as I became engrossed in the workpapers, I heard another knock. I looked up to see Anita Cline, one of my audit seniors. Anita was also the source of most of my tension headaches.

As busy as I was, I really didn't feel like dealing with Anita today. She was a very capable auditor, and she did good work. She was, however, the type of person who had driven me out of executive management. A dark cloud followed her everywhere she went. She saw everything from a negative perspective. She always had a problem, usually very trivial, and every time I met with her she had at least one complaint. The old half full – half empty analogy did not apply to Anita. To her, the glass was completely empty.

I took a deep breath as I reluctantly waved her into my office. I became even more concerned when she sat down. That meant it would be one of her longer bitching sessions.

"Rob, I have a problem I need to talk to you about."

"Oh, what a surprise!" I replied in as sarcastic a tone as possible.

"I'm having problems with the troops."

She said it as though she were the CEO of a fortune five hundred company and had several thousand employees under her. She had only three.

My management style is simple. Let everyone do what they want, when they want, as long as they produce. Pass out job assignments, be available for advice, and stay out of their way. Somehow, this approach did not work with Anita.

As she described one of her ridiculous encounters with a staff auditor, I began to think of how much I dreaded the seemingly endless number of years I had to work until retirement. After about a minute, I tuned her out. Finally, she stopped talking. I assumed the silence had been preceded by a question. This was my opening to get her out of my office.

"I agree with your recommendation, Anita. Go to it," I replied, having no idea what that might involve. It worked. A beaming smile spread across her face, as she left the office.

As I flipped through the work papers, I wondered what I had just agreed to. I was sure I would hear from her three employees later in the day. But for now, my problem was solved.

My luncheon meeting with our firm's senior partner, Stan Henson, was at Dierdorf and Harts, an upscale steakhouse across the street from the office. Once a month or so, Stan invites each of the managers to have lunch with several of the partners. Stan feels this is a good way for the partners to really get to know what is going on, and it makes the managers feel part of the ownership of the firm.

Other than Stan's luncheons, I rarely dined with the partners in the firm. It's not that I don't like them. With a couple of exceptions, I believe the partners in our firm are good, quality individuals. It's just that I prefer a quick hamburger or sub sandwich to the two-hour lunches the partners enjoy. I would rather spend the extra hour working, so that I can leave the office earlier in the evening and spend more time at home with my family.

A couple of the partners have told me that I need to play the game and interact more with the higher-ups. One even had the nerve to ask me why I didn't want to be successful, like him. This was the same partner, who prided himself for the long hours he put in. While he lived in a million dollar house and belonged to the most expensive country club in St. Louis, he had been divorced three times and hadn't seen his two kids in over five years. I guess his definition of success was a little different than mine.

Due to my own stubbornness, I have never been good at playing the game of office politics. In my naïve way of looking at the world, I believe the quality of your work and value to your employer should count for more than who you eat lunch with or how good a schmoozer you are. I have learned over the years that this is not the case. I am often dismayed at how twisted our values are both in our personal lives as well as our business lives.

Even though I do not enjoy office politics, I am politically savvy enough to know that I should never turn down Stan Henson for lunch. Besides, I really do like Stan. I respect him for his knowledge and his management abilities. He is very demanding, but he is fair and honest. When he tells you something, you can count on it being true. He is also very ethical, and he made sure the firm steered clear of the lucrative consulting engagements that have plagued other accounting firms. Stan believes firmly in the AICPA audit standard that states that auditors should be completely independent of their clients. Unfortunately, many of the other CPA firms have placed monetary concerns above ethics, and many investors and employees are now paying for this greed. It is difficult for me to believe that an audit firm would forsake professional ethics and turn a blind eye on fraudulent accounting practices to keep from rocking the boat, so they can retain their lucrative consulting fees. It is a good feeling to know that, as long as Stan is in charge, my firm will never be linked to accounting scandals, such as those that occurred at Enron, World Com, and HealthSouth.

The first part of the luncheon meeting was typical. We discussed the usual topics: the recent spate of murders; how the Cardinals were doing the first week of the season; Ram's trade rumors; potential new clients; staffing issues, etc.

During dessert, however, Stan sprung a surprise. He tossed a brochure across the table towards me. Apprehensively, I picked it up, opened it, and realized it was a brochure of the Bombay Club of Key Largo, Florida.

"What's this, Stan?"

"I just thought you and your wife needed a vacation, Rob."

"Uh Huh. Tell me what's really going on. I know the firm is too cheap to spring for a vacation. There has to be a catch."

"Okay. As you know, with the new government push toward enforcing the fraud and abuse statutes in physician offices, along with the new HIPPAA regulations taking effect, physician clinics are going to have a real need for specialized consulting services. In addition, with the three percent reduction to the physician fee schedule planned by CMS, physicians will need help finding ways to make up for the lost revenues. I think there is a tremendous market out there, and you and your staff have the expertise to provide services to that market. Most of the larger firms have not been interested in physician clinics because individual clinics tend to be smaller clients. We can possibly develop a niche in this market."

"That sounds good, Stan, I'm all for it. What does that have to do with Key Largo?"

"Well, the American Medical Association is having a regional conference at the Bombay Club next month. I would like for you and your lovely wife to accompany Carol and me to this convention. This presents the perfect opportunity to begin showcasing the services we can provide. We will set up a booth in the exhibit hall. And, we'll dazzle those physicians and pick up some business. We'll even manage to have a good time in the process."

"Stan, you know my social skills leave a lot to be desired. I am sure someone else in the firm would do a better job than me. Besides, the last thing on earth I want to do is to mingle with a bunch of arrogant surgeons."

"Yes, I am aware of your social phobias. However, you are the best man for the job. Since we will be one of the sponsors of the convention, the AMA has also asked us to be a guest speaker for one of the breakout sessions. The topics they want discussed involve the new regulations governing fraud and abuse, the new HIPPAA regulations, and new ways to maximize physician reimbursement. I can think of no one better to make that presentation than you. You know the healthcare regulations better than anyone in the firm."

Great, I thought. *At least Stacy will be happy. She's been begging me to take her on a Caribbean cruise. I think she will find five days in Key Largo as a good substitute.*

"Rob, in addition to the potential revenues we can generate from the convention, it promises to be interesting as well. The keynote speaker will be Senator Jim Bryant. You realize he is considering running for president in 2004. Just think, in a couple of years, you may be able to tell people that you once met the President of the United States."

Oh boy, I thought, sarcastically. I am not much into politics. Truth is, I find most of the candidates phony. I really had no burning desire to meet Jim Bryant or any other politician for that matter.

"You forget, Stan, that Jim Bryant is a Sikeston boy. I remember him from way back when he was our county prosecutor. I was only around twelve at the time, but I followed the case that started his political career. Do you remember Darrell Rogers, Stan? Jim Bryant was responsible for convicting him and, ultimately, for his execution."

"Yeah, I remember the execution very well. I don't think Missouri has ever had as much opposition to an execution as we did with Darrell Rogers. I'm no bleeding heart, but I remember feeling sorry for him after watching that British documentary. I am all in favor of the death penalty, but it sure seemed like he did a lot of good while he was in prison. It's a shame to waste a life that could do more good. I'm sure there were a lot of inmates in the general population that deserved to be executed more so than Darrell Rogers. By the way, what do you personally think of Jim Bryant, Rob?"

"Oh, about the same as I feel about any politician, I guess. I always thought he was the type to say anything or do anything to advance his political career. But then again, most politicians are like that. He tends to be conservative, which I like. I guess he's okay."

"Rob, you are about as cynical as they come. I really need your help on this though. I think this is an excellent chance for the firm to pick up some additional revenues."

I could not think of a more intimidating scenario in which to be a guest speaker. Although I have spoken at numerous conventions in front of healthcare finance professionals, I have never spoken before a large group of physicians. I also knew the Bombay Club was a very exclusive club in Key Largo, Florida; not particularly my kind of place.

I knew Stan well enough to know when he would compromise and when he would not. In this case, I sensed that I'd better not try to wiggle out of it. I decided to make the best of it. No matter how miserable I was while I was there, I knew it would be a good experience for me. Besides, I would have a very happy wife when I broke the news to her.

That night after the choir concert, I told Stacy of our upcoming trip to Key Largo. As expected, at first she was ecstatic. Within minutes, however, she began fretting.

"Rob, what if your parents can't keep the kids, then what are we going to do? You do realize I have nothing to wear for the trip, don't you? I am definitely going to have to go shopping this weekend. I simply do not have clothes suitable for that place."

In my mind, I began to calculate how much this "free" vacation would cost me.

Chapter 14

South County – St. Louis

Ricky pulled into his apartment complex and parked his black, Jeep Cherokee. He walked into his building, checked his mailbox, and started up the stairs to his second floor apartment. At the top of the stairs, he saw Debbie Riley, his twenty-six year old neighbor.

"Hello, Debbie. It's going to be a nice, cool evening, isn't it?"

"Oh, hi Ricky. Yeah, the weathers nice, I guess. It's not like I can enjoy it with that monster out there on the loose. I'm afraid to leave my apartment."

"I heard there was another murder last night," Ricky said. In a sympathetic voice he continued. "Don't worry, Debbie. I'm sure you're safe in this building. Have a good night."

Ricky smiled to himself as he unlocked his apartment door. *She may not realize it, but she really is safe as long as she lives next door to me,* he thought.

Ricky grabbed a soda out of the refrigerator and sat down in his recliner. He flipped the TV on to channel 9, the local CBS affiliate.

As he expected, the six p.m. news lead story was the latest murder in South County. Ricky smiled as he relished the attention.

He listened intently as he heard the news anchorwomen, Melissa Grogan, describe the viciousness of the murder. The anchorwoman looked sad as she described the latest victim: a thirty-year-old, successful, advertising executive; engaged to an engineer at Boeing; described by family and friends as fun loving and compassionate.

Melissa Grogan then recapped the nine previous murders. She discussed the fact that all of the victims had been successful, professional women. She then described how the city was living in fear, and women were flocking to obtain gun permits to protect themselves. She then referred to the killer as a monster, with no conscience.

Ricky stared at the anchorwoman and spoke to himself: "Be careful lady. You might just say something you will regret."

The news then switched from the anchorwomen to on location interviews of various St. Louis residents. The concerned citizens discussed how afraid they were; how they would kill the guy if they could get their hands on him; how shocked they were that this kind of evil existed in their society.

The next segment of the news included an interview with the St. Louis Police Chief, Bob Recker. It was obvious to Ricky, by the way he played to the camera, that he enjoyed the spotlight. With a concerned expression, he stated that they still had no legitimate suspects. He reiterated, though, that the St. Louis Police Department and the FBI were working together, and they would catch the killer. He suggested that everyone be sure to keep their doors and windows locked at night. He also reiterated that anyone, who might have information regarding the murders, should call the police department immediately.

I wish you luck, Chief Recker, Ricky thought to himself. *You are going to need it because I am just getting started.*

* * *

During the first few months following his parole in December 1991, Ricky maintained a low profile. It had taken all the energy he could muster to resist the temptations. The anger had built during the twelve years he spent in prison, and he was about to explode when he was released. Ricky was smart, however. He knew if he killed right away, he would become an immediate suspect, since the police usually looked first at previously convicted killers just released from custody.

Another reason he waited was that he had discovered that he was being followed. He first noticed someone following him two weeks after his release. He realized the guy was a professional because he had been very discreet. He also suspected that he was not associated with law enforcement. While in prison, he had heard from fellow inmates that a detective named Eric Lowe had been snooping around the prison, asking questions about him just prior to Darrell Roger's execution. He later learned that Eric had been hired by the BADP to prove Darrell's innocence. His first assumption was that Eric Lowe suspected him of Lora Smith's murder. He then concluded that Eric Lowe had informed the BADP of his suspicions, and as a result, the BADP also suspected him of the murder.

Ricky learned that Eric Lowe had then been murdered. He assumed Eric Lowe's murder was simply a coincidence. He also assumed the person now following him was Eric's replacement, hired by the BADP. He mistakenly assumed the BADP was now following him, trying to prove that the State had executed an innocent man. Little did Ricky know that the BADP knew nothing of Ricky Henry, and the person following him was really Roy Weston, who worked for Congressman Jim Bryant.

After his parole, Ricky moved to St. Louis, and with the help of his parole officer, he landed a decent paying job in the maintenance department of an auto parts manufacturer. While in prison, he had perfected his mechanical skills by working on the prison's kitchen equipment, boilers, mechanical equipment, and prison vehicles. He had also taken several repair courses and had become an accomplished mechanic by the time he was released.

For the first few months following his release, he played the part of the perfect citizen. He worked hard and did little else but go to the grocery store, the bank, and perform the functions that are necessary in everyday life. He wanted to defer any suspicion that he was a threat. He laid low until he was certain he was no longer being followed. Only then, did he begin the plan he had orchestrated while in prison. He would have his revenge on the people in the world out to destroy him; women in power.

When Ricky was first released, he was tempted to go after Regina Phillips immediately. He had been obsessed with her during his twelve years in prison, and he had dreamed of the day when he would be free to make her pay for what she had done to him. He changed his mind, however, when he thought the BADP was on to him. He knew it would be too risky, and if Regina were murdered, they might make the connection to the murder of Patricia Wells and the car accident. Besides, by waiting he would have something to look forward to.

He did keep track of Regina, however. He made it a point to know what was happening in her life – her work schedule; her closest friends; the clubs she belonged to; the boards she served on. He enjoyed following her, anticipating the final moment they would share together.

Once, he even broke into her house, stood at her bedroom door, and watched her sleep. He was so close, just a couple feet away from her. It would have been so easy, and he was tempted, but he maintained his self-control. Before he left her house that night, he took a necklace and a pair of her underwear, just as a reminder.

Since he was forced to wait for Regina, he transferred his built up rage to other women, who reminded him of her. After waiting six long months, he finally felt it would be safe to strike.

His first victims were from rural areas in Illinois. He knew he would be less likely to be a suspect in another state. The Illinois victims were random and simply served to extinguish his rage. The only thing these victims had in common was career success. Each woman was a successful professional or executive.

With each killing, his confidence grew until finally he felt comfortable striking in the St. Louis area. Unlike in Illinois, the victims in St. Louis were carefully selected and the murders were well planned.

He spent weeks selecting his first St. Louis victim, first narrowing it down to five, then finally choosing a hospital executive. She happened to be the Chief Operating Officer of a prestigious St. Louis hospital. Of all the women in positions of power, Ricky detested lawyers, doctors, and hospital administrators more than any other. He specifically blamed these people for his father's death and his mother's downhill slide into alcoholism.

The hospital executive made a fatal mistake in a crowded hospital elevator that resulted in her being St. Louis victim number one. With Ricky standing in the elevator no more than two feet away, she lit into a cardiology technician, humiliating him in front of the six other people sharing the elevator. Within twelve hours of the incident, her naked body was found bound to her bed.

This occurred twelve years ago, and it marked the beginning of Ricky's terror on the city of St. Louis.

* * *

Ricky switched stations, and found that the local NBC news affiliate was also covering the murders. The importance of the timing of the murders was being analyzed. Experts and profilers were being interviewed; all of who agreed that the killer's rage was intensifying. They discussed the fact that the murders began infrequently, about two years apart. Now, they were occurring only one month apart.

Ricky smiled. He had them all fooled. *What idiots*, he thought. If only they knew the whole truth. They had no idea that he was also responsible for the five murders in Southern Illinois that occurred in 1992. Back then; his modus operandi was different, so the police had not yet connected those killings to the ones in St. Louis. He knew, however, that they would eventually tie all the murders together.

He switched the channel back to Channel Nine and Melissa Grogan. She was now interviewing the mayor of St. Louis. It was fifteen minutes into the thirty minute newscast, and the only story reported so far had been the murders. There had been no mention of national news events, sports, or weather. Ricky was dominating the news. He was a celebrity. He was more important than anything or anybody else in St. Louis. He was even more important than the city's beloved Cardinals baseball team.

He laughed out loud. *Now, I'll give them a real story to report. Ms. Grogan seems to enjoy the spotlight. She relishes attention. I think I'll help her out and make her a real celebrity. I will make sure no one ever forgets her.*

He stared at her face on the screen before him. His adrenaline started pumping, and his hands became sweaty as he thought of the pure pleasure he would enjoy in the near future. He had just chosen his eleventh St. Louis victim.

Chapter 15

May 13, 2003

The sun was high and bright as Stacy and I drove our rented Ford Taurus down Highway One through the southern portion of the Florida Everglades. We crossed Florida Bay, and instead of turning right to go to Key West, we made a left turn and were soon on the island of Key Largo; the northern-most island in the Florida Keys.

We were surprised at how desolate the island was as we drove north on 905. There were swamps on both sides of the road, and we were surprised to see several alligators along the way. There was no sign of civilized life except for a few locals fishing off the side of the road. After driving for what seemed like an eternity, we thought we were lost.

It was not uncommon at all for me to get lost while driving. Stacy was used to this by now, and she had come to expect it. My sense of direction was not very good, and I was often too stubborn to ask for help. Most of the arguments between Stacy and I occurred in the car, while we were attempting to find our vacation destination. I guess Stacy sensed that I was not in a good mood, so she this time she kept her comments to herself. Just as I started to stop the car and pull out the map, we saw a small sign directing us to the Bombay Club. For once, I had not been lost after all.

We made a left turn and drove on a narrow road through dense woods for two or three miles. Finally, we came to a guard station, which I assumed represented the entrance to the private resort. We gave our names to the guard, and as we drove through the gate we entered, what I would describe as, paradise.

It was amazing that such a beautiful place could exist on the edge of a swamp. It was by far the most beautiful place either of us had ever been. It was how I pictured the Garden of Eden to have looked. Everything was a dark green; flowers were blooming everywhere; and there were hundreds of full-grown palm trees. At the tip of the resort was a white sand beach overlooking the Atlantic Ocean. A man-made lagoon was located on one side of the resort, with dozens of hammocks. An Olympic-sized swimming pool, with hot tubs on either side, was located on the other. I could easily understand why the bluebloods would want to make this their seasonal residence.

To my frustration, none of the buildings were marked. I guess the resort assumed all residents and guests knew where everything was located. We drove around for thirty minutes, and had to ask three workers for directions before we finally found the building in which to register.

I parked the rental in a lot adjacent to the registration building. Our car looked a little out of place among the Lexus, BMWs, Jaguars, and Cadillac's that filled the parking lot. We entered the building and walked to the front desk to register. As I waited in line, I noticed a middle-aged lady sitting in one of the lounge chairs, staring at me. She was giving me a look over; her piercing, nosy eyes roving up and down my body, checking me out. She had a disgusted look on her face, the same kind of look my son has when we set a plate of vegetables in front of him. At first, I thought my zipper might be undone. After verifying that wasn't the case, I realized that it was my choice of clothing that was displeasing to her. I guess my taste was not quite up to her standards.

As I looked around the room, I noticed that the men checking in all wore suits or sports coats with ties, and were sporting Rolex watches. The women's fingers were adorned with diamonds that stood out from fifty feet away. I knew for sure then that this was a place for the well-heeled. I also realized that the exorbitant dress I was observing would not go unnoticed by Stacy. I knew I was in for a tongue lashing for my selection of clothing attire.

It didn't take her long. As soon as we were outside the registration building, she lit into me.

"Rob, I told you to go shopping. I warned you about this. Carol Henson told me this was an exclusive place. In exclusive resorts, people dress up. You are going to embarrass both of us with the clothes you brought. Just because you're an accountant, doesn't mean you have to act like one."

"Stacy, I hate the word 'exclusive.' That implies that it is only good enough for certain people. Besides, the brochure said the dress here is casual. To me, that means shorts and a T-shirt."

There was a brief period of silence, and I thought I might have scored some points. I was wrong.

"Please tell me you brought something other than shorts and T-shirts. Surely, you aren't that stupid. Rob, you should know not to believe everything you read in those brochures. Most people who belong to this club are millionaires. They don't wear wrinkled shorts, bought from who knows where, and shirts with ducks on the pocket."

"Well, with the money you spent on clothes for this trip, there was none left for me anyway. Besides, I brought two suits for my presentation. I can just wear one of them to the reception tonight."

Stacy scowled at me when I turned down the bell hops request to carry our bags to the room. As I unlocked the door to our room and rolled the suitcases through the entrance, she had her hands on her hips.

"Rob, people staying in places like this do not carry their own bags."

"There is a first time for everything, dear," I replied.

As I looked around our luxurious and grossly overpriced room, I was pleased to find a mini bar. Although I am not much of a drinker, I figured I needed something to loosen me up for the beachside reception we were attending in a couple of hours.

After a hot shower and a couple of Heinekens, I was ready to face the members of the American Medical Association.

Senator Jim Bryant picked up his cell phone on the second ring. "What have you found, Roy?"

"Jim, I still don't know if it's Ricky Henry."

"Are you telling me it could be Ricky? You followed him for six months after his release from prison, and you told me then that he was no threat, that you didn't think he would kill again. Now, you're telling me he may be the serial killer they are looking for in St. Louis."

"Jim, all I can tell you is he did nothing suspicious during the six months I tailed him. We both thought it was senseless to continue our surveillance. Besides, it may not even be him."

"Okay, Roy. Go over it with me one more time."

"Jim, we know the ten women were killed with a knife; the same type of knife Ricky used to kill Patricia Wells and Lora Smith. We also know that Ricky lived in St. Louis during the time each of the ten murders occurred. The killer broke into the victims residence through a window, just like the Wells and Smith murders. Finally, the women murdered in St. Louis were all career women, who had been very successful; just like Patricia Wells and Lora Smith."

"What's your gut feeling Roy?"

"I hate to say this, but I think it might very well be Ricky. From what we know of him, everything fits. The good news for you is the police know nothing about him. He is not even on their list of suspects."

"How did you let this happen, Roy? You're supposed to be the best. You realize we may be responsible for the deaths of ten women. How am I going to be able to sleep at night? I need to know for sure if he is the killer. I want you to follow him day and night, until we know. Most importantly, do not let him kill again."

"Consider it done, Jim. I will let you know as soon as I know something."

As Jim ended the call, he slammed the phone on the ground.

His wife, Taylor, heard the noise and called out from the shower. "Is everything all right, Jim?"

"Yeah dear. Everything is just terrific."

Jim wished Natalie were here instead of Taylor. Now that he planned to run for the Presidency, he would be forced to tone it down with Natalie. He knew a scandal would destroy his chances and would ruin everything he had worked for.

It would almost be worth it, he thought. He found himself thinking more and more of Natalie these days. Whenever he had a bad day, like today, he would find comfort with her. She had been his life raft for the past three years. She also understood and respected the need to be discreet. Natalie never asked for commitment; she was content just being with him.

As Taylor walked out of the shower draped in a Bombay Club towel, he tried to hide his resentment toward her. He knew Taylor was necessary for him to make it to the White House. Somehow, he would have to put up with her and convey to the public the appearance of a perfect marriage.

He walked over to the mini bar and opened a miniature bottle of red wine. "Would you like some wine, sweetheart?"

"No, none for me, thanks."

He took his wine over to the window in his suite and looked out over the Atlantic Ocean. He thought once again about Darrell Rogers. The case which had started his political climb, was now his albatross. Instead of being so obsessed with obtaining a conviction, he should have investigated properly when he began having doubts about Darrell's guilt. Maybe, then they would have caught Ricky and ten murdered women would still be alive.

He drained the glass of wine and then went back to the mini bar for another.

Chapter 16

As Stacy and I were walking down to the beach for the evening reception, we saw Stan and Carol.

Stan gave Stacy a hug and told her how good she looked.

"Isn't this a fabulous place, Stacy?" he asked.

"It sure is Stan. Rob and I are really going to enjoy ourselves. Thanks so much for bringing us here."

"Rob, aren't you a little hot in that suit and tie? Why didn't you just wear a light sports coat?"

All of a sudden, I wished I had listened to Stacy. My ignorance when it came to appropriate clothing attire was astounding. Suddenly, the phrase "it is better to be overdressed than underdressed" popped into my head.

"I just wanted to impress these doctors with our professionalism, Stan. We want them to think we're in the big leagues; not a bunch of smucks."

"You're right, Rob. Tomorrow night, I think I will wear a suit and tie. You can't be too formal at this place."

"My thoughts exactly." I winked at Stacy, and she glared at me.

I had to admit that the place was beautiful, and the setting was magnificent. The club had tables set up on the beach, and each table had a lit candle in the center. The sun was setting in the background, and the ocean view was stunning. The spread of food was unbelievable. A band was playing beach music over by the pool.

I knew Stan wanted me to be social, to get to know some of the doctors. So, Stacy and I decided to sit at a table with some physicians and their spouses. We tried, as best we could, to join in on their conversation.

I quickly learned that the company at our table consisted of a neurosurgeon from Boston; a cardiac surgeon from Richmond; and an endocrinologist from Atlanta. The three physicians were accompanied by their wives, although none of the wives were doing any of the talking.

It took ten minutes before the cardiac surgeon stopped talking long enough for me to introduce Stacy and myself to the group. They were all very cordial as I shook hands with each of them, and explained what I did and why we were at the conference. Shortly after my introduction, the cardiac surgeon resumed where he had left off. It amazed me at how he held their attention as he complained over and over again how the government was screwing him on his fees.

"A physician just cannot make a decent living anymore in this country" he lamented. "The government keeps reducing our fees, and at the same time they keep adding costly regulations to our practices. As if the governments not bad enough, then we have to deal with the trial lawyers. Those scumbags are responsible for my malpractice insurance premium doubling last year."

That last comment got the other two physicians adamantly involved in the discussion. It was unanimous. Trial lawyers were the scum of the earth.

The endocrinologist then went on a tirade about how the Medicare and Medicaid programs are now denying payment for lab tests and procedures because they do not consider them medically necessary. "Just last month, we received thirty-seven denials on lab tests alone. The government is now in the business of practicing medicine," he said.

I perked up a bit. The endocrinologist had given me an opening. I was well versed on the government's new medical necessity guidelines for laboratory tests. Just as I tried to get a word in, however, the neurosurgeon interrupted and began preaching about how his practice was being hurt by the increasing number of uninsured patients he was treating.

"I just can't keep providing free care to these patients. The physicians in this country are going to starve unless the government does something to ensure we are paid for treating the uninsured. What little we make on our paying patients, the government takes half of it back in taxes."

"Yeah, if I had it to do over again, I wouldn't have gone into medicine," the endocrinologist commented. "You just can't make a decent living anymore as a physician."

Just as I started to pull my handkerchief out and wipe my eyes, the conversation changed drastically. The cardiac surgeon then forged into a discussion on travel. He began by describing the exotic places he and his wife had traveled to the past few years: Venice, Morocco, Paris, the Cayman Islands. He then described how he and his wife were becoming tired of spending so much of their time in their vacation home on Nantucket. They were considering purchasing a place in

Palm Beach, Florida. That way, they could go back and forth between Nantucket and Palm Beach on their yacht.

The practical accountant in me tried to make sense of this. The surgeon claimed he could not make a decent living; yet he owned a house in Boston, a vacation home in Nantucket, and a yacht. He is planning to purchase a house in Palm Beach. He also apparently spends a great deal of time traveling around the world. I wondered how much he made before the government started "screwing him". I also wanted to ask him how many weeks a year he worked. I almost made the suggestion that if he spent more time in his office and less time vacationing, he might make more money. Under normal circumstances, I wouldn't have been able to resist, but I knew Stan was counting on me to pick up some of these arrogant jerks as clients.

Just as I thought I could take no more, I received a reprieve. I heard a large commotion, and as I glanced over toward the pool to see what it was, I saw Senator Jim Bryant and his wife. They were followed by several aids as they made their way to the speaker's podium that had been set up for the reception.

As he was introduced, Jim Bryant received a standing ovation from the thousand or so AMA members and spouses that were present. The spokesman for the AMA introduced him as the next President of the United States.

I must admit that I was somewhat interested in what he had to say. I had a certain sense of pride knowing that a resident from my small hometown had done so well. I vividly remembered shaking his hand as a kid when he spoke at my school.

Jim Bryant had a certain aura of power about him. He conveyed self-confidence. He was very eloquent, had a good sense of humor, and a certain charisma. He had also mastered his political skills, and he certainly knew his audience. During his speech, he promised to reform Medicare, improve physician payments, secure meaningful tort reform, and eliminate the ridiculous government regulations that are so burdensome to the medical profession. With each promise, the island shook with applause. He received no fewer than ten standing ovations during his twenty-minute speech.

For such highly educated professionals, they sure are naïve, I thought. *If he would have passed around a plate, I believe everyone here would have emptied his or her pockets for his campaign fund.*

A couple of hours later, as Stacy and I made it back to our room, I finally began to relax. All I had to do now was give my two-hour presentation in the morning to the fifty physicians who had signed up to attend. Next, I had to man our exhibition booth with Stan for three hours, and then my obligations would be over. By four o'clock the next day, I would be free to enjoy this paradise. I planned on spending tomorrow evening and the following day lying on the beach, swimming in the pool, and walking around the beautiful resort.

Chapter 17

As Roy Weston finished unpacking his suitcase, he thought of the undesirable job that was ahead of him. He remembered how bored he had been eleven years ago when he had to follow Ricky around for six months. Six months of surveillance and not a bit of action. Ricky had done nothing during those six months. Roy was a man of action and became bored very easily.

Although Jim Bryant paid him very well, he no longer needed the money. He was now set for life, thanks to the Columbian job. Three years ago, he was paid one million dollars by a Columbian drug cartel for assassinating a new drug lord and his associates because they were perceived as new competition.

Roy remembered the rush he had received as he weaved in and out of danger in the Columbian jungles. That job had represented his proudest moment and his most difficult. He showed true brilliance when he planned his attack at precisely the same time the drug lord and all his associates were having a meeting at the smuggler's house. They never suspected a thing when the bomb exploded. All thirteen of them were killed at once. Less than one week after accepting the engagement, Roy had wiped out the competition.

Roy was here now only because he felt some obligation to Jim Bryant because of their past relationship. The Bryant family had been good to him and had provided work for him when he was just getting started, so he felt he owed them. Roy was always loyal to his clients; that was one reason he was so much in demand.

He also knew it was very possible that Jim Bryant would someday be President of the United States. Roy knew all of Jim's dirty secrets, and he knew Jim would be willing to do just about anything to keep him happy. He could picture himself as the director of the CIA. He often dreamed of the missions he would control. The sky would be the limit. As CIA director, Roy would make sure that America would never suffer another attack like we experienced on nine-eleven.

Despite his commitment to Jim Bryant, Roy still considered this job beneath him. Ricky Henry was small potatoes. Roy was a trained assassin of drug lords, mob bosses, dignitaries, even presidents. Ricky Henry was just a two-bit killer, if anything at all. The worst part of this job was that he had strict instructions from Jim Bryant not to kill Ricky until he had proof that Ricky was, in fact, the serial killer. Roy knew that Jim was still in denial. Jim did not want to admit to himself that ten murders had occurred that he could have prevented, had he not been so zealous to convict and execute Darrell Rogers.

The truth was that Roy suspected Ricky of the St. Louis murders all along. He hadn't dared tell Jim because he knew Jim would have him tailing Ricky again. Roy knew Ricky was clever, and would probably never be caught by the police. He really didn't see that Ricky was much of a threat to Jim. Unlike Jim Bryant, Roy wasn't bothered by the murders or the guilt associated with knowing he could have prevented them.

Although Roy preferred taking Ricky out right away, he would defer to the wishes of his employer. He would follow Ricky until he had proof he was the killer or until he caught him in action. Then he would kill him and find a new engagement more suitable to his abilities.

Roy rented a vacant apartment within a mile of Ricky's apartment complex in South St. Louis County. At five-thirty a.m., Roy broke into Ricky's car and placed a tracking device under the dashboard. He then waited in his Explorer for Ricky to leave for work. Just minutes after he saw Ricky pull out of his apartment complex, he then slipped into his apartment and placed a microscopic camera under Ricky's dining room table. The camera was positioned so that Roy would be able to see the front door to know when Ricky left or when he had company. He also placed a motion detector just above Ricky's doorframe that would trigger an alarm in Roy's apartment. Roy would know exactly when Ricky left his apartment.

While he was in Ricky's apartment, he performed a complete search of the premises, hoping to find some evidence of the murders. As expected, he turned up nothing. Ricky was not the type of serial killer to keep trophies around. *Ricky may be insane,* he thought, *but he is certainly not stupid.*

Roy left and drove back to his own apartment. He would take it easy the rest of the day, until it was time for Ricky to leave from work. At four p.m., he would be at the auto parts plant, so he could follow Ricky as he left work. He hoped Ricky would strike again soon, so that he would have sufficient proof for Jim Bryant. He was anxious to finish this job.

Chapter 18

Ricky looked down at his watch and saw that it was only three p.m. He still had another hour to go. Begrudgingly, he looked at the next work order in the pile and was instantly relieved because it was a job he could finish in less than an hour. At least he would be able to leave on time today.

Ricky knew the plant as well as anyone. He had been working here for over twelve years now. With the exception of Walt Reed, the maintenance supervisor, he had more seniority than anyone else in the maintenance department. He had never even considered leaving the plant. With his criminal conviction, he knew he would have difficulty finding another job. He was also aware that he would never be able to find a job that paid as well as this one did. Over the past twelve years, he had earned some pretty decent raises, and his salary was very good for a person without a college degree. Although money meant very little to him, it was important to have sufficient savings in the event he was forced into becoming a fugitive.

No one at the plant was aware that he had been in prison, except the plant manager and the director of personnel. He had never given anyone reason to believe he was anything but an average, hard working, normal guy. Although most of his fellow workers considered him quiet and somewhat of a loner, they all got along with him. He even took the new guys under his wing and helped them learn the ropes.

His coworkers were amazed at how strong and agile he was. Although he was of average height and had a slim build, he was extremely strong.

Walt considered him his best employee. He was intelligent, dependable, and conscientious. Several of Walt's men had problems with attendance and tardiness. Walt noticed that productivity often suffered on Mondays, since many of his workers dragged in with a hangover. Not Ricky. He was always on time, never sick, and never goofed off. He worked from the time he clocked in until the end of his shift.

Walt knew that Ricky was a little odd and never socialized with the other men after work. He had been a model employee, though, with the exception of one incident. A couple years ago, the plant hired a new female safety officer, Suzanne Hobson. Suzanne's job was to develop and implement the plant's safety policies and to make sure the plant was abiding by all State and OSHA regulations. She was also responsible for making sure employees were following procedures recommended by the plant's workers' compensation carrier. She was given complete authority to correct any practices she deemed were unsafe.

During one of her inspections, Suzanne noticed that some of the workers in the maintenance department were taking the safety guard off one of the machines while they were servicing it. She held a department meeting and notified them that they must, at all times, make sure the guard was in place while working on the equipment.

Ricky resented being told what to do by Suzanne, and he refused to comply. He informed Walt that it would slow him down, and that he was not in danger if he failed to use the safety guard.

Walt informed Ricky he had no choice, and he would follow the safety policy or be written up for insubordination. Ricky complied, but he began making derogatory remarks about Suzanne to other employees. Suzanne then began to see Ricky quite often around the plant. He seemed to be following her, and when she would look at him, he would glare at her in an intimidating manner. Suzanne became afraid of him, and she finally reported him to Walt and to the director of personnel. Ricky was then told that if he continued to talk about her or gave her any trouble, he would be terminated.

After that, Suzanne never had any additional problems with Ricky at the plant. Unfortunately though, Suzanne was employed only a short time after the incident. Less than a year after the incident with Ricky, she died of a massive cocaine overdose. The death was ruled a suicide.

Suzanne's friends, relatives, and co-workers swore she never used drugs. Her sister had spoken to her just hours before her body was found. According to her sister, she was not depressed and had, in fact, been excited about the trip to Las Vegas the two had planned for later in the month. No one understood what happened that night. No one, that is, except Ricky.

Ricky was relieved when it was finally four o'clock and his shift ended. He had big plans for this evening, and he was anxious to get started. As usual, on the day of a planned attack he had been excited and had trouble concentrating on his work.

He walked to the time clock and swiped his badge, officially ending his workday. He then opened the refrigerator in the break room, grabbed his lunch sack, and headed through the back door to the employee parking lot. As he climbed into his black, Jeep Cherokee, he glanced in his rear view mirror and noticed a red Explorer parked in the back row of the parking lot. It looked like the same Explorer he saw last night at the grocery store and the night before at the gas station. Although he wasn't completely sure at the time, he felt then that he was being followed.

He swung his SUV around to the back of the parking lot and made a mental note of the license number on the Explorer. It matched the number on the Explorer he saw at the grocery store. Now, he knew for sure he was being followed. He then slowly drove past the vehicle to get a look at the passenger. As he drove past, the man slowly sank down in the driver's side seat in an attempt to keep Ricky from seeing him. He was too late, and Ricky was able to catch a quick glimpse of him, noting the man appeared to be middle-aged and was wearing sunglasses and a Cardinals baseball cap.

The first thought that crossed Ricky's mind was that the police had found something, and they now considered him a suspect in the murders. He was convinced the man in the Explorer was an undercover detective. Just as he began to think that his whole plan was in jeopardy, he realized that if the police had real evidence he would already have been arrested; not followed. The police must know something, though, or he wouldn't be under suspicion.

Pulling out of the parking lot, Ricky tried to think of something he might have left behind after the murders that could possibly have led the police to him. He could think of nothing. He had been so careful; so meticulous. Where had he made a mistake?

He thought of his plans for Melissa Grogan tonight. Surely, he could ditch the detective and keep his date with Melissa. Besides, he wasn't sure he could wait even if he wanted. The desire was so strong he could no longer put it off. For the past three nights, he had been having those awful dreams; the cold, night sweats.

His father was in his dreams again; asking for revenge. He could not let him down. For his sake, he had to punish them, and he had to do it soon. It had to be tonight. He would just have to find a way to lose the detective.

He knew that it was extremely risky now to remain in St Louis much longer. Leaving St. Louis, without first having his rendezvous with Regina Phillips, was out of the question, however. He would just have to expedite his plans. He became excited, as he now realized that Regina would have to be next, after Melissa Grogan. The moment he had waited for so long would be here very soon.

Chapter 19

Melissa Grogan slammed on her brakes as a green, Ford Taurus cut in the lane directly in front of her. Melissa pounded on her horn, pulled up in the lane beside the poor guy and gave him the finger. She then floored the accelerator to eighty- five for two additional miles before taking the downtown exit. As she swerved in and out of traffic on Tenth Street, narrowly missing two pedestrians, she herself received the bird several times. She didn't care. She was already extremely late, and she didn't feel like getting chewed on again by the station manager.

As Melissa sped up the ramp in the parking garage, she narrowly missed hitting a car exiting the ramp onto the blue level. She finally made it to her destined spot, on the garage's orange level. She then wheeled her BMW into a "no parking" zone next to the entrance to the walkway, leading to the station. As she slammed her car door shut and sprinted through the door, she heard someone call her name.

The parking attendant had reluctantly followed her into the building in a futile attempt to have her move her car. "Miss Grogan, you know you can't park there. That spot is reserved for emergency vehicles only."

"Go screw yourself," replied Melissa. "Get a real job!"

The attendant knew better than to press the issue. He had been chewed out numerous times by Miss Grogan. He knew when to leave well enough alone. "This job ain't worth it," he muttered.

Melissa stormed into the station like a hurricane, yelling for makeup and her script.

Neil Johnson, the station manager, shook his head as he heard Melissa stomp down the hallway. He would give anything if he could figure out a way to get rid of her. She was more trouble than all the other newscasters combined. He knew the prima donnas were all high maintenance, but she was in a league of her own.

The trouble was that ever since Melissa became the anchorwoman of the six and ten o'clock news, the station had dominated the ratings. For some unknown reason, St. Louisans loved her. Neil knew that, no matter how much trouble she caused, the owners of the station would never let him fire her. They were more likely to get rid of him than her. Like it or not, she was making money for the station, so she was untouchable. So, day in and day out, he had to put up with her relentless demands and tirades. He was hopeful that, due to her enormous popularity, she would eventually be recruited to a larger market, such as New York or Chicago, or to a national network like CBS. Anytime Neil interacted with the big boys, he was sure to mention how good Melissa was, just hoping they took the bait. Unfortunately for Neil Johnson, it had yet to happen, and he was stuck with her. Neil dreaded facing her now, but he knew it was part of the job.

"You're late again Melissa. There is no way you have time to properly prepare the questions you're going to ask the Congressman during the live interview. Or did you forget that we have the interview set for tonight?"

"Neil, when are you ever going to stop worrying about me? Don't you know by now that this station would be nothing without me. Unlike some of the other idiots you have on the air here, I don't need an hour to prepare for a simple interview. One of these days, I'm finally going to leave this hick station and work for a real news news organization."

Not soon enough for me, thought Neil.

Neil tried his best to control his temper, but with each passing day it became more difficult. Melissa Grogan made Martha Stewart look like a nun. He remembered when Melissa first approached him for a job. At that time she was a nobody, just trying to land a spot as an investigative reporter, practically begging for a job. She was humble and appreciative in her first couple of years with the station. That was then and this is now. Things sure changed.

Her big break came when she taped an investigative series on city government. As part of her investigation, she uncovered the corruption that existed at that time at city hall. Melissa learned that the mayor and city comptroller were receiving kickbacks from contractors in exchange for being awarded lucrative city building projects. As a result of Melissa's reporting, the mayor, comptroller, and two aldermen received prison sentences, and several other key city employees were terminated. Melissa became an instant celebrity in St. Louis. In addition to being given the news anchor position, the station rewarded her by selecting her to host a one-hour talk show each Thursday night.

As her popularity grew, so did her ego and her demands. After she became the lead news anchor, she suddenly realized her husband wasn't up to her standards. He wasn't quite on her level, intellectually or socially. She divorced him and began dating one of the star players of the St. Louis Blues. She also gave her husband full custody of their four year-old son. She had no time to raise a kid; she needed to devote her full attention to advancing her career.

The weekly, live talk show had provided Melissa a forum in which to criticize the St. Louis Police Department for the way they had handled the investigation of the serial killings. She had been relentless in her attack, and the station had received numerous complaints about her from city hall.

Melissa was barking off her final orders to the stressed out staff when the producer started counting down the final seconds to the broadcast. As he counted down to five, Melissa's scowl began fading. When he reached one and the green light went on the camera indicating they were on the air, Melissa was all smiles. She was gracious as she welcomed the viewers and thanked them for tuning in to Channel 9. She was the ultimate professional as she highlighted the top stories of the day. Of course, the lead story was the status of the police investigation of the serial killer.

To her viewers, she was a beautiful, intelligent, caring news reporter. To many, she was like a trusted member of the family. She was in their living rooms each night at six o'clock and again at ten o'clock, informing them of what has occurred in their hometown.

After delivering the ten o'clock news and insulting most of the news staff, Melissa finally prepared to leave for the evening. She slid into her BMW and pulled out of the parking garage at exactly eleven-thirty.

Melissa lived in Webster Groves, one of St. Louis' oldest suburbs. Her neighborhood consisted of beautiful large, restored homes built a century ago. The area was well maintained, with beautiful trees, shrubs, and flowers.

As she pulled into her garage, she was still fuming over her recent argument with Neil Johnson. Just before she left the station, Neil informed her that she had to tone down the criticism on her talk show of St. Louis Police Chief, Bob Recker. The political brass at city hall could make it very difficult for the station by refusing interviews and access to city officials. Melissa hated office politics. She felt the public needed to hear the truth, no matter how unpopular it was. To her, the fact that the police had no leads after ten murders was inexcusable. Someone should be held accountable.

The more she thought of Neil Johnson, the angrier she became. She knew the station had never fully appreciated what she had done for them. Without her, they would still be lagging at number three in the local ratings.

I think its time to put out some feelers, she thought. After all, her popularity was at an all time high. It would be a perfect time to make a move. She had always dreamed of living in New York; Boston wouldn't be bad either. She preferred the east coast because the exposure was greater, and she would have a better chance of being noticed by one of the major networks.

Melissa opened the back door leading from the garage into her kitchen. She set her purse on the kitchen table. She immediately went to the refrigerator, opened a bottle of Amstel Light, and walked to the bathroom to run the bath water. A nice long bubble bath would feel good and would release some of the tension.

She undressed, but before she stepped into the bathtub, she walked through the house making sure all her doors and windows were locked. Like everyone else in St. Louis, she was terrified of the serial killer. She knew it was irrational; with over two and a half million people living in the St. Louis area, the chances of her being a victim were extremely slim. Nevertheless, she was not going to take any chances. Besides, she fit the profile of the other victims. Like all the previous victims, she was a highly successful, professional woman; the exact type the killer seemed to find attractive.

After satisfying herself that the house was secure, she sank into the hot bath and took a long swig of the beer. Within minutes, she began feeling better. Why shouldn't she feel good? She was only thirty-two, and already she was the top news anchor in the nation's eighteenth largest television market. She was also dating Bart Stevens, the NHLs second leading goal scorer. She knew there were even better things ahead in her future.

She smiled as she thought of Bart. Their relationship had begun heating up recently. She liked the thought of someday being married to a sports superstar. The Blues season had just ended. Once again, a good season ended on a sour note as they were bumped early in the playoffs. She didn't mind because that meant Bart would have more time to spend with her.

She climbed out of the tub and decided to give Bart a call. She knew he would still be up because his hockey schedule had him used to going to bed late at night.

With a towel draped around her, Melissa walked into the kitchen and grabbed the cordless phone. As she punched in the numbers, she realized there was no dial tone. She then tried the phone in the living room. It too, was not working. There must be a problem with the phone lines. Angrily, she threw the phone to the carpet. She made a mental note to contact the regional manager of Southwestern Bell in the morning to give him a piece of her mind. Maybe she would even do a segment on her talk show about the declining quality of services provided by telephone and utility monopolies. She had no use for incompetence.

She took a deep breath and came to the conclusion that she could officially call this a rotten day. Nothing seemed to have gone right since she woke up this morning. She decided she would go to bed. Tomorrow would be better.

She walked into her bedroom to put on a nightshirt. As she reached into her dresser drawers, the lights suddenly went out. The house became pitch black. Panic swept over her. Her first thoughts were of the killer. Could he be in her house? Frantically, she tried to rationalize the situation. She made an effort to convince herself that an accident in the neighborhood probably had knocked out the phone and utility lines.

With her legs feeling wobbly, she slowly began walking toward the kitchen, finding her way by feeling the walls. After what seemed like an eternity, she finally made it to the refrigerator. She took two steps to the right of the refrigerator, where she knew the flashlight should be. She knelt down and was relieved when she felt the flashlight. She pulled it from the electrical outlet, turned it, on and immediately scanned the kitchen and living room. She saw no one. Slowly and carefully, she shined the flashlight into the family room and dining room. Still nothing.

Just as she began to relax and breath easier, a phone rang. She shrieked in fear. Then she realized it was just her cell phone. With the flashlight guiding the way, she walked over to her purse on the kitchen table and grabbed the phone.

"Hello."

The voice on the other end replied in a soft, hoarse whisper. "I enjoyed your coverage of me tonight. I happen to be one of your biggest fans. You look better in person than you do on the air; especially wearing that purple towel."

"He's in the house!" Melissa screamed.

Melissa threw the cell phone to the floor, but she couldn't move. She was paralyzed; her legs felt like rubber. Her whole body was shaking in terror.

Think, she thought. *Don't panic.*

She began to regain her faculties. She first turned off the flashlight, so he couldn't see her. *Where is he?* she thought.

If she could just get to a door or window, she could get out and run to the neighbors. She was in the kitchen, and the closest door was the one leading to the garage. If she could just get to the garage, she could push the garage door opener and run outside to the safety of her neighbors.

Melissa slowly took two steps, then stopped to listen. There was no sound. As she felt the hutch with her hands, she knew she was next to the door leading into the garage. Quickly, she flung open the door and ran into the garage. She felt for the button to open the garage door. After feeling around the wall for a few seconds, she found it and pushed. The garage door did not open. She pushed the button again. Nothing.

She sank to the floor as she realized the automatic garage doors would not work with the electricity shut off. Melissa knew she could not open the garage manually. She wanted to cry, to scream, but she knew she couldn't.

The resolve that made her so successful as a reporter started to kick in. *I'm not going down without a fight*, she vowed. Quietly, she opened the door leading back into the kitchen. She decided to turn on her flashlight and make a run for the front door.

She flicked on the flashlight, and as she directed the beam to the front door, she immediately sprinted across the kitchen, through the living room, towards the door. Just before she reached for the doorknob, she was grabbed from behind and knocked to the floor. The flashlight fell from her hands and, once again, she was in complete darkness. Despite her efforts to kick and claw, she could not prevent her attacker from lifting her off the ground. He was strong, and no matter how hard she fought, she could not shake free from his grasp.

As she was thrown onto her bed, Melissa swung and kicked furiously, successfully landing two blows to the attacker's face. He was unfazed, however. Despite her fighting, he managed to tie her to the bed, binding her hands and feet to the bed posts with duct tape. She was now powerless. There was nothing she could do. Sweat began to pour out of her body as she began thinking of what lay ahead for her. After covering the murders as a reporter, she was aware of the horrible deaths the other victims suffered.

He left the room for the breaker box to restore electricity to the house. When he returned to the bedroom, all the lights were now on. He walked up to Melissa and removed her towel, exposing her body. For the first time, Melissa then saw the man who had been the subject of her news reports nearly every night the past few years. She immediately noticed a large scar on the side of his neck, and another smaller scar above his nose. She also noticed his eyes. They appeared cold and lifeless.

He stood over her, looking down at her body, and spoke for the first time. "I've been waiting a long time for this, Melissa. You looked so powerful and important on TV. Somehow, you don't look so powerful now. You see, Melissa, you and women like you, think you're too good for people like me. You think you can control everything, make your own rules, and stomp on anyone who gets in your way. You're used to having your own way, always getting what you want. Laws don't apply to you; you just buy your way out of trouble. I have been put on this earth to enact justice. I am here to protect the poor, common man from people like you."

"Melissa, I am the one with the real power. I decide who lives and who dies. I'll let you in on a little secret. The ten murders you have been reporting are just the tip of the iceberg. Do you remember the five unsolved murders that occurred a few years ago in Southern Illinois? I believe you even mentioned them recently during your newscast. I happen to be intimately familiar with the details. You may also be interested to know that I first started my mission over twenty-five years ago in Sikeston. It's too bad you won't be able to report this new information. That would make quite a story, wouldn't it? Well, unfortunately, tomorrow night you won't be delivering the top story, you will be the top story."

The despair Melissa had been feeling now turned to anger. She was seething with hatred. "You're just a loser, who couldn't make it in the real world, so you have to blame others for your failure. You're pathetic. You're not man enough to date women, so you have to kill them."

He moved to the front of the bed, and bent down near Melissa's face. He felt her hair and softly touched her cheeks. Melissa then spit in his face.

He responded by quickly turning around and grabbing the knife. Melissa knew it was over. She prayed it would be quick and painless. As she closed her eyes for the inevitable, she suddenly heard a deafening, crashing sound. She realized that someone had broken through the window in the living room.

As she opened her eyes to see the person she hoped could save her, she instead saw the steel blade of the knife just before it touched her neck. She then felt nothing but the wetness of her blood dripping down her neck onto her chest. Just before she lost consciousness, she saw the killer leaving though her bedroom window.

Seconds later, Roy Weston appeared in her bedroom, but Melissa never saw him.

Chapter 20

Roy Weston was upset with himself for allowing Ricky to spot him in the parking lot at the auto parts plant. It was a mistake that only an amateur would make. He should have known better. He had been careless. Maybe, he was taking this job a little too lightly. Anyway, his mistake had been costly, and now Ricky knew he was being followed. Ricky would now be extra careful, making his job that much more difficult.

This job was turning out to be much harder than he expected. Ricky was turning out to be a major pain. It would be so much easier if he could just take him out now. But instead, Jim Bryant had to be certain that Ricky was the killer before he would allow him to do his job. In his opinion, this was a big waste of time. He didn't understand why he couldn't kill Ricky now and then wait to see if the killings suddenly stopped. That would be the easy way.

The only way to prove Ricky was the killer now was to catch him in the act. At the same time, he had to somehow prevent Ricky from actually committing the murder because Jim Bryant did not want any more victims. He would have to stop Ricky, kill him, and then dispose of his body and any evidence that could tie him to the serial killings.

To Roy, all this concern was unnecessary. In his line of work, death was usually the end product of a job well done. He had seen hundreds of fellow comrades killed in the jungles of Vietnam. He had participated with other soldiers in wiping out an entire North Vietnamese squad. He had lived the mafia code, in which human life had little value. Compared to what he had seen during his lifetime, these ten murders were nothing. He didn't understand why Jim Bryant was making such a big deal about saving the eleventh victim. He was especially baffled by Jim's insistence on making sure Ricky was the one, before taking him out. It angered Roy that Jim Bryant was such a wuss. *Maybe he isn't fit to be president after all*, he grumbled.

As Ricky pulled out of his employer's parking lot, Roy followed, making sure he went straight home. Once he saw Ricky enter his apartment, he then went back to his own apartment. At first, he thought it would be another uneventful evening. Realizing he was now under suspicion, Roy did not think Ricky would attack again for some time. He was surprised when he was awakened at eleven fifteen that night by the alarm. Ricky had left his apartment.

Roy immediately ran to his car and, using the tracking device, soon caught up to Ricky. He kept a safe distance behind, so that Ricky would not spot him again. In the event he lost him, he was protected because the tracking device would work as long as he was within a five-mile range. Even if he lost sight, he would still know Ricky's general location.

Ricky exited off Interstate 55 and headed north on Interstate 270 for eight miles, and took the east exit on Interstate 44. As Roy made the turn onto the Interstate 44 exit, he encountered an unexpected problem. A car, several hundred yards in front of him, switched lanes directly in front of an eighteen-wheeler. The car forced the driver of the massive truck to slam on his brakes, making a hideous screech that could be heard for miles. In an attempt to avoid the car, the trucker also turned sharply to his left, toward the inside lane. The trucker lost control and the truck flipped, effectively blocking all four lanes. The two cars immediately behind the trucker could not stop in time and rammed into the truck.

Roy slammed his brakes, effectively managing to keep from hitting the car in front of him. As his car came to a sudden stop, he surveyed the scene in front of him. It was total chaos. The interstate was completely blocked, and people were scrambling out of their cars to check on the trucker and the passengers in the other two wrecked cars. Ricky had been ahead of the accident and was now out of sight. Roy checked his equipment and saw that Ricky was now at least two miles ahead.

Roy was furious. He attempted to cut through the median to get around the accident, but the two cars in front of him effectively blocked him. He was still several feet back on the onramp, with no way to access the median.

He stormed out of his car, opened the door of the empty car in front of him, found the keys still in the ignition, and drove it out of his way. Fortunately for the driver, he was a good Samaritan and had vacated his car to help the victims of the accident.

The driver in the other vehicle was not so lucky. Roy walked up to the second vehicle in his way, a Lincoln Navigator. Unfortunately for the driver, he was still sitting in the driver's seat. He didn't take too kindly to being ordered to move his SUV. When he refused, Roy grabbed him by the collar, pulled him out of the vehicle, and slammed his face against the hard pavement. Roy then climbed in, put the vehicle in reverse, and rammed it into the concrete barrier that separated the interstate from the adjoining neighborhood. The rear of the Lincoln

Navigator was smashed. Not that the poor owner would notice. He was too busy picking up fallen teeth and trying to stop the blood that was pouring profusely from his mouth.

With his path now cleared, Roy drove along the median, around the chaos, and was soon back on the interstate in pursuit of Ricky. As he checked the tracking device, he realized that Ricky was now out of range. He had lost him.

This was not turning out to be one of his better days. First, he had allowed Ricky to spot him. Now, he had managed to lose him on a routine tailing. Fairly certain that at this late hour, Ricky was out for a kill, Roy knew he had to find him soon. He did not want to explain to Senator Bryant how he had allowed Ricky to kill yet another victim.

Roy cursed himself as he came to the realization that he may not find Ricky in time to prevent another murder. He wasn't particularly concerned about the victim, but he was worried about Jim Bryant and the impact this botched job would have on his reputation. The esteemed reputation he held among the ranks of corrupt politicians, the criminal underworld, and third world dictators was now in jeopardy. He had to find Ricky soon.

Roy had no idea if Ricky had stayed on the interstate all the way to downtown, or if he had taken one of the exits leading to one of St. Louis' many suburbs. Thinking of Ricky's prior patterns, he decided he would probably head for the suburbs. His best bet was to take each exit and drive along the major thoroughfares until he received a signal on his equipment.

The first exit was Lindbergh Boulevard. He drove several miles in each direction from the interstate. No signal. He then drove back to the interstate and took the next exit. Same result. Finally, after exiting onto Elm Street and driving north, he hit pay dirt. Ricky was in Webster

Groves. Roy now knew his general location. Now, all he had to do was find him before it was too late.

The detector was very accurate and would direct him to within one hundred yards of Ricky. Roy drove to the general location indicated by the equipment. Then he drove around the neighborhood until he spotted a black Jeep Cherokee, parked on the street. The driver's license matched. He had found Ricky, now all he had to do was find the right house.

With his 38 Special in hand, Roy jumped out of his Explorer and eased up to the house in front of Ricky's truck. It was unlikely that Ricky would park directly in front of his victim's house, but he had to be sure. Several lights were still on in the house. As he peaked in each of the windows, he noticed nothing that looked suspicious. He then went to the next house.

With each house, Roy became angrier. Where was he? He had now covered a two square block area and had seen no evidence of Ricky. Two hours had now passed since he lost Ricky at the accident. He was beginning to think it was too late to save the victim. He decided to check a couple more houses and if he was unsuccessful, he would give up. Then he would go back to his vehicle and wait for Ricky. He would follow Ricky home, kill him, and dispose of his body where no one would ever find it. At least the night wouldn't be a total failure. He would have definitive proof for Jim Bryant that Ricky was the killer, and he would have eliminated him once and for all. Ricky would no longer pose a threat to Jim Bryant.. Surely, Jim wouldn't be too upset about this last victim.

As he crept along the front of a white ranch, he tripped over a barberry bush, causing sharp thorns to pierce the skin on his arms. He swore to himself that this would be the last house. He peered in the front window and saw nothing. As he walked to the back of the house, he noticed a bedroom light still on.

The bedroom window was covered with mini-blinds, so it was difficult to see in. He noticed a slight crack in the blinds towards the bottom of the window. He crouched down and peered through the crack. He saw a bed, then as his eyes scanned toward the end of the bed, he saw what looked like duct tape over a foot. He immediately ran to the next window and looked in. This room was dark, but he could see through it into a lit hallway. He saw what appeared to be a man walking from the hallway toward the lighted bedroom. It had to be Ricky.

Roy ran to the back, then to the front of the house, trying both doors. They were locked and dead bolted. Knowing he didn't have much time, he kicked in the front window, and ran immediately to the bedroom.

He saw the woman but didn't see Ricky. Ricky had already made it out through the bedroom window.

Roy immediately saw the blood gushing down her neck and knew he had been just a few seconds too late. He climbed out the window and ran as hard as he could back to Ricky's SUV. By the time he rounded the corner to the street where the truck was parked, he saw Ricky drive away.

Chapter 21

The frantic nine one-one call came in at five minutes after two. The caller gave her address and pleaded with the dispatcher to hurry because her neighbor's house had been broken into, and the intruder had just left through the bedroom window. "I'm afraid my neighbor may have been attacked!" she screamed.

The patrol car and ambulance arrived at exactly the same time, just three and one-half minutes after the call. Jerry Brown was the first officer to enter the bedroom, and he was horrified at what he saw. He knew immediately it was the serial killer. Like all the others, the woman was taped to the bed, with her throat slashed. The officer noticed that the victim looked familiar. Suddenly, it registered.

"Get in here, Stan! It's Melissa Grogan from the news. Get those paramedics in here, now!"

The paramedics ran into the room and felt the body to see if there was a pulse. "We have a live one here! We have a faint pulse, but she has lost a lot of blood. She is not breathing. We have to intubate her."

Within seconds, the proficient paramedics had the ET tube down her throat and into her trachea. The endo-tracheal tube was connected to an ambubag, and one of the paramedics was squeezing the bag to supply air to her lungs. They placed her on a stretcher, and within ten minutes were pulling into the emergency room at St. John's hospital.

Meanwhile, a massive search was underway at the crime scene. No fewer than six police cars were now parked in front of the house, and the officers spanned out over the neighborhood hoping that the killer was still in the area. After a thirty-minute search, they knew they had lost him once again.

When the dispatcher relayed the news that the victim was still alive, St. Louis police chief Bob Recker was immediately called at home. Within thirty minutes of the phone call, Chief Recker was sitting in the surgery waiting area, hoping that Melissa survived the emergency surgery.

Three hours later, Melissa regained consciousness. Her eyes were very heavy and groggy, and she had no idea where she was. The first thing she noticed was the discomfort she felt from the various tubes that seemed to be stuck in every orifice of her body. She wanted to immediately pull out the NG tube that was taped to her nose, with one end extending down into her stomach and the other attached to a wall suction unit.. She tried to reach the tube, but she couldn't because her wrists were restrained to the side of the bed.

She also felt the discomfort of the ET tube that was placed down her throat, connecting her to the ventilator that was whirring in the background.

"Where was she? Why couldn't she move?"

As she began to regain her senses, she saw a nurse hover over her, adjusting her IV lines. The nurse looked at her, noticed her eyes were opened, and smiled. "Hi, Melissa, you are a real fighter."

Melissa tried to speak, but found it impossible with the tube stuck down her throat.

The nurse then went outside the room, and she and a man began whispering. The nurse came back and removed the restraints from Melissa's wrists. The man, who had been talking with the nurse, then came over to Melissa's side.

Chief Recker looked down at Melissa, and thought of how ironic the situation was. Here lie his biggest critic, a victim of the monster he had been unable to stop. She epitomized his failure.

"Melissa, this is Chief Recker."

Melissa looked at the man and recognized him immediately. She wondered why the police chief was here.

Suddenly, it started to come back to her. She began to remember the terror. Her eyes rolled in the back of her head, and she began shaking uncontrollably as she relived the attack. She tried desperately to pull herself out of the bed.

The nurse immediately injected Valium into the IV line to sedate her. Within seconds, the Valium began to kick in, and Melissa began to relax.

"Melissa, this is very important. You can help us catch this monster. You are the only person alive who can identify him. We are going to need you write down a description. Please think of anything you can remember about him."

Chief Recker handed her a pen and notepad, and Melissa slowly wrote down three words: "scar on neck."

"That's good, Melissa. What else can you remember about him?"

Melissa tried to write something else, but she was fighting the effects of the drug, and her eyes were becoming heavy.

Just as the Chief began to ask Melissa questions about the killer's height and hair color, she closed her eyes and dozed off. The doctor then came into the room and forced Chief Recker to leave, saying that Melissa needed her rest.

"Is she going to make it, Doctor?"

"It's too early to tell, Chief. She is sure one tough lady, though. If anyone can pull through this, my bet would be on her."

As Chief Recker left the hospital, he felt that for the first time since this nightmare began, he finally had a real clue.

Chapter 22

May 14, 2003

    Senator Jim Bryant stared in disbelief as he watched the Fox News Channel. The situation was spinning out of control right in front of his eyes. He watched as Britt Hume described the latest attack in St. Louis: victim number eleven. The story was capturing a great deal of national attention because the victim was a very popular news anchorwoman. Jim almost fell out of his chair when the station switched to a news conference, and the St. Louis police chief announced that the latest victim had survived the attack and was still alive. Jim started shaking when the chief stated that the killer had a large scar on his neck. The chief went on to say that they hoped to have a better description from the victim later in the day

    With shaking hands, the senator poured himself another shot of brandy. The liquor was not helping. He could not stop shaking, and he was sweating profusely. For the first time in his life, he felt he was not in control. His dream was slipping away.

Late last night he had been awakened by a phone call from Roy Weston. Jim had been furious when Roy explained to him that Ricky had killed another victim. That was bad enough, but then Roy informed him that Ricky was still alive and had gotten away. Now, he was hearing on national news that the victim was alive and had provided a description of the killer.

Jim poured himself another drink, and punched in Roy's cell phone number. He wanted to scream at Roy, to let him know how incompetent he was. The truth was, however, that he was afraid of him. He was afraid to push him too far. Killing came as easy for Roy as swatting flies did for most people. Jim certainly didn't want to make him too angry. Unfortunately, he still needed Roy to help him get out of this mess.

"Roy, are you watching the news?"

Roy was agitated as he thought of the great senator sitting in his fancy mansion, wasting his time. "No, Senator. I don't have the luxury of watching television. I'm just a little busy. In case you forgot, I'm trying to locate Ricky."

"Well, Roy, the description of the victim you gave me last night was just a little off."

"Oh, how's that, Senator?"

"THE VICTIM ISN'T DEAD, ROY! SHE IS ALIVE AND SHE HAS DESCRIBED RICKY!"

"Say that again."

"Melissa Grogan is still alive, and she has provided a description of Ricky to the police. She identified the scar on Ricky's neck. Roy, I don't care how you do it, but you have to get rid of her today. You also need to eliminate Ricky before he becomes a suspect. Do you understand? Am I making myself clear?"

"Well I'll be damned. We have quite a situation, don't we Senator? I'll take care of it, don't you worry."

Jim slammed the phone down and wondered how he had allowed this situation to get so out of control. He reflected on the case, twenty-four years ago, that started this avalanche of events. He recalled the one mistake he made at the time; how he had convinced himself to proceed even though he had doubts about Mrs. Hammond's testimony. At the time, it seemed like no big deal. That one small mistake, however, had indirectly resulted in so many deaths. It had forced him to commit murder, and to jump into bed with a thug like Roy Weston.

Jim knew it was a waste of time to dwell on past mistakes, though. It was now time for damage control. It was still possible for him to be President if he could stop the damage now. He knew he must get rid of Melissa Grogan before she could provide additional information. She was the only witness linking Ricky to the murders. Reluctantly, he had been forced to give Roy the order to kill her. The killing needed to take place immediately.

Jim now knew for sure that Ricky was responsible for at least ten murders, plus the attack on Melissa Grogan. Was that all? There was no telling how many other murders that psychopath had committed that the authorities did not know about.

Now that the police had a description, it was very possible that Ricky could become a suspect. Ricky would have to be disposed of before that happened. With Melissa and Ricky out of the picture, there would be no way to link Ricky to the crimes. There would also be no reason for the police to conduct an extensive background check on Ricky, and therefore, they would never associate him with the murder of Lora Smith.

The problem was that Ricky could not be located. He did not return to his apartment last night after the attack. Roy had assured

Jim that he would find Ricky before the police did. Once again, Jim found himself relying on Roy Weston. Somehow, he didn't feel quite as confident in Roy's abilities as he had previously. Jim never liked Roy; he saw him as nothing more than a cold-blooded killer, but he always viewed him as being the best in the business. Now, he wasn't so sure.

Chapter 23

Key Largo, Florida

    I glanced at my watch and was glad I only had thirty minutes left to go. As I looked out at the thirty or so physicians attending the meeting, I swore to myself that I would never again speak before a group of doctors.

    The agenda for the presentation included three topics: legal issues involving healthcare fraud and abuse; new government patient privacy regulations; and changes to the Medicare physician fee schedule. I was now two and one-half hours into my presentation and I had yet to complete all the points on the first topic.

    There were three physicians in attendance that felt the need to respond to each point I made during the presentation. Each time I made a point, at least one of the three (usually all three) felt the need to expand on the point, disagree with it, or bring up another issue that may or may not be related to the point I was attempting to make. All three seemed to take particular exception to my interpretation of the anti-kickback and Stark laws. These laws impose restrictions on payments made by hospitals to physicians.

I have never understood why some people always feel the need to impress others with their knowledge (or lack of knowledge) of the subject matter. There was certainly no shortage of egos in the conference room.

Since I had only thirty minutes to go, I made the decision to jump ahead to the one issue I felt the group would be most interested in. I decided to skip the rest of the legal discussion and the privacy regulations, and end the day talking about ways to maximize reimbursement to offset the reductions in the Medicare fee schedule. As I suspected, this seemed to garner some interest.

For the first time all day, pens and notepads appeared on the tables and doctors began taking notes. I had struck gold. As I expected, my audience was genuinely interested in ways to make more money.

Once again, I was superceded by one of my three friends. The most vocal of the three was a bald-headed and seriously overweight cardiologist. Just as I was describing the correlation between written documentation and reimbursement, the doctor interrupted me. He gave me a condescending look that indicated that I wasn't fit to serve him his coffee, much less to have the gall to tell him how he should improve his practice.

In an eloquent manner, he informed the group that documenting in patient charts was nothing more than a bunch of nonsense required by bureaucrats and accountants as a way to justify their existence. "No one ever looks at our documentation, anyway," he stated. He then described how doctors should make up for the loss in revenues by demanding more from the hospitals. "After all", he said, "we control whether or not they have any patients."

He then went on to explain how he had convinced his hospital to begin paying him to be the medical director of the hospital's cardiology department. He explained that he avoided violating the anti-kickback and Stark laws by having a management contract with the hospital.

As he spoke, I could feel the energy building in the room. Ears began to perk up. The yawning stopped. Many in the audience were already figuring how much they would demand from their hospitals. They were dreaming of newer cars, boats, and larger houses.

To the chagrin of my portly friend, one doctor had the audacity to ask me what I thought about the concept of a management contract to get around the kickback and Stark laws. I explained that it was fine as long as the precise duties were defined in the contract, and the payment to the doctor was based on the fair market value of the services provided to the hospital. I also explained that the hospital should perform an annual evaluation of the physician's performance in carrying out these duties. The physician or hospital should also maintain a log of hours worked to support the compensation.

"Hogwash!" yelled the Cardiologist. "You're not saying that we actually have to work for the hospital to earn these fees, are you?"

"Of course, I am," I replied.

"That's ridiculous. As long as the payment is coming from the hospital and not the government, they don't care. Besides, the government has cut our fees so much we have to find some way to make up for these lost revenues."

By now, I was biting my tongue to be civil to this pompous prick. When I suggested that he make up for the lost revenue by working harder and seeing more patients, he turned bright red.

I realized that the meeting would continue to disintegrate, so I decided to end it. I politely thanked the doctors for attending. Just as I began packing up my materials, I remembered the instructions from Stan. I knew I'd be in hot water if I didn't make his sales pitch. Reluctantly, I passed out my business cards and asked everyone to contact me if they ever needed consulting services in the areas discussed during the meeting. I skipped right past the cardiologist when I passed out the cards.

Two physicians came up to me after the meeting and asked a few questions regarding the fraud and abuse regulations. They were genuinely concerned with certain transactions they were considering. After talking with them for ten minutes or so, I felt much better about the meeting. At least it wasn't a total waste.

I was relieved when I was finally able to leave the conference room. Carrying the laptop and projector, I walked along the path, through the various flower gardens, back to my room.

For the first time during the trip, I was totally relaxed. With a pina colada in one hand and the latest John Grisham book in the other, I was in heaven. It was a few minutes after four, and I had fulfilled my commitments. I had survived the disastrous speaking engagement that morning, and I had endured three long, boring hours manning the firm's table in the exhibition hall. Due to the fact that our giveaways were not as lavish as most of the other vendors, we had very few doctors stop by our booth.

Stan would not admit that he had made a mistake in selecting a box of golf balls as an enticement for doctors to visit our booth. The CPA firm across the hall from us was giving away leather briefcases filled with boxes of Godiva chocolates and a bottle of wine. Their booth had doctors lined up ten deep. An architectural firm, specializing in designing physician office buildings, was giving away certificates for four hours of deep-sea fishing. They, too, had a steady stream of doctors interested in their services (although I doubt very seriously many of the doctors were in the process of building new office buildings). Meanwhile, due to the inadequacy of our giveaways, we had only seven visitors during the three hours we sat at the booth.

Stan was so upset with the lack of interest in our firm that he decided to go back to his room to sulk. Despite Carol's objection, he decided to fly home first thing in the morning, a day earlier than he had originally planned.

I, on the other hand, was not about to leave early. This was one of the few times that Stacy and I had a chance to be by ourselves without the kids. Besides, I figured there wouldn't be very many times during our lives that we would be able to stay in a private resort in the Florida Keys. We might as well take advantage of it.

Our normal family vacations centered around a beach, usually Myrtle Beach, Virginia Beach, or Gulf Shores. With the sugar white sand, hundreds of palm trees, lagoon, and hammocks, this place was different than the beaches we were used to. This place compared quite favorably to the beaches in the Caribbean.

The one thing that stood out to me was the people lying around the beach and the pool. They were mostly women. I guess the men were busy playing golf or deep-sea fishing. Nearly all the women were extremely attractive and physically fit. The setting could have passed for a Sports Illustrated calendar shoot.

Most of the men I remembered seeing around the resort were much older than these women appeared to be. Also, the men, as a whole, did not strike me as being particularly fit. Most of the men appeared to be in worse shape than I was. Considering my current condition, that is pretty pitiful. I wandered how many of these women had married for money. I also wondered which of these women was married to my friend, the overweight cardiologist.

Stacy seemed to be enjoying herself swimming laps in the Olympic-sized pool. Unlike me, she was into exercise. She swam up to the edge of the pool, near my lounge chair. "How about getting me another margarita?" she requested.

I slowly made my way over to the tiki bar, where all of the chairs but one were occupied. I pulled out the last chair and sat down. A Jamaican bartender appeared and took my order for a frozen margarita. The view from the tiki bar was fabulous, and I realized I could sit right here the rest of the day and be totally content.

The only thing I thought was out of place was the TV that was sitting on a shelf above the numerous liquor bottles. The TV was tuned in to CNN. I thought the idea here was to escape from the problems of everyday life. The last thing I wanted to do was to watch the news, which tended to be depressing.

While I was waiting for the margarita, I tried to divert my attention from the TV, but when I heard the TV reporter say she was providing an update on the serial killings in St. Louis, I quickly became interested. As I paid the bartender seven dollars for Stacy's drink, I heard the reporter say that the latest victim had survived the attack. She went on to say that the victim was a popular reporter for the local CBS affiliate. The attack occurred around two o'clock the previous night, and a neighbor who heard a noise had called nine one-one. When the ambulance arrived, the victim was barely alive. She is now in critical condition at St. John's hospital in St. Louis.

The reporter went on to say that the police had finally received a break in the case because the victim was able to provide a sketchy description of the killer. "According to our sources, the victim described the killer as having brown hair, medium height, a lean build, and a large scar on the right side of his neck."

Even though it was eighty- five degrees outside, I suddenly felt a chill. The hair on my arms stood straight up, and I had goose bumps. Memories that had been buried for years in my subconscious were awakened. My mind raced back twenty-five years to my childhood. I thought of Ricky. I relived that day I played football in my backyard with him. I remembered seeing him that night, hiding behind the shrubs, after he had killed Mrs. Wright's dog. I recalled his expression as he was led to the police car after killing Frank. As I tried to picture Ricky's face, I visualized his cold eyes and his hideous-looking scar. Could this be the same scar the victim was describing? Could Ricky be the killer?

For the first time in many years, I thought of Carla. I wondered where she lived and what she was doing. Could her brother, my former neighbor, be a cold-blooded serial killer?

I immediately left the tiki bar, and with her drink in hand, I headed back to the pool and Stacy. No longer could I enjoy the beauty of our surroundings. I kept thinking of Ricky and wondering if my imagination was running wild. My mind began to rationalize, and I knew the odds of Ricky being the killer were practically zero. After all, Ricky probably doesn't even live in St. Louis. Something inside me, though, kept telling me it was him. I knew that I had to find out for sure if he was the killer.

About a month ago, I had watched a St. Louis news special on the serial killings. The reporter had interviewed an FBI profiler, who worked in the agencies' serial crimes division. According to the FBI expert, the killer was probably a loner, who felt he had been victimized by women in positions of power. The killer's victims had all been successful women.

Ricky certainly fit the profile. From what I remembered as a kid, he was definitely a loner. I thought of the two women Ricky blamed for destroying his life: the lawyer responsible for the accident that killed his father, and the prosecuting attorney who covered up the fact that the driver was drunk at the time of the accident. I thought of the seven-year old boy who lost his father, and I thought of the abuse he suffered at the hands of his stepfather. I wondered if he harbored such deep resentment that he was capable of these crimes.

As I stared out over the ocean, I tried desperately to remember everything I knew about Ricky. I remembered as a kid having a horrible thought that kept popping up in my head. I always wondered whether Ricky had murdered the drunk driver who killed his father. Knowing that he had killed both his stepfather, Frank, and the dog, made me realize that he was certainly capable. I also knew the woman's murder was never solved. At the time, I dismissed it believing my imagination was getting the better of me. Now, I wasn't so sure.

As I reflected on the year when Ricky and Carla lived behind us, I thought of all the strange things that occurred in our neighborhood: the murders of Frank, Mrs. Wright's dog, and Dr. Lora Smith. I knew Ricky was responsible for Frank's death, but could he have also killed the doctor? To this day, something always bothered me about the man who had been convicted of her murder. Darrell Rogers just didn't seem like he was capable of cold-blooded murder. Could Ricky have been the real killer and gotten by with it all these years?

I thought of whether or not I should go to the police with my suspicions. I would not be able to live with myself if Ricky was indeed the killer, and I just sat back and allowed him to kill again. At the same time, Ricky had lived a hard life and, if he was innocent, I certainly did not want to create unnecessary trouble for him. I also felt I owed it to Carla to have more evidence than simple intuition before I assumed her brother was a killer.

I made the decision that I would not go to the police unless I had credible evidence that pointed toward Ricky.

Chapter 24

Savannah, Georgia

John Granado and Vinnie Ballmerito sat in the late model, blue Chevy Caprice directly across the square from Carla William's house. They were fortunate in finding a vacant house this close to Carla. The elderly lady living in the house was out of town visiting her daughter. Due to the large trees, her driveway was well hidden from the street, and it offered a perfect view of the front of Carla's house. It was a hot, humid night in Savannah, and between the heat and Vinnie's cheap cigarettes, John began feeling dizzy.

This was the first time John had worked with Vinnie. If he had his preference, he would rather be working alone. Roy Weston had insisted that he bring Vinnie along with him for the job. Vinnie was the son of a friend of Roy's, and apparently Roy owed this friend a big favor. So, like it or not, he was stuck with him.

Last night, John had been hired by Roy Weston to help him catch Ricky Henry. Roy was convinced that Ricky would not return to his apartment in St. Louis, and he felt there was a good chance that Ricky may pay his sister a visit in Savannah. Roy still had unfinished business to take care of in St. Louis, so he hired John to go to Savannah to keep an eye on Ricky's sister, Carla Williams. Roy trusted John, which was important because no one could ever find out what they were doing.

Earlier in the day, John had planted a bug in Carla's phone, so now they were set. All they had to do now was watch and wait.

Years ago, John worked with Roy for the Balducci crime family. They stayed in touch over the years and had helped each other out from time to time. John retired from the organized crime business after his boss, Big Bill Lombardo, was convicted of murder. After Lombardo's downfall, John felt there was no longer any future in the mob, so he decided to get out before he became a target of the prosecuting attorney at the time.

John had managed to squirrel away approximately three hundred thousand dollars while working for the Balducci family. Ten years ago, John left New York and moved to Richmond, Virginia, where he used his savings to start his own home security company. During his years with the mob, he specialized in surveillance. As a result, he became an expert at breaking into homes. There wasn't a security system around that he couldn't solve. He was now using that experience to design and install systems to provide protection from people like himself. His company had become quite successful.

The success of his business had changed John for the better. For the first time in his life he was earning an honest living, and he had become a respectable citizen. He became an avid reader and took great pride in being able to have intellectual conversations with his wealthy clients. He even joined the Chamber of Commerce and the Lions Club.

At first, John turned down Roy's offer. After all, he was no longer a thug. He was now a legitimate businessman; a pillar of the community. He was earning a good, honest living. He reconsidered, however, when

Roy told him his client was willing to pay him two hundred thousand dollars if he killed Ricky. He would still be paid one hundred grand, even if Ricky never showed up. He was looking to expand his Richmond business, and he could use the extra capital, so he accepted the offer. Besides, he figured he would be doing society a favor by getting a serial killer off the streets. Roy refused to disclose the identity of the client, but John guessed that he was high profile.

All John and Vinnie had to do was observe Carla Williams in case Ricky attempted to contact her. If they spotted Ricky, they had instructions to kill him and dispose of the body so it would never be found. It had been over ten years since John had killed another human being, but he figured it was like riding a bike; once you learn, you never forget how to do it.

Roy had provided them with a background report on Carla. Carla had been living alone ever since her husband, Tony Williams, died of pancreatic cancer two years ago. She had met Tony, who was fifteen years her senior, while she was attending college at the University of Georgia. She married him right after her college graduation. Tony was a very successful antiques dealer in Savannah, and owned a retail business on Bay Street. Soon after their marriage, Carla became actively involved in the business. When Tony died, She took over. She was now a well-respected antiques dealer in her own rights.

Carla was thirty-nine years old; three years younger than her murderous brother. She was strikingly beautiful, a fact that did not go unnoticed by Vinnie. John was worried that Vinnie might try something with her. Based on what he had seen so far of Vinnie, he didn't think rape was beneath him.

Carla's house sat on the northern end of Oglethorpe Square. Like most houses in downtown Savannah, it had historic significance, having been built in 1835. The house was a two-story Colonial and contained fifteen rooms.

During the day, John would keep an eye on Carla in the antiques store, while Vinnie watched the house. The plan was that they would meet back at the car in the evening and take turns sleeping until the next morning. John was not at all thrilled to have to spend so much time with a thug like Vinnie. Vinnie was twenty-five years younger than John and had no respect for his seniors. In addition, he was hot-tempered and ignorant. Vinnie had recently been booted from the Army, and apparently was in desperate need of cash. As a result, John was now stuck with him.

John looked over at Vinnie with disdain. Vinnie was wearing a sleeveless T-shirt, and he was sporting a tattoo on his arm that said "Life Sucks". He had a *Hustler* magazine in one hand and a Budweiser in the other. John was beginning to become bored, so he debated whether or not to engage Vinnie in a conversation. He finally decided that talking with him had to be better than the awful silence of the past two hours.

"Vinnie, did you know that Savannah has twenty-four public squares? It's the only city in the world built around public squares. It was the intention of Oglethorpe, when he founded Savannah in 1736, to establish a city like no other in the world. For all these years, the citizens have continued to honor his wishes."

"Great, John. Like I give a crap. All I know is this place is hot! I don't understand why you think it's so special. All I see is a bunch of old houses and trees with moss hanging down."

"That figures. That's what's wrong with the younger generation. You don't appreciate anything. Did you know that nearly all of these houses were built before the Civil War? Sherman's army spared Savannah from destruction, and most of the original houses have been preserved. These streets look very similar to the way they looked before the Civil War. It's a shame we won't have time to take a tour."

"Are you crazy? What's with you John? Are we here to do a hit or are we going to start a boy scout troop? Roy told me you're one of the best, but you act more like a history teacher than a trained assassin. Are you sure you worked for the Balducci family?"

John's anger began to build. He didn't like the idea of this punk questioning his abilities or his toughness. If he didn't have to answer to Roy Weston, he would have taught him a valuable lesson. He knew, however, there was a strong likelihood that he would be spending the next couple nights with him in this crowded car, so he decided to make the best of the situation and be somewhat civil.

. "Yeah, I worked with the family for fifteen years. I actually played a role in Big Bill Lombardo's rise to the head of the family. I participated in the murder of Paul Conigliaro in 1985 that made Big Bill the boss."

Vinnie seemed genuinely impressed. "You mean you actually knew Big Bill?"

"Of course, I knew him. He was a personal friend of mine. I saw him at least monthly."

Vinnie gave John a look that indicated that he didn't believe a word of it. He then grabbed a joint from the pocket in his jeans and started to light up.

John could contain himself no longer. If Vinnie had a question regarding John's toughness, John certainly answered it. A vicious left hook landed squarely on Vinnie's jaw. The blow snapped his head against his seat and, like a rubber band, sent his head crashing into the dashboard.

Vinnie was stunned. When he finally regained his faculties, he gave John a dazed look, indicating that he couldn't believe what had just happened.

"You're dumber than I thought, Vinnie. Do you want to blow this job by getting us arrested? There are cops all over the historic district. Besides, I hate that dope. I don't know what you young punks see in that stuff. And another thing, get rid of that beer. I need you to be alert in case Ricky shows up."

"I think you broke my jaw! My lips cut, and I'm bleeding."

"Don't be a wuss. I can see why the army got rid of your sorry ass. If you plan on working for Roy Weston, you are going to have to toughen up."

Vinnie was quiet for the next thirty minutes. John didn't know if his jaw hurt too much to talk, or if he were afraid to. In any event, John now had his respect.

John looked down at his watch, which indicated it was now fifteen minutes until ten. He glanced over at Vinnie and saw that he had fallen asleep. John shook his head in disgust. The work ethic of this new generation just wasn't what it should be.

It had been so long since he had done a surveillance job that he had forgotten how boring they were. Just as he began to think it was a long shot that Ricky would appear, Carla's phone rang. His heart skipped a beat as he adjusted the volume on the receiver.

"Hello."

A man answered in a raspy voice. "Carla, its me. Can I come see you?"

"Oh, Ricky, is that you? It's so good to hear from you. Where are you?"

"In Savannah. I'm two blocks from your house."

John sat straight up in his seat. "Get up deadbeat! Ricky's here."

Vinnie slowly rubbed his eyes, grunted, and then started to close them again.

For the second time within the past two hours, Vinnie was hit with a strong left hook. This time the blow was to the nose.

Vinnie let out a yelp. "I think you broke my nose! I need to go to the emergency room."

"The only place you'll be going is to the bottom of the Savannah River if you don't quit your whining. Be alert; Ricky's on his way."

John scanned the area, but saw nothing. He then reached under the seat and grabbed his pistol. Vinnie pulled out a handkerchief from his back pocket and pressed it against his nose to stop the bleeding. He tentatively turned his head to look at John and saw John's gun. He started to perk up. Finally, he was going to see some action.

Suddenly, John spotted a black Jeep Cherokee. His palms began sweating. He looked at the picture of Ricky that Roy had given him, just to be sure the driver was, in fact, Ricky. The Cherokee passed directly behind them, but because of the inadequacy of the street lighting, John could not tell for sure if it was Ricky.

The Cherokee pulled up to the curb in front of Carla's house, and a thin man, with black jeans and a black shirt climbed out. The man walked up to the front door and, within seconds, was let inside the house.

"It's him," said John.

John grabbed the cell phone and punched in Roy Weston's number to notify him that they had located Ricky and should have the job completed soon.

"What are we waiting for?" asked Vinnie. Let's go get Ricky, so we can get out of here."

"We can't yet. We have to do this without Carla's knowledge. We'll have to get him when he comes back out."

"What if he decides to spend the night?"

"Then we'll wait until morning."

John shook his head. It was hard enough to eliminate someone without a trace, but now he had to do it while babysitting this idiot. John wondered again what this kid's father must have done for Roy Weston to be so indebted to him.

May 15, 2003

About an hour after sunrise, the front door of the house opened and Carla came out alone. There was no sign of Ricky. It appeared he was going to remain in the house.

John reached over and shook Vinnie. Still half asleep, Vinnie started to grumble. Then he remembered that he was in the car with John, and he quickly held up his hands to block any potential left hooks. He was now wide-awake and alert. "Yeah, John. What can I do for you?"

John smiled and said: "I need you to walk over to the antique store and make sure that's where Carla is going. Radio me as soon as you know. Then keep an eye on her to make sure she doesn't come back."

"What are you going to do?"

"As soon as I hear from you, I'm going in to get Ricky."

Vinnie started to protest, but then remembered why his jaw and nose were aching, and decided against it.

Less than twenty minutes later Vinnie was on the radio indicating that Carla was, in fact, at her store.

"Vinnie, as soon as I finish I will radio you and you can help me dispose of the cargo."

John took a deep breath, opened the car door, and slowly eased through the backyards of the nineteenth century mansions that surrounded the square. Once he reached the side of the square where

Carla's house was located, he walked down the alley until he reached her back yard.

Holding a cup of coffee in one hand and a set of binoculars with the other, Ricky peered through the lens outside Carla's living room window. He could see the man getting out of the car. He could also see the bulge in his back. Ricky knew it was a gun. He was now certain the police had found something definitive to tie him to the murders. Why else would the police follow him halfway across the country? The two men must be here to arrest him. He was surprised, however, that there were only two. He also couldn't figure out where the second man had gone. Maybe he was already waiting outside the house.

Ever since the disaster at the reporter's house, Ricky had been extremely cautious and observant. He first noticed, who he assumed were the undercover officers, last night shortly after he entered Carla's house. From an upstairs bedroom window, he noticed the two men sitting in a parked car in a driveway across the square. Due to the darkness, he was unable to get a good look at them.

He then left the house, being very careful not to be detected, and crouched behind a bush within fifty feet of the car. His suspicions were confirmed when he noticed the man sitting in the driver's seat had a pair of binoculars pointed towards Carla's house. Strangely, the man on the passenger side had appeared to be holding a handkerchief against his nose.

Ricky kept the binoculars focused on the man until he could no longer see him. He then calmly walked to the dining room window where he spotted him again. The man was heading toward the kitchen door in the back of the house. Pulling the knife from the back of his jeans, Ricky calmly walked through the kitchen to the back door. Just prior to reaching the back door, he spotted a lug wrench on top of Carla's refrigerator. He slid the knife behind his back in favor of the lug wrench. Standing against the wall to the right of the door, he could hear a clicking sound as the man picked the lock.

The door slowly opened, and the man cautiously pushed the door forward. Ricky was now behind the door and out of view. The man slowly walked through the doorway. Waiting until he could see his back, Ricky swung the lug wrench, hitting the man squarely in the back of the head. The man instantly fell to the floor. Dazed, the man started to raise his head. Ricky stepped in front him and hit him again with the lug wrench. This time he was knocked unconscious.

Ricky then placed his hands under the man's arms and dragged him downstairs to Carla's basement. The basement was unfinished and was only used for storage. Using a rope he found in an old supply cabinet, Ricky tied the man to an old cast iron stove. He then pulled the man's wallet out of his back pocket.

He was surprised to find that the wallet did not contain some form of police identification. He found a business card and matched it to the man's driver's license. The card and license indicated that the man's name was John Granado. His residence was in Richmond, Virginia. Apparently, the man was not a police detective, but owned a company specializing in home security.

Ricky was relieved. He wasn't being followed by the police after all. So who was this guy and his partner, and why were they following him? He knew they had to be linked to the man in St. Louis, who had disrupted his plans at Melissa Grogan's house. As he looked down at John Granado, he smiled because he knew he would soon find out who was after him.

* * *

Vinnie was angry. After trying to radio John for over two hours, he decided to walk back to the car. He was bored, hungry, and in pain. Even after taking four Tylenols, his nose and jaw still hurt like heck.

He decided this surveillance crap was for the birds. He didn't care how good the money was, he simply could not spend all day in miserable heat, sitting on a bench watching the front of a store. He had to have some action. Despite his heavy debts, he decided this would be his last job for Roy Weston.

After being kicked out of the army, he had racked up some heavy gambling debts that he had been unable to pay off. His father had arranged for him to earn some fast cash by convincing Roy Weston to hire him. With the money he made on this job alone, he would be able to pay off over half of his debts. He would have to figure out another way to come up with the rest of the money.

As he approached the car, he worried that John may pop him again for leaving Carla at the store. He looked through the window of the car, and saw that John was not there. "He must be in Carla's house", he thought. If he went to the house now, maybe he could get in on some of the action.

Vinnie crossed the square, calmly walked through a yard, and made it to the alley behind Carla's house. He walked down the alley until he was directly behind her house. Hunched down so that he wouldn't be seen, he made his way to her back door. As he looked through the glass into the kitchen, he felt a sharp jab in his left arm. He immediately looked down and saw a needle sticking out of his arm. Suddenly, he became dizzy, his vision blurred, and he passed out.

An hour later when Vinnie opened his eyes, he let out a piercing scream. John was seated in a chair directly in front of him, covered in blood. Three of his fingers were missing, and Vinnie could tell that his throat had been slashed.

Vinnie jerked as he felt someone pat him on his back. "I hope you will be smarter than your partner. I'll give him credit, he's a tough son-of-a-gun. It seemed kind of senseless, however, for him to have endured all that pain when all he had to do was tell me who employed him."

The man was now in front of Vinnie, waving a bloody knife in front of his face. Vinnie's eyes widened in horror, and within minutes he told Ricky everything he knew about Roy Weston. True to his word, Ricky made Vinnie's death quick and painless.

Ricky cleaned up the mess in Carla's basement and disposed of the two bodies in the Savannah River. He then left a note for Carla, telling her he was sorry, but he had to leave to take care of urgent business.

He was relieved that he was now free to go back to St. Louis. He now knew for sure he was not a police suspect. Compliments of Vinnie, he had learned that a trained assassin, named Roy Weston, was the man who was trying to kill him. Although he still didn't know who had hired Roy, he was determined to find out. With a piece of paper containing Roy Weston's address in his shirt pocket, he began the long drive back to St. Louis.

The hunted was now the hunter.

Chapter 25

Roy Weston was a bundle of nerves. What should have been a routine, easy job, was turning out to be extremely challenging. During the past twenty-four hours he had been on an emotional roller coaster. His normal calm, cool demeanor had taken on an edgy, nervous twist.

He was elated when John phoned late last night, notifying him they had located the suspect. He thought for sure that John would complete the job, and he would never have to worry about Ricky again. Twenty-four hours had passed, however, and he had not heard from John. Something had gone wrong.

Roy was beginning to really dislike Ricky Henry. Not only had Ricky made a fool of him and harmed his impeccable reputation, he had also, more than likely, killed one of his few friends. Over the course of his thirty-plus year career, Ricky Henry was turning out to be Roy's most capable adversary. This had become personal.

To make matters worse, Senator Bryant had been calling every hour wanting an update, demanding to know if he had caught Ricky.

With each call, the Senator was losing more and more patience. Roy was really starting to become sick of the Senator.

Convinced that John and Vinnie had succumbed to an unpleasant death at the hands of Ricky, Roy knew it was now even more critical to dispose of Melissa Grogan, the only witness who could identify Ricky.

Donned in a white lab coat, Roy parked his Explorer in the employee parking lot at St. John's Mercy Hospital. It was fifteen minutes before midnight, so he knew the skeleton, night shift would be working.

Roy reached into the glove box and retrieved a full syringe of morphine. Placing the syringe into the right pocket of his lab coat, he locked the vehicle and walked to the emergency room entrance. With the lab coat, stethoscope, and hand-held transcription device in hand, he looked like one of over a hundred staff physicians, residents, and medical students that routinely wander the halls of St. Johns. At night especially, the majority of nurses on the floors were contract nurses, who were not familiar with the hospital's medical staff. The staff at the ICU nurses station did not even look up as Roy walked by them on his way to room 212.

The patient in room 212, Mrs. Jones, was selected by Roy because of her location. From her room, the staff would not be able to see Melissa Grogan's room. Roy smiled as he approached the patient's bed. To him, the elderly woman already looked half-dead. She was gaunt, extremely pale, and had numerous tubes sticking out of her body. He could hear the beep of a cardiac monitor and the whirring sound of a ventilator.

"Hi, Mrs. Jones, it's time for your pain medication. Trust me, after this, you won't feel any more pain."

Mrs. Jones looked confused as Roy pulled the syringe out of his pocket. Instead of adding it to the IV line as the nurses had been doing, he injected the lethal dose directly into her arm. He placed the syringe back in his pocket and immediately walked out of the room. He then entered a supply closet, where he tried to appear as though he was looking for a supply.

Within minutes, an alarm sounded at the nurse's station. "Code, room 212!" yelled one of the nurses. The code was then announced on the overhead paging system, and suddenly the ICU was in total chaos. Nurses, residents, and respiratory therapists all converged on room 212.

Roy calmly walked out of the supply closet and down the hall toward Melissa Grogan's room. He was almost knocked over by a nurse wheeling a crash cart toward room 212, but due to the urgency of the situation, she paid no attention to him.

Melissa Grogan had been awakened by the activity and was straining her head to see through the glass partition, which separated her room from the hallway. As Roy entered her room, he was startled when she began to speak. "What's going on?" she asked.

Her alertness and the clarity of her voice surprised Roy. Apparently, she was in much better condition than the hospital and police were leading the media to believe. He was glad he hadn't waited any longer.

If she suspected anything when Roy entered her room, she didn't show it. He closed the curtains and calmly walked over to the side of her bed. He pretended to check the tubing from her IV infusion pump. He then felt the NG tube as if he was checking to make sure it was placed correctly. Next, he lifted her head and told her he needed to reposition her pillow. Instead of placing the pillow back under her head, he pushed it firmly over her face and applied pressure. Melissa kicked and tried to scream, but the pillow reduced the sound to a slight muffle. As he held the pillow to her face with one hand, he held down her arms with the other hand, to keep her from knocking over any equipment. Within one minute, the kicking and sounds stopped. Melissa's body became limp.

He checked for a pulse. Finding none, he slipped out of the room. Crouching down out of the view of the security camera, he made his way to the stairwell. Within five minutes, he was in his truck pulling out of the hospital parking lot.

Chapter 26

Three days later: May 17, 2003

Although it was still only May, the temperature hovered near ninety degrees as I pulled out of the Scott County Courthouse in Benton, Missouri. It had cost me twenty-five bucks and over two hours of my time, but the dated copier had provided me with a complete copy of the transcript of Darrell Roger's trial.

I was surprised that Stan didn't ask a barrage of questions when I informed him that I needed to take the week off for personal reasons. I was relieved because I wanted as few people as possible to know about my suspicions.

To an almost annoying extent, Stan insisted on knowing what was going on in the personal lives of his managers. He always believed a happy personal life was necessary for a successful career. The only reason I could come up with as to why he didn't demand to know what was going on, was that he was still so distraught over the disaster at the exhibit hall that he really wasn't paying attention to my request.

Anyway, he granted my request, and I now had the entire week to try to investigate whether or not Ricky could be the serial killer.

Since school had just let out for the summer, Stacy and I decided to take the kids and spend the week at my parent's house in Sikeston. I felt the best place to start my investigation was with the Lora Smith case in Sikeston.

The first thing I did last night, after arriving back in St. Louis from Key Largo, was to check the St. Louis area telephone directory to determine if Ricky lived in St. Louis. The directory listed fifteen Ricky, Rick, or Richard Henry's. Ten of those identified a Mr. and Mrs., so I ruled those out on the assumption that Ricky never married. I then called the remaining five.

When they answered, I decided to tell them I was a county clerk, attempting to recompile some old county records that had been destroyed in a fire. Then I planned to ask them if their father's name was Tom Henry, and if they had grown up in Murray, Kentucky.

I ruled out the first person I called, due to the fact that he had a British accent. The second person sounded much too old and told me he had never even heard of Murray, Kentucky. On the third call, an answering machine picked up. A gravely voice came on: "This is Ricky. I'm not in right now; leave your name and number and I will call you back. If this is Ardin Automotive and it is a maintenance emergency, beep me at 314-636-4357."

The hair on my arms stood up. The voice certainly sounded familiar. Would I remember Ricky's voice after twenty-five years? I was excited because Ardin Automotive had been a client of mine at my former accounting firm. I decided I would call first thing in the morning to see if I could find more information on the Ricky Henry that worked there.

This morning, before loading up the van for the trip to my parents house in Sikeston, I called the assistant controller of Ardin, Dan Ricker. Dan and I had gone out to lunch a few times while I worked on their audit, and I hoped he still worked there. I was pleased when I asked the switchboard operator for him, and she put me right through.

After a few pleasantries, I asked Dan if he could bend the rules a little and provide me with some personal information on one of their employees. He agreed, and within a couple of minutes he had accessed the company's personnel database.

Ardin Automotive did, in fact, have an employee named Ricky Henry. His date of hire was December 17, 1991. This meant that he lived in St. Louis during the period of time the murders occurred.

I then asked Dan for his date of birth. The Ricky Henry working at Ardin had a date of birth of October 12, 1960. My heart skipped a beat because I knew that would make him about the same age as the Ricky I knew.

When Dan told me his pension beneficiary was a Carla Williams, who lived in Savannah, Georgia, I knew for sure it was my former neighbor. Although I didn't know Carla's married name, I knew the probability was almost zero of there being more than one Ricky Henry, who was trained as a mechanic, born in 1960, and had a next of kin named Carla. I was convinced this was the Ricky Henry who used to be my neighbor. Now, I needed to find out if he was, in fact, responsible for these murders.

As I drove down Highway 61 south toward Sikeston, I glanced at the inch high trial transcript of the Lora Smith murder, lying on the passenger seat. I planned to read as much of it as I could tonight. Before then, I hoped to obtain as much information as I could possibly find concerning the murder of Patricia Wells. Seeing that it was only one-thirty in the afternoon, I made the decision to make the one-hour drive to Paducah, Kentucky; the town where the murder occurred. I would probably have enough time to visit the Paducah library and review the newspaper coverage of the murder from the library archives.

As I pulled into my parent's driveway, I saw my kids playing in the front yard with the water hose. I smiled as I remembered how I used to play in that same yard when I was their age. I had a lot of special memories of the house and neighborhood, and I was glad Mom and Dad never moved. As I watched the kids, I thought of my childhood friend, Steve. I also thought of Carla and Ricky. Could Ricky have been so messed up as a kid that he could have turned into a serial killer? If so, should I have seen the signs?

I tried to put those thoughts out of my mind as I climbed out of the car. I was a little perturbed to see five empty Mountain Dew cans in the grass, near where the kids were playing. They were my mother's only grandchildren, and she tended to spoil them and let them have whatever they wanted. I frowned as I thought of spending an hour in the car riding to Paducah with three kids on a caffeine high.

"Go get changed kids if you want to ride with your mom and me to Paducah."

"What's there to do in Paducah, Daddy?" asked Bobby.

"I think your mom and the girls want to go to the mall shopping. I'm going to the library."

"Yuck. I think I'll stay here with Papa. He said he might take me fishing at the complex."

"Suit yourself, sport. Catch some big ones, and we'll have a fish fry later this week."

Actually, I was sort of relieved that Bobby decided not to go. With Bobby and Amanda, the combination of too much Mountain Dew and a car ride was bound to be lethal. I could picture them fighting the entire trip, and I really needed some quiet time to begin to process what I was learning about Ricky.

Sitting in a plastic chair in the corner of the library, I waded through two microfilm reels of newspaper editions from 1977, before I hit pay dirt. The front page of the September 24, 1977 edition of the Paducah Daily News contained, in large print, the headline: "Prominent Local Attorney Found Murdered in Home."

The newspaper article described the murder as brutal. Patricia Wells had been stabbed repeatedly in her home shortly after midnight. The police stated that robbery did not appear to be a motive, since cash and jewelry were left in plain view at the crime scene.

The victim, Patricia Wells, was described as a civic-minded mover and shaker, active in Paducah's social circles. The article went on to describe her numerous civic involvements and good deeds.

The second page of the article identified some of the details of the murder. I learned that Patricia Well's killer had apparently gained entry to the house by climbing through a bathroom window. I felt a knot develop in the pit of my stomach as I realized the many similarities between this murder and the St. Louis serial killings. Like the Wells murderer, the serial killer also gained access by climbing through windows. He also used a knife, and displayed uncontrollable anger by stabbing his victims numerous times.

Despite my attempts to rationalize these similarities as nothing more than coincidence, I couldn't help but realize that the evidence was all pointing toward Ricky. I shuddered as I thought of the fact that I may have once lived next door to a monster.

I reviewed the news articles covering the next month, reading each story pertaining to the murder. I learned nothing new about the case except for the fact that the police never had a viable suspect. Originally, the police believed the killer was a former client of Ms. Wells, who had been upset with her representation of his case. This suspect was a man she had represented years before, who had been paroled just prior to her murder. The man had insisted that he was innocent, and he blamed Patricia Wells for his conviction. After a brief investigation, the man was cleared as a suspect in Patricia's murder when his alibi checked out.

I made copies of the articles and left the library feeling more frustrated than ever. Should I go to the police now or should I keep digging in hopes of finding something that proved Ricky was not the killer? Unfortunately, I chose to wait. That decision will haunt me the rest of my life.

Chapter 27

The adrenalin rush kicked in as Ricky drove across the Poplar Street Bridge, connecting East St. Louis with downtown. Ricky had been homesick, and seeing the Arch and the downtown skyline brought back the pleasant memories the city had provided him.

It was now eight in the morning and rush hour was in full force. Fortunately, Ricky was driving west on Interstate 40 and was heading away from downtown and the heavy traffic. With one hand on the steering wheel, he used his other to reach into his pocket and pull out the sheet of paper containing the information on Roy Weston. Thanks to the assistance provided by the late Vinnie Ballmerito, he had the address of Roy Weston's apartment. He read the address and realized it was a street he had never heard of. He decided he would stop at a convenience store and purchase a city map to find the location of the street. Besides, he had been driving fourteen straight hours and could use a cup of coffee.

He took the Grand Street exit, drove east past St. Louis University, and two miles later pulled into the parking lot of a gas station. The neighborhood around the gas station looked rundown. Several homeless men were sitting in front of the empty, dilapidated buildings. The gas station had bars over the windows.

He climbed out of his vehicle, stretched, and walked toward the station. In the parking lot of the building next to the gas station, he noticed a homeless man, sitting on a curb, slouched over, with his elbows resting on his knees. He noticed the man was missing his right hand.

Ricky entered the station, purchased a map, a bag of donuts, and two cups of coffee. He then walked over to the man. Reaching in his pocket, Ricky took out a twenty-dollar bill and tossed it to him. The man looked up, amazed. Ricky then flashed a grin, and handed him one of the coffees and the bag of donuts. He then sat down next to the man and talked for about ten minutes.

After spending the past three hours napping in Forest Park, Ricky now felt refreshed. The familiar feeling of excitement and nervousness was now spreading throughout his body. The feeling became stronger the closer he came to Roy Weston's apartment complex.

He turned off Brighton Street into the complex. He then parked in a lot in front of Building C; the building next to Roy's. Dressed in black jeans and a black shirt, he casually walked around to the back of Roy's building.

Ricky had already been to Roy's apartment complex earlier in the day. Using his newly purchased city map, he had found the apartment complex easily. He had been surprised when he realized it was in South County, within a mile of his own apartment. He laughed to himself as he realized Roy must have had his apartment bugged.

He knew Roy's temporary residence was in apartment # 7. During his earlier visit, he wanted to make sure Roy hadn't changed his residence and was still living here. This was confirmed when he saw a red Explorer with the same license number he had seen that day in the parking lot of the plant.

To understand the layout of the building, he had entered it and walked to the outside of Roy's apartment door. He could smell coffee brewing. He also heard the phone ring and a man pick up, who identified himself as Roy.

During his earlier visit that day, Ricky also learned that a woman in her early thirties lived in apartment #6, the one next to Roy's. As he watched her leave her apartment, he felt those all too familiar feelings. The feelings of anger, then of desire. He could tell she was one of those snooty executives because she wore a fancy business suit and drove a fancy sports car. Shortly after she left, he broke into her apartment. He found out she was a nurse manager at a St. Louis hospital. The feeling of rage swept over him as he read the numerous diplomas and certifications plastered on her bedroom wall. The rage slowly gave way to ecstasy as he anticipated the hours ahead. This night would bring double pleasure. He would satisfy his craving, and at the same time, rub it in Roy Weston's face.

He still did not know who had hired Roy Weston or why he was being targeted. After tonight, however, Mr. Weston would have no doubts that he had messed with the wrong person.

Apartment #6 was on the second floor of the building. Each individual apartment in the building had a private balcony. The balcony for apartment # 6 was located in the back of the building. Ricky used the wooden railing on the first floor balcony to propel himself up to the second floor balcony. Within seconds, he was in the nurse manager's apartment.

An hour later, he used the woman's kitchen sink to wash her blood from his knife. Using the cleansed knife, he removed a lock of hair from her dead body. He then removed one of her shoes and placed her hospital ID badge and the lock of hair inside the shoe.

Having seen Roy leave his apartment earlier in the evening, Ricky decided he would have some fun. With the shoe in hand, he entered Roy's apartment through the sliding glass doors leading from the balcony. He placed the shoe on Roy's dining room table, with a note:

"Roy, I was in the neighborhood and thought I would pay you a visit. I'm sorry I missed you. Best Regards. Ricky."

Ricky then rummaged through drawers and cabinets, looking for information. He had learned from Vinnie Balmarito that Roy was a trained assassin, who had been hired to kill him. Vinnie, however, was unable to tell him who had hired Roy. It was obvious to him that Vinnie had been telling the truth. Roy had not disclosed to anyone the identity of the person who had engaged his services.

Ricky's search proved successful. In the kitchen, he found a notebook in a drawer next to the refrigerator. Flipping through the pages, he found a cell phone number. Beside the number were the words: "JB. Private."

Using Roy's phone, he quickly dialed the number. After eight rings, a man, who was clearly irritated at having been disturbed, answered.

"Yeah. What do you want?"

Ricky could hear clanging in the background, of what sounded like ice being dropped into a glass. "Who am I calling, please?"

"You are calling a United States senator. I hope this is important!"

"Oh, it's very important, Senator," answered Ricky.

Ricky hung up the phone and smiled. It all made perfect sense now.

Carrying two sacks of groceries, Roy trudged up the flight of stairs to his apartment. He cursed as he dropped one of the bags while fumbling for his keys. Angrily, he watched as three oranges bounced down the stairs.

Having regained possession of the oranges and two sacks, he kicked the door open and walked inside. As he set the bags on the kitchen counter, he noticed a woman's shoe on his dining room table. Puzzled, he lifted the shoe and noticed a picture ID and a stand of blond hair. He immediately recognized the picture as that of his neighbor.

With a sense of dread, he immediately went to her apartment. After making sure no one was looking, he opened the unlocked door. He knew exactly what he would find as he headed for the bedroom. Just as he expected, the woman was lying in her bed in a pool of blood.

Roy had never been so humiliated. This punk was not only beating him; he was taunting him. "He will pay," pledged Roy.

Reluctantly, Roy picked up the phone. He wasn't looking forward to telling Senator Bryant the latest news.

Chapter 28

The Southern Baptist Convention was reaching its climax. The keynote speaker, Senator Jim Bryant, stepped up to the podium to a thunderous ovation. He smiled and waved to the sixty thousand Baptists gathered at Atlanta's Georgia dome. He knew it was essential for him to win the support of the Christian Coalition and the ultra conservatives. Judging by the reaction of his audience, he was certainly succeeding.

He began his speech by introducing his wife, Taylor Bryant. With his voice choking, he informed the crowd that she was the love of his life: his support and inspiration. He pulled a handkerchief out of his back pocket. Wiping his eyes, he told the crowd that he thanked God each and every day for her. Without her, he would be nothing. It was quite a performance.

Over the next hour, he hammered home his beliefs; his values. He envisioned a better tomorrow for his country. He wanted to bring family values back as the cornerstone of our culture. He wanted to make people accountable for their actions. He wanted an America where we could walk the inner-city streets without fear of being mugged. He wanted the entertainment industry cleaned up; where families could watch television together without being embarrassed by the content.

With each point, he pounded the podium with his fists. He had the crowd worked up to a frenzy. He said all the right things; even though, deep down, it meant nothing to him. Truth was, he could care less about family values or personal responsibility. He simply saw this position as his best chance of becoming the next president of the United States.

After shaking what seemed like thousands of hands, he finally managed to reach the tunnel where the limousine was waiting. He was glad to be out of there. He didn't think he could have managed that fake smile a second longer. In the back seat, he immediately found the bourbon and poured himself a shot. After slugging it down, he poured himself another.

By the time he reached the Marriott hotel, he was feeling relaxed. His heart began racing as he thought of Natalie and of what lie in store later in the night. First, he had to get rid of Taylor.

He realized Taylor was a necessity. During the campaign, he would have to present the perfect image, and unfortunately she would be the centerpiece. He also needed the support and endorsement of her father. Jack Carter carried enough influence in the Southeast to win several states for him. He could ill afford to have Jack Carter against him.

He heard the water running in the bathroom sink as he unlocked the door to his hotel suite. With a toothbrush sticking out of her mouth, Taylor mumbled. "Honey, is that you?"

"Yes, dear."

"You were great tonight. Did you really mean what you said about me?"

"Of course I did, darling."

He pecked her on the cheek, and looked at her through the bathroom mirror. She was certainly not unattractive. He couldn't figure out why he was so repulsed by her. Maybe it was the fact that she couldn't bear him a child. Maybe he resented her so much because she had denied him his legacy.

As much as he would like to, he knew he could not divorce her: at least not until after he completed his Presidential term. Divorce was out of the question for the candidate representing morality and family values. Besides, he knew she was an asset on the campaign trail. She was smart and well educated. She even looked like a first lady. She was polished, refined, and said all the right things. The media loved her.

That was her problem, he thought. She was too perfect, never took risks. She was too predictable, and she lacked spontaneity.

Just one of her many habits that annoyed him was when she flossed her teeth and tried to carry on a conversation. She rubbed the floss back and forth between her teeth and mumbled incoherently: "Jim, let's order a bottle of wine from room service and watch a movie tonight."

"Oh Taylor, that sounds so good. I'd give anything to be able to relax and watch a movie with you, but I promised the governor some time on my schedule. Tonight is the only time I can meet with him. Sorry dear."

"That's okay. Just make sure you capture his endorsement. We're going to need his support if we are to take Georgia in the primary. Remember, he likes your position on capital punishment, but thinks you have gone too far with your campaign reform initiative. Don't forget, he has plans to run for the Senate next year, and he believes your proposed limits on contributions will hurt his chances. If it comes up tonight, you need to tone it down."

"Good idea. I'll definitely take a more moderate approach to my position on campaign reform, if the Governor brings it up."

He knew Taylor had good ideas and generally offered sound advice, but he resented her constantly telling him what to do. He was determined not to let her get to him tonight. There was no way she was going to ruin this evening. He had no intention of seeing the good Governor. He had better plans.

As he left the suite, he checked the hallway. After confirming there was no one in sight, he walked down the hall until he reached the third room. He lightly tapped on the door. Natalie opened it, wearing the negligee he had bought her for Christmas.

He smiled and looked up and down, admiring her body. It was so perfect, just like her. He had been seeing Natalie now for several years. He knew it was risky, but they had been careful. He knew just one slip up and his presidential hopes would be ruined. A scandal would ruin his political future, but he knew they would never get caught. Unlike Bill Clinton, Gary Hart, and some of the other politicians wrecked by sex scandals, he was too smart.

He wished he could give her more. She certainly deserved better than being reduced to a mistress. He couldn't, however, and she understood. She always understood him.

He opened the mini bar and began preparing drinks. Just as he was placing the ice in the glasses, his cell phone rang. Angrily, he walked over to the phone and picked it up. After a few seconds, he set the phone down and poured the drinks.

"Who was on the phone?" Natalie asked.

"Just some nut who happened to get my number. It happens all the time. Some kooks think it's fun to call and harass a busy United States Senator. This guy even disguised his voice in an effort to scare me."

"Well if your not worried, I guess I'm not worried," she said as she slowly walked to him.

She placed her arms around him, and he slid his hands around her back. Just as he began to untie the negligee, the phone rang again. This time he was furious. Why couldn't he ever have some peace?

He grabbed the phone. "This better be good," he yelled into the receiver.

"Well it's not good, Senator, but you need to hear it anyway."

"What now Roy? Please tell me you've located Ricky and everything is going to be okay."

"Oh, we located Ricky alright. He paid my neighbor a visit."

"What do you mean he paid your neighbor a visit. You don't mean?"

Before he could complete the sentence, Roy cut in. "Yes, unfortunately that's exactly what I mean. He murdered my neighbor to prove a point that he is invincible; that it will do us no good to try to stop him."

"I'm beginning to think he's right. Is he in any danger of being caught by the police?"

"No, he's too smart and careful for that. I don't think we need to worry about that right now. We have other more pressing problems."

Jim drained his drink and walked over to the mini bar. "What other problems?" he asked, anxiously.

"I'm afraid he may know who you are, Senator. After killing my neighbor, he broke into my apartment. I had a notebook with your initials and telephone number in it. Have you received any unusual calls within the past hour?"

Jim didn't respond. He just sat on the edge of the bed. His complexion was white as a sheet.

"What's wrong, Jim?" asked Natalie.

He couldn't speak. He wanted to tell her. He wanted to cry and bury his head into her shoulders for protection. But, he couldn't. No one, not even Natalie, could ever find out the awful things he had done.

He knew he was being punished for what he had done to poor Darrell Rogers. Now, he not only had to be concerned about losing his career and reputation, he had to fear for his own life. He had a psychopath after him, who was intelligent and cunning enough to beat and humiliate one of the best assassins in the world.

He picked up the phone again and dialed Roy's number. He then asked Roy to find him the best bodyguard in the business. He only hoped that would be enough. It was apparent to him that Ricky was intelligent and would stop at nothing to get what he wanted. His life was in grave danger.

Chapter 29

May 18, 2003

It was a sunny Tuesday morning. Stacy, Mom, and the kids decided to go to the park. I was alone in my dad's study, summarizing the information I had on the Patricia Well's murder. After staying up most of the night reading the information, I was now pretty sure that Ricky was responsible for her murder. I had no proof, however, and did not feel the police would show much interest with the limited information I had gathered.

Since I also suspected Ricky of Dr. Lora Smith's murder, I decided I would see what I could dig up on her case. Earlier this morning I had gone to the Sikeston library and copied the newspaper articles from 1978 for the days immediately following Dr. Smith's murder. Between the newspaper articles and the trial transcript, I hoped I could find something I could use.

As I read the articles, it brought back memories from so long ago. I remembered the day of the murder as though it were just yesterday. In a way my innocence was shattered that day. It was my first real exposure to the evil that exists among us. I realized for the first time that bad things really did happen to good people.

I vividly remember playing ball in the front yard with my best friend, Steve, when we heard the siren. We immediately rode our bikes to Dr. Smith's house. I recall the sick feeling I had when I saw Dr. Smith's boyfriend being consoled on the front porch. I remember watching the news coverage of the murder that night and how I had trouble sleeping.

As a twelve year old at the time, I guess the part that bothered me the most was the accused murderer: Darrell Rogers. He seemed so normal, like someone you ran into every day. He had a wife and young daughter; a good job. I remember thinking that if he were capable of doing this, anyone could.

After reading the newspaper articles, I started reading the trial transcript that I picked up from the Benton courthouse yesterday. As I began reading, something grabbed my attention. I noticed that Mrs. Hammonds was a key witness at trial. She was the only witness who actually saw Darrell Roger's at Dr. Smith's house. I remembered Mrs. Hammonds because I mowed her yard one summer. I smiled as I recalled how spunky and funny she was. I always liked her.

Mrs. Hammonds was around eighty years old back when I mowed her yard some twenty-five years ago. There was no way she was still alive. I did remember, though, that she had a son who lived in Memphis. Maybe he was still alive.

I remembered Mrs. Hammonds being a very religious woman. She used to have a large sign in her front yard, that I constantly had to move to mow around, advertising the Methodist church.

Within minutes, I had the church secretary on the phone and, fortunately, Mike Hammond's Memphis phone number was listed in the church directory.

Mr. Hammonds was more than willing to talk with me. He told me the only thing he remembered his mother discussing with him was the fact that she saw a built-in toolbox in the back of Darrell Roger's truck. She had been upset that the prosecutor, Jim Bryant, would not allow her to mention this during her testimony.

Mr. Hammond's also suggested that I discuss the case with the private investigator, who had been working on behalf of Darrell Rogers.

"I didn't realize there was a private investigator," I said.

"Yeah, he came around a few months before Mom died. That would have been about twelve years ago. Mom died in 1991. Some British group, who was attempting to prove Darrell's innocence, hired the investigator. Mom told me the P.I. was very excited when she told him about the toolbox and the fact that Jim Bryant did not want her to mention that during her testimony. I thought it was strange that she never heard from him again."

"I wonder why Jim Bryant tried to prevent your mother from mentioning the toolbox. Do you have any idea?"

"No, unless Darrell didn't have a toolbox on his truck. If Darrell did have a toolbox, I would think Jim Bryant would have wanted Mom to mention it because it adds more validity to her eyewitness account. Mom was certain she saw the toolbox. If it so happened that Darrell did not have a toolbox on his truck, then maybe it wasn't him that mom saw that night. If that is the case, then either Jim Bryant didn't believe Mom when she said she saw the toolbox, or he believed her and didn't want the jury to find out. I don't believe he would have deliberately withheld evidence from the jury. Surely, Jim Bryant wouldn't convince a witness to alter her testimony. You do know that he is running for president of the United States, don't you? It makes me proud to know that my mom knew him so well."

As I thanked Mr. Hammonds and hung up the phone, something was bothering me. I remembered Ricky owning a truck, but I couldn't remember the color or whether or not it had a toolbox. I did remember that he was a mechanic, so it would make sense that he would have a built-in toolbox in the back.

That evening, I decided I would look through our old photo albums to see if we had an old photograph showing Ricky's truck. I was dreading this because the photo albums were in one of the dozens of boxes stacked in my parent's attic. Finding them would not be a pleasant experience.

Later that night, I pulled on the overhead rope to lower the ladder, and I climbed up into the attic. With a flashlight in my hand, I crawled from box to box looking for the old photo albums. The attic was cramped with only about three feet of space separating the plywood floor from the ceiling. The attic had no circulation and soon I was sweating. Many of the boxes were located in a portion of the attic where there was no plywood floor, so I had to crawl across the insulation making sure I stayed on the floor joists to keep from falling through the ceiling. After breathing in a lung full of dust and bumping my head three or four times, I finally found the box containing the photographs.

As I climbed down the ladder with the box, I brought a great deal of insulation down with me. I was wringing wet with sweat and the insulation sticking to my skin felt like sandpaper. Bobbie thought it was funny that my hair, skin, and clothes were covered with the white insulation. He thought it looked like snow. It didn't feel like snow; it itched like crazy.

After a quick shower, Stacy and I began looking at each album in an attempt to find a picture of Ricky's truck. Mom approached us and immediately wanted to know what we were up to. Stacy and I had previously agreed that we would not tell her or Dad what we were doing. We didn't want to worry them unnecessarily. We had disguised our visit as nothing more than a few days away from the city. I told mom I was reminiscing about old times and wanted Stacy to see some of our old family pictures. Looking at the pictures did bring back many pleasant memories of past vacations and of friends I haven't seen in years.

In the second to the last album, we actually found several pictures of Carla. One of the pictures was of Carla in her front yard. My stomach suddenly knotted up as I saw, in the background of the photograph, a blue pickup truck parked in Carla's driveway. The pickup had a white toolbox attached under the rear window.

As I stared at the picture, I was in shock. I didn't want to believe it, but I knew it was true. I was absolutely convinced now that Ricky was responsible for the murders. The question I had to answer now is whether I had enough information to be taken seriously by the police. The police would only consider facts, not my intuition. In the case of Lora Smith's murder, I knew the police would not be too anxious to admit they had made a mistake that led to the execution of an innocent man. Even though the murder occurred twenty-five years ago, they probably still had officers on the force who were also there at that time. It would make the Sikeston Police Department look bad.

I also knew the political ramifications of accusing Ricky of Lora Smith's murder. If the media caught wind of this, it could ruin Jim Bryant's chances of becoming president. I knew how powerful and ambitious he was. The more I thought of going to the police, the more nervous I became.

On a notebook, I jotted down the facts I had obtained so far that implicated Ricky as the killer of Patricia Wells, Lora Smith, and the serial murders. 1. Ricky lived only two blocks from Lora Smith's house at the time of the murder. 2. Ricky drove a blue pickup with a built-in toolbox, which matched the description of the vehicle Mrs Hammonds described. 3. Ricky was known to be violent. This was supported by the fact that he killed his stepfather and my neighbor's dog, just because the woman yelled at him. 4. The details of the Lora Smith and Patricia Wells murders were very similar to the serial killings in St. Louis. The method of entry and the weapon were the same for all murders. 5. Ricky had a motive for killing Patricia Wells. She was responsible for the death of his father. 6. Like Patricia Wells, the other victims were all successful women. 7. Ricky had easy access to each of the victims. Ricky lived in the vicinity of each victim at the time of the murder. 8. The latest St. Louis victim, Melissa Grogan, described her attacker as having a large scar on his neck and a raspy voice. That description certainly fit Ricky.

As I reviewed my list I realized that, other than the physical description by Melissa Grogan, there was nothing definitive tying Ricky to any of the murders. Even Mrs. Hammond's description of the toolbox could not be confirmed since it was not in the trial transcript. I realized I needed more evidence.

I was now at a dead end. Where would I obtain more evidence? Just as I was beginning to become frustrated, I remembered that Mike Hammonds had mentioned a private investigator, who had been hired to find evidence to prevent Darrell Roger's execution. Since Mr. Hammonds did not remember his name, I knew it might be difficult to locate him. I asked myself who would know about him.

Suddenly, a newspaper article I read the night before popped in my mind. The story described Lisa Roger's reaction to her husband's guilty verdict. She had been devastated. I realized that she would know about the investigator.

I felt sorry for Lisa Rogers. I could not imagine what she had gone through; watching her husband be convicted and later executed for a crime he didn't commit. I remembered Mom and Dad talking about how many people had shunned her after the conviction, effectively forcing her to move out of town.

I wondered how she was doing now; if she had been able to put this behind her. Would it make her feel better knowing that I also believed Darrell was innocent? I knew I would want to know that if I were in her position. I decided I would pay Lisa Rogers a visit.

Chapter 30

"May I help you, sir?"

Ricky smiled at the hotel clerk. "I need a room, please. I will be staying two nights. "

While trying not to stare at the unsightly scar on the guest's neck, the slightly overweight, middle-aged clerk smiled back. "You're in luck, sir. Up until last night we were booked up. The American Legion had their annual meeting at the convention center across the street. In fact, all the Drury hotels in the St. Louis area were booked up. Tonight, though, we have plenty of rooms. I'll get you a room with a nice view of the river, Lacledes Landing, and the Arch.

Ricky pulled out his MasterCard and paid for the room. Within minutes, he was in his room unpacking his suitcase.

He knew it was too dangerous to return to his apartment, so he decided to play it safe and stay in a hotel. Besides, he would not be in St. Louis very long. He had one loose end to tie up, then he would be heading to Washington D.C. He was looking forward to paying a visit to his favorite United States Senator.

He walked over to the window, where he caught a glimpse of the Mississippi River in the near distance. To his far right, he could see the bright gleam of the sunlight bouncing off the Arch. On his left stood renovated warehouses that, over a century ago, stored cotton, tobacco, and coffee. Now, the buildings were used as restaurants and nightclubs. He had been in the nightclubs on the Landing before. One of his previous victims was a regular of one of the clubs, and he had watched her dance the night away on several occasions. Now, as he looked down at the building, he was once again reminded of her.

This time, Ricky was not here for the nightclubs. He was here because the hotel was just three blocks from Regina Phillip's office building. Tonight, he would rest, watch a little TV, and wait anxiously for tomorrow morning. The day he had waited for all these years had finally arrived. His heart began racing, and his hands became sweaty as he thought of Regina.

By eleven o'clock in the morning, he would be waiting outside her office building. When she left for lunch, he would follow her and watch her eat. He would find a table close to her, and he would savor the moment. In the afternoon, he would ride the elevator to the forty first floor. He had been there several times before, and it always excited him. If questioned, he would tell the receptionist that he had gotten off on the wrong floor. He would be there long enough to feel her presence; her power. It would charge his batteries and would be a prelude to their meeting later that night. To Ricky, the anticipation was almost as pleasurable as the act itself.

Tomorrow night, he would follow Regina home from work. Her husband frequently traveled during the week, and in all likelihood, she would be alone. He would wait outside her house until the time was right. Then the fun would begin. Finally, his father would be able to rest in peace.

A couple of hours later, Ricky reached into his shaving kit, pulled out a bottle of sleeping pills, and popped three in his mouth. Tomorrow would be a big day, and he needed a good night's sleep. The pills helped to keep the nightmares away. Without them, he knew he would have the same horrific dream he had been having nearly every night the past few weeks. For some reason, the most recent dreams had been much worse than the usual ones.

These latest dreams began with a picnic. His family was lying on a blanket next to the lake, eating his mother's fried chicken. His little, three year-old sister, Carla, had said something funny and his mom and dad were laughing. He was seated in his mother's lap, and the warm sun was shining on his face.

Next, the dream shifted to his father's gravesite. He was holding his mother's hand, trying not to cry. He pleaded with God not to let them put his daddy in the ground. God wouldn't listen. He tried to stop them from throwing dirt on the casket. His daddy wouldn't be able to breath. The man with the shovel pushed him down. From the ground, he looked up and saw Patricia Wells and Regina Phillips, dressed in black, standing behind a tree, laughing. Flaunting the fact that they had gotten away with it.

The dream would continue. Now, he was two year's older, living in a musty smelling house. He was covering his face in defense as Frank swung the strap over and over again. He felt the sting but tried to put it out of his mind. Out of the corner of his eye, he could see his mother passed out on the couch, her empty glass lying on the floor.

The dream ended with him waking up in a cold sweat. The dream always resulted in a massive headache that would not go away until morning. He knew after he killed Regina Phillips that the nightmares and headaches would stop.

* * *

Shattered Lives

Roy Weston hung up his phone. Finally, he had located Ricky. He had been alerted that Ricky's credit card had been used to charge a room at the St. Louis Drury Inn Convention Center. This time Ricky would not get away from him.

Roy was not surprised that Ricky had selected downtown as the place to stay. He knew that Regina Phillips worked downtown. During the months he had followed Ricky just after his release from prison, he learned that Ricky was infatuated with her. He also knew why. He had learned that Regina Phillips was responsible for Patricia Wells getting off scot-free after the accident that killed Ricky's father.

The only thing that surprised him was that Ricky had waited so long to kill her. The only reason for this that Roy could come up with is that he enjoyed the anticipation and didn't want it to end. It was kind of like saving the best food on your plate for last. Anyway, Roy decided it was senseless to try to rationalize the thoughts and actions of a madman.

Roy was now convinced that the timing was right, and Ricky was finally going after Regina. That was the reason he had chosen a hotel so close to her office. It was time to put an end to Ricky, once and for all.

Chapter 31

I found out from one of my mother's friends that Lisa Rogers now lived in Cape Girardeau, Missouri. Before I placed the call, I debated on how I was going to break the news to her. It's not an easy thing to tell a woman that you have strong evidence that suggests that her husband was wrongly executed.

I am not known for my tact or my sensitivity. Normally, I don't mince words, I get right to the point in a conversation. In this case, even I realized it would not be appropriate to begin the conversations with: *Hi, Mrs. Rogers, this is Rob Gipson. I know you don't know me, but I happen to know who really committed the crime for which your husband was executed.*

I decided the best way to handle it was to first tell her I believed her husband was innocent, and that I had discovered information that might be helpful. Then, I thought I would explain that I had reason to believe that the person responsible for Lora Smith's murder was also responsible for numerous other murders.

When she answered her phone, my voice began to crack. I was extremely awkward as I tried to repeat the words I had rehearsed. When I finished, I wasn't sure if her reaction would be one of sadness, anger, or elation.

As expected, at first she was shocked. After a long silence, she explained that I was the first person since Darrell's execution to show any interest in the case.

She then muttered that she knew this would eventually happen; that the truth would finally come out. I couldn't tell if she was speaking to herself or to me, but it was clear that she did not know quite how to process this new information.

After the initial shock, she became excited. She demanded to know the details. When I told her I would rather discuss it in person, she insisted I come over right away.

Cape Girardeau was a quick thirty-minute trip from my parent's house in Sikeston. Lisa Rogers lived in a nice, brick ranch home near Southeast Missouri State University. As I walked up the sidewalk leading to her front door, I couldn't help but notice her immaculate yard. The shrubs were all neatly trimmed, and the street and sidewalk were perfectly edged. Flowers were blooming all around her house.

I was nervous as I rang her doorbell. In less than ten seconds, she opened the door and welcomed me inside. Although I had never met her before, I did see her numerous times on TV and in the newspaper during the trial. I remembered that she was a very attractive woman. As I saw her now, I noticed that she had aged very well. She was even prettier than I remembered.

Although now fifty-one, she looked much younger. She had a very warm smile and a radiant glow that seemed to brighten up the room. This was in direct contrast to my earlier impression of her as the sad and bashful wife of a murderer.

I had expected her to be bitter and angry for the miscarriage of justice done to her and her family. She was anything but bitter. After spending just ten minutes with her, it was obvious that she had not dwelled on the past and instead had gotten on with her life.

I learned that after Darrell's conviction she and her daughter, Sara, had moved to Jefferson City to be closer to the prison. She had taken a job as a waitress, and with the help of Darrell's mother, she and Sara had managed to make ends meet. After the execution, she received one hundred thousand dollars in life insurance proceeds on Darrell's policy. With the life insurance funds, they were able to buy the house in Cape. This allowed them to be closer to Darrell's mother.

As I stood in her kitchen and watched her start the coffee maker, she explained how she and Darrell had become close to the Lord in the last few years of Darrell's life. After his death, she made the decision to spend the rest of her life doing the Lord's work. At first, she began doing volunteer work at her church and the homeless shelter. A few years ago, she became the full-time, paid youth minister of the First Baptist Church of Cape County.

She led me into a sunroom that had been added to the back of her house. After pouring us both a cup of coffee, she politely asked me to explain how I had become involved in the case and the facts I had uncovered that made me convinced that Darrell was innocent.

I walked her through the chain of events. I began by explaining that I had grown up in the same neighborhood in Sikeston, where she and Darrell had lived. I told her I remembered the trial very well. A teardrop slid down her cheek as I expressed how sorry I had felt for her and her daughter after the trial.

As I told her about Ricky, she never said a word. She would nod from time to time, letting me know she followed what I was saying. I described the similarities between the St. Louis murders and Lora

Smith's murder. I also explained my theory that Ricky had murdered Patricia Wells on year before he murdered Lora Smith. I mentioned that Ricky matched the description that the surviving victim gave of her attacker, and that Ricky lived near each victim at the time of the murders.

Then I went over the most compelling piece of information I had: the toolbox described by Mrs. Hammonds. When I told her that Ricky had owned a blue truck, containing a built-in toolbox, she began crying. As she sobbed, she told me that it was now in God's will for the truth to come out.

"This is where I need your help," I replied. "We need something to corroborate the toolbox. I know from talking to Mrs. Hammond's son that a private detective was working on behalf of your husband. Apparently, Mrs. Hammons mentioned the toolbox to the detective. Mr. Hammond's impression was that the detective felt the toolbox was important to Darrell's case. I was hoping you might know who he is, and how we can get in touch with him."

"Yes, Rob, I knew the detective. His name was Eric Lowe. At one time he worked for the Sikeston Police Department. A British organization called the BADP, whose purpose was to abolish the death penalty throughout the world, had taken a special interest in Darrell's case. They believed he was innocent and wanted to prove it so that they could use him as an example of what is wrong with the death penalty. They hired Eric Lowe to prove Darrell's innocence."

She took a sip of her coffee and continued. "Eric Lowe began the investigation, but then took off unexpectedly. He told the BADP he could no longer work the case due to personal reasons. The next thing we knew he had skipped town, and we could not locate him. The BADP believed he found something and then used it as blackmail. We know that shortly after telling the BADP that he was quitting the job, he came into a great deal of money. He then went on a wild spending spree. A couple of months later, the BADP called me and told me he had been murdered in South Carolina."

She continued. "We believe the money and murder are too coincidental. Someone very powerful and influential was responsible for giving him the money and for killing him. We believe the same person is somehow tied in with Darrell's case. We tried to get the authorities involved, but they were not interested. Neither the Feds nor the local police had much use for the BADP. They were even less interested in what I had to say."

"Did the BADP have a feeling for who may be responsible?" I asked.

"Yes, they did. They actually suspected that Jim Bryant was behind this. I know it sounds farfetched, but according to the BADP, Jim Bryant is not the moralistic, family values guy he portrays to the public."

"Hardly any of them are," I agreed.

"The BADP dug up some information on our good senator. Apparently, he lives a double life. The one you see in public is different from the one he lives in private."

"Surprise, surprise. Surely, you're not suggesting that a politician would not be genuine" I replied, sarcastically.

"All politicians have big egos, but Jim Bryant is eaten up with his. He also craves power, and according to the BADP he will do anything to get it."

"The question is, Lisa, would he go so far as to allow an innocent man to be executed? If what you are implying is correct, it would also mean that he was responsible for the murder of Eric Lowe. Do you and the BADP believe he is capable of that?

"Up until today, I did not believe so. Now with the information you have just presented, it is all starting to make sense. Eric Lowe somehow figured out that Ricky Henry had killed Lora Smith. He also knew that Jim Bryant had encouraged Mrs. Hammonds to withhold information during her testimony at trial. Instead of seeking justice, he used the information to blackmail Jim Bryant. After the payoff, Jim Bryant saw him as a continual threat and had him murdered."

Although I wasn't sure I believed it, I had to admit that Lisa's theory made sense. What if her theory was true? My stomach muscles tightened as I thought of the ramifications. Our nation may be in the process of electing a psychopath as president.

Worse yet, what if he found out Lisa and I suspecting him? If Lisa was correct, he had already murdered once because he felt threatened. We could be next. What had I gotten myself into?

Chapter 32

May 19, 2003: St. Louis, Missouri

I have never considered myself a particularly brave person; nor have I been prone to take excessive risks during my lifetime. Somehow though, here I was, with Lisa, standing outside the door of a serial killer's apartment. With sweat pouring down my face and hands shaking so badly that I could barely hold the keys, I finally managed to unlock the door.

I was somewhat proud of my ingenuity. I had obtained the keys by telling the manager of Ricky's apartment complex that I was Ricky's brother and was worried about him. The manager was more than willing to allow us to inspect the apartment. He complained that Ricky had not paid last month's rent. Anything I could do to help collect the past due rent would be greatly appreciated.

Apparently, Ricky had vacated the apartment suddenly, leaving behind his furniture, clothes, and television set. It was obvious; also, that Ricky had not been back to the apartment because his mailbox was overflowing. The mail carrier had left a notice on the box stating that all future mail could be picked up at the post office. The manager told me if someone didn't remove the furniture and belongings from the apartment within the next week, he was going to have them hauled off to the county landfill.

Even though I knew Ricky would not be in the apartment, I was still a little apprehensive. I knew, however, that Lisa and I needed something definitive to give the police. As much as I dreaded it, I knew our best bet was to search Ricky's apartment.

As I unlocked the door, I hesitated before opening it. Lisa shoved me to the side and forcibly opened the door.

"What were you waiting on?" she demanded.

"Well, I guess I wanted to make sure there wasn't a knife waiting on the other side of the door for me," I replied.

"Oh, give me a break. You know Ricky's not here."

I was a little embarrassed that I'd let a woman take charge of this situation. I had even tried to convince Lisa not to come, but she had insisted. Now that she was here, I was amazed at her resolve and courage.

The front door opened into the living room. As I followed Lisa inside, my first observation was of how clean and neat Ricky kept the apartment. There was nothing out of place, and the apartment looked spotless. This surprised me. Apparently, Ricky was a clean freak. We quickly walked through the apartment, checking out the living room, kitchen, bathroom, and bedroom. Lisa appeared to be much calmer than I was. I couldn't help but be nervous. I halfway expected to find body parts or a wall plastered with pictures of dead women. I was relieved to find that the apartment looked the same as any ordinary apartment; only cleaner.

After failing to find something obvious, we decided to split up for a more thorough search. I agreed to search the kitchen and bathroom.

Lisa said she would search the bedroom. I began by opening the kitchen cabinets. Every minute or so, I looked over my shoulder toward the front door, just to make sure Ricky hadn't sneaked in carrying a knife. After a few minutes, I began to relax a little.

The cabinets contained the usual plates, glasses, and cups; all neatly arranged. Satisfied there was nothing useful in the cabinets, I moved to the drawers located on either side of the sink. The farthest drawer to my right, and next to the refrigerator, contained the utensils. Hoping to find several large knives he had used as murder weapons, I was disappointed to note there was nothing larger than a steak knife.

As I began searching the next drawer, the refrigerator kicked on. The sudden, unexpected noise sent me reeling backwards. As I spun around to see if anyone was behind me, I ran into Lisa, practically knocking her over. We both yelled.

"What are you doing?" I yelled.

"Just checking to see if you found anything. Why did you run into me?"

My face flushed, and I tried to conceal my embarrassment. "I heard a noise."

Lisa laughed. "A little jumpy, are we?"

"Yeah, I guess my training as an accountant didn't exactly prepare me to track down a serial killer. In the accounting profession, you are seldom placed in life or death situations. When I heard the noise, I became a little spooked."

It is amazing at how a man's pride is a greater force than fear. Suddenly, I was no longer nervous. I was angry at myself for being such a wuss. At that moment, a part of me wished Ricky would walk into the apartment, so that I could redeem myself. I was now more determined than ever to do whatever was necessary to find new evidence.

Finding nothing in the kitchen or bathroom, I moved into the bedroom to check on Lisa's progress. I saw her sitting on the floor going through some information she had pulled from the dresser drawers. Instead of disturbing her, I decided to check out the bedroom closet.

Consistent with everything else in the apartment, the clothes and shoes in the closet were neatly arranged. What I noticed most was that there were so few clothes. Mostly blue and black jeans and T-shirts. There were only three or four button down shirts. Ricky was partial to dark colors. At least half of his shirts were black.

Looking up, I noticed a shelf above the hanging clothes, just a few inches below the ceiling. I grabbed a chair from the desk and stood on it to reach the shelf. The shelf was still too high for me to see anything, so I had to feel around with my hands. Starting from the right I began moving my hands across the plywood, feeling to see if there was anything on the shelf.

When my hand hit the far-left wall, I noticed the drywall was not level. As I pushed against the wall, a portion of the drywall caved in. Feeling the hole, I reached in as far as I could and felt an object. By instinct, I jerked my hand back through the hole.

"Lisa, I think I've found something. There appears to be a box hidden behind the wall."

"Can't you pull it out?" she asked.

I took a deep breath and, mustering all the courage I had, I put my hand back into the hole and felt for the box. I said a short prayer, pleading that there were no body parts waiting for me through that hole. I was relieved when my hand touched nothing but the box. I was able to grip the lid and pull the box out of the hole.

I waited until I had climbed down from the chair before I looked at the box. It was an old shoebox, and judging by the weight, it appeared to be full of papers. I set it down and Lisa and I looked at each other, both afraid of what might be inside.

Deciding to redeem myself for the embarrassing scene in the kitchen, I quickly pulled the top off. I was relieved that the inside of the box contained only newspaper clippings and loose photographs. After we spread the contents out on the floor, we placed the articles in chronological order. They were all from the Tyler, Kentucky newspaper and covered the years from 1968 to 1978.

Two of the clippings were of the car accident from 1968 that resulted in the death of Ricky's father. One, describing the accident, had a large picture of Ricky and his father. In the photograph, seven-year-old Ricky was sitting on his father's lap, smiling as though he didn't have a care in the world. The article accompanying the photograph described the accident as a head on collision. It made no mention of the fact that the Henry's truck was parked on the side of the road. The article made note that Tom Henry was pronounced dead at the Tyler hospital, and that the boy, Ricky, was in critical condition. The article identified Patricia Wells, a prominent local attorney, as the driver of the other vehicle. She was listed in stable condition. There was no mention of her blood alcohol content.

The second clipping, from the following day's edition, quoted the prosecuting attorney, Regina Phillips, as saying she would not seek charges against Patricia Wells concerning the accident.

A couple of the clippings covered Patricia Well's murder in 1978. The remainder of the articles seemed to follow the career of Regina Phillips. One was an editorial praising her moral character and her desire to seek justice. Written over the editorial in red ink was the word: "LIES."

The last clipping described Regina's resignation from the prosecutor's office in Tyler to work for a law firm in St. Louis. Handwritten in the right margin of the clipping were two addresses: one appeared to be a business address in downtown St. Louis; the other a residential address in St. Louis.

Along with the newspaper clippings, there were three photographs. They were of a middle-aged woman. One of the photographs had St. Louis' Trans World Dome in the background. Since the dome was not completed until 1996, I knew this was a fairly recent picture.

Lisa and I compared the woman in the photograph to the picture of Regina Phillips in the newspaper. Even though the photograph was taken at least eighteen years after the newspaper article, it was obvious it was Regina Phillips. She had aged very well.

"She may be his next victim!" I said. "He's apparently on the run, and I doubt he would leave town with her still alive."

"I'd say its almost a certainty," Lisa agreed.

"It's probably time for us to go the police, Lisa. It may be the only way to save Regina Phillip's life."

"Do you think they will believe us?"

"I think it's a long shot. They will probably blow us off. Even though we have circumstantial evidence tying him to the Patricia Wells and Lora Smith murder, the St. Louis police are not going to be very concerned about two murders that occurred twenty-five years ago in Paducah, Kentucky and Sikeston, Missouri. Especially, since a man has already been convicted and executed for one of the murders. They will only be interested in the St. Louis murders, and our problem then is that even with these newspaper clippings and photographs, we have no hard evidence suggesting that Ricky is responsible for the St. Louis murders. All we have is the physical description given by one of the victims."

"Rob, what about Senator Bryant? Should we mention our suspicions that he killed the person blackmailing him for his wrongful conviction of Darrell?"

"I think we would lose credibility for sure if we brought that up. It's so shocking to think that a senator would be capable of murder that no one will take us seriously. They will think we are lunatics if we accuse a United States senator of murder without any hard proof. They will probably equate us with the likes of people who still think Elvis is alive or people who believe they have been abducted by aliens."

We both agreed we would go to the police and give it our best shot. If that didn't work, we would have to personally convince Regina Phillips that she was a target of the serial killer.

Chapter 33

Roy Weston took another sip of coffee as he stared at the monitor in his apartment. *Who are these two, and what are they looking for?* he thought.

Thanks to the hidden cameras he had placed throughout Ricky's apartment, he was now watching a man and a woman pilfering through Ricky's closets and drawers. He knew the man's name was Rob and the woman's name was Lisa. Unfortunately, during their conversations, they did not use each other's last names.

Roy watched with interest as the man pulled a box down from a shelf in the bedroom closet. He was immediately disappointed for failing to find the box himself when he had searched the apartment. He watched them sort through the contents of the box and listened intently to their conversation. He was surprised when he heard them refer to Ricky as a serial killer. He was astounded when they mentioned Senator Jim Bryant. Somehow, they had figured the whole thing out and they were going to the police with it. This was turning out to be a disaster.

He knew he had to stop them before they made it to the police station. He hesitated a little as he grabbed his gun. He looked at it and winced. He could kill a man without any hesitation or guilt; that had never been a problem. But a woman; that was a different story. He was an old softy when it came to women; especially pretty ones. Despite having killed numerous times, the only women he had ever killed were the two at St. John's hospital: Melissa Grogan and the elderly woman. Those killings hadn't bothered him. The older woman was on her deathbed anyway, and Melissa Grogan was alive only because he had personally intervened and stopped Ricky before Ricky had a chance to finish her off.

This was different. He would have to kill a perfectly healthy, attractive woman. He had always hoped this day would never come. He knew he had no choice, however. Like it or not, the assignment required it of him.

The woman knew too much. He had no idea who this Lisa was, but he could never allow her to talk to the police. She would lead the police to Ricky; then to Jim Bryant; and finally to himself. It was a matter of self-preservation. He would have to kill her.

He cursed himself for being so sensitive. It was a weakness, and in his line of work you cannot afford to have weaknesses. *No more Mr. nice guy,* he muttered.

As he slammed his apartment door shut, he cursed Ricky Henry. This two-bit killer had managed to outsmart him, humiliate him, and was now forcing him to violate his sacred principles. He couldn't wait to get his hands on Ricky.

As he swung into the parking lot in front of Ricky's apartment, he was almost sideswiped by a green minivan. Roy had to turn the wheel hard to the right to keep from missing the van. He glared at the van and saw that the male driver was having an animated discussion with his female companion. He was obviously not paying attention to his driving. Angrily, Roy pounded his horn. If it weren't for more pressing matters, he would have chased him down and beaten the crap out of him.

Roy swung into the parking spot nearest to Ricky's apartment. Placing the gun into the back of his jeans, he entered the building and ran up the stairs. Deciding to hurry and get it over with, he quickly opened the door. Seeing no one in the kitchen or living room, he hurriedly checked the bedroom and bathroom. His pulse quickened as he realized they had already left the apartment.

The minivan. They must have been the man and woman in the minivan, he thought.

He sprinted to his truck and within minutes, he was on Interstate 55 heading north toward the downtown police station. The speedometer reached eighty-five; still no sign of them. He knew from the conversation he had overheard in Ricky's apartment that they were planning to go to the downtown police station. A sense of panic struck him as he realized he must find them before they reached the station.

He pulled off the interstate onto Memorial Drive. There was still no sight of a green minivan. The light at the Walnut intersection was red, but he ran right through it causing a car to slam on its brakes to avoid hitting him. He turned left onto busy Market Street, going sixty. Running through two additional red lights, he had to do some fancy maneuvering to avoid hitting several cars. Horns were blaring, and he received the finger at least a dozen times. Fortunately, there were no police in the vicinity. He turned left on Tenth and right on Clark. The station was several blocks directly in front of him, and still he did not see the van.

Just as he was beginning to think he was mistaken; that the minivan was not the correct vehicle, he saw it turning onto Clark Street just three blocks ahead of him and one block from the station. He slammed on the accelerator, passed two cars and caused a car in the opposite lane to run off the road and crash into a light pole behind the city hall building.

He finally reached the police station, but he was too late. They had parked, were already out of the minivan, and were walking toward the front door.

Roy knew he had to act quickly. It would be too late once they made it inside the building. He stopped his truck directly in front of the station. He saw that Rob was opening the front door for Lisa. He had to do something drastic to stop them from getting inside.

Fortunately, the green berets had provided Roy with the training necessary to take decisive action in the heat of battle. He saw a police officer walking up behind Rob and recognized an opportunity. Just as Rob entered the building, Roy instinctively shot the officer. The officer fell immediately to the pavement. A second and third shot then hit the glass door just as Rob stepped inside the building.

Due to the silencer, no one heard the shots. The shattering of the glass, however, was heard as was the scream of the officer. Total chaos ensued. What was left of the front door was shattered as several officers ran through it, ducking to avoid any future gunfire.

Before he sped down the street, Roy caught a glimpse of Rob and Lisa running out the door and down the stairs. Apparently, Roy's shot had missed them both. He had accomplished his objective, however. With an officer down, the police station would be in turmoil for the rest of the day.

Because the silencer was used, no one could tell from what direction the shots were fired. Fortunately for Roy, a man was standing in front of the police station at the time of the shooting. The officers immediately assumed he was the shooter, and by the time they realized he did not have a gun, Roy was safely out of sight.

He drove around downtown for a few minutes until he reasoned that it would be safe to return to the scene. As he approached the station a few minutes later, he smiled as he witnessed the chaos he had created. He realized there would be no police reports taken today. He had averted a catastrophe.

A group of officers were erecting barriers to the parking lot. A second team was stringing yellow crime scene tape across the front walkway. Roy assumed Rob and Lisa would be unable to get their minivan out of the parking lot. He was surprised when he saw it in his rear view mirror turning off Clark Street.

"I guess they didn't want to stick around to get shot at again," he mused.

Twenty minutes later, he watched the minivan pull into a driveway in a residential area of South County. Roy soon realized it was Rob's house. He had his gun out, but put it back under the seat when he saw three children come out of the house.

He didn't care what the stakes were, he would not risk the life of a child. Even Roy Weston had his limitations.

Lisa and I were still shaking when we pulled into my driveway. Neither of us knew if we had done the right thing by leaving the police station. Truth is, we both panicked. We were pretty sure that we were the intended targets, and we felt our chances of living through the day would be better if we made it out of there. Someone obviously had seen us at Ricky's apartment. Since we had no idea who we were dealing with, we didn't know now if we could trust the police.

One thing I knew for sure was that if we were, indeed, the intended targets, my family might be in danger as well. Lisa and I decided we should get Stacy and the kids out of town as soon as possible.

I pulled Stacy into the bedroom and shut the door. I explained what had happened and that they might be in danger. It took me awhile to convince her to take the kids to my parent's house in Sikeston. She begged Lisa and I to go with her and the kids. I assured her that we would as soon as we warned Regina Phillips.

Reluctantly, she agreed. Within ten minutes, I was relieved as she and the kids backed out of the driveway. At least they would be safe.

Next, I tried to convince Lisa to leave. "There is no sense in both of us sticking around and being in danger. You need to go home or stay with your daughter," I said.

"No way, Rob. I have a bigger stake in this than you do. It was my husband who died as a result of this. I am in this for the duration. No one wants justice and answers more than I do. If it means risking my life, then so be it."

With that decided, we both agreed it would be safer to leave the house. If someone were looking for us, this would be the first place they searched. I grabbed the phone book and the cell phone, and we climbed back into the minivan. As we drove off, neither of us noticed the red Explorer that followed us.

With one hand on the steering wheel, I punched in the number as Lisa called it o After three rings, a receptionist came on the line: "Michaels, Raper, Conway, and Phillips. Can I help you please?"

"I need to speak to Regina Phillips, please."

"One moment please, while I connect you with her secretary."

The phone rang again and within a few seconds, a pleasant voice came on. "Regina Phillips office. This is Nancy. May I help you?"

"Yes, my name is Rob Gipson. I need to speak with Mrs. Phillips. It is very important."

"Can I tell her what this is regarding, sir?"

With mounting frustration, I replied. "Please tell her this is personal, and it is imperative that I speak with her immediately."

"Just a moment, Mr. Gipson."

After being placed on hold for what seemed like an eternity, Regina Phillips came on the line. In a tone that suggested that I had just interrupted something important, she spoke. "Regina Phillips here."

"Mrs. Phillips, my name is Rob Gipson. It is very important that I meet with you today. I am afraid you may be in some …."

Before I could complete my request, she cut me off. "Mr. Gipson, I don't believe I have you scheduled on my calendar today. I am afraid I'm terribly busy. You will have to talk to my secretary to schedule an appointment."

Before I could respond, she had transferred me back to Nancy. When Nancy came on the line, she had Mrs. Phillip's calendar out. "Mr. Gipson. Mrs. Phillips has an opening at three o'clock on July 19."

I was astounded. "But this is only May."

"Mrs. Phillips is a very busy attorney."

"Look Nancy. I need to see her today. It's for her own good."

Apparently, my latest comment was mistakenly perceived as a threat. Before I could utter another word, Regina Phillips was back on the line informing me if I ever tried to call back she would have me arrested and prosecuted for harassment. When I heard the click on the other end, I was furious.

I turned my head and looked at Lisa. "Here we are trying to help this woman and she hangs up on me. You know, I'm starting to side with Ricky. I don't think I like Regina Phillips. She wants us to leave her alone, maybe we should oblige her."

Lisa smiled as if to let me know she knew I wasn't serious. The problem was that I was only half kidding. I'm not sure I was willing to potentially risk my life for an arrogant primma donna like Regina Phillips.

"Rob, you know you wouldn't be able to live with yourself. Besides, I have an idea. Give me the phone."

I handed the phone to her, anxious to see what she had up her sleeve. So far, nothing Lisa did surprised me. I had known her only a short while, but already I was amazed at her resolve and spontaneity.

Lisa flipped through the yellow pages until she found the section listing the attorneys. She scanned the section until she found a quarter page ad for the law firm of Michaels, Raper, Conway, and Phillips. She read the ad and informed me that the firm specialized in medical malpractice, product liability, and bankruptcies.

Without hesitation, Lisa hit the redial button and soon had the receptionist back on the line. Within seconds, she was speaking with Nancy.

"Yes. My name is Rita Pounds. Ms. Phillips was recommended to me by my divorce attorney. I recently had a hysterectomy at St. Vincent's Hospital. I developed an infection, and when I went to Good Hope's emergency room, they X-rayed me and found that two sponges were left in me from the surgery. I had to be operated on again for the sponges to be removed. I spent three weeks in the hospital and have lost two month's wages."

Nancy perked up. "Just a second, Ms. Pounds, Mrs. Phillips will be right with you."

This time there was no delay. Regina Phillips was on the phone immediately. No, it would not be a problem. She could see her within the hour. All of a sudden, her schedule was not quite so busy.

She smiled as she placed the phone on the dashboard. "How did you come up with that?" I asked, still amazed.

"The one thing I have learned throughout my husband's horrible ordeal and my own personal experiences is that lawyers love money. In fact, I am convinced that some of them have a sixth sense. They can smell it."

"A few years ago, I had a hysterectomy and my obstetrician mistakenly left two sponges inside me. I developed a horrible infection and missed several weeks of work. The attorneys were like lap dogs at my feet. I don't know how they found out about it, but I received visits from three of them before I was even discharged from the hospital. They were practically begging me to sue the doctor and the hospital. They said I had an airtight case. It was a no-brainer. It would be easy to prove negligence. According to the attorneys, I would take them to the cleaners because juries are not sympathetic to doctors and hospitals. Juries perceive them as greedy and arrogant."

"I wasn't about to sue, however. It was a simple mistake that could have been made by any doctor. I don't believe it is Christian to take advantage like that. One of the attorneys wouldn't let it go. Told me I was making the biggest mistake of my life. He said I didn't know how lucky I really was. I had won the lottery but was refusing to cash in my ticket."

"Can you believe it? I had been lying in a hospital bed with a one-hundred-five degree fever, and this greedy bastard was telling me how lucky I was."

"So, I decided to take a gamble that Regina would be one of those attorneys who would salivate at the chance to sue a doctor and a hospital. Fortunately, she didn't disappoint me."

As I watched her manipulate her way into the appointment with Regina Phillips, I realized I had never been around a woman quite like Lisa Rogers. Until this moment, I had not fully appreciated her beauty. Her intelligence and determination made her that much more attractive.

Within fifteen minutes, we were pulling into the parking garage adjacent to the Metropolitan Building. The building, which towers over sixty stories, is the tallest in St. Louis. Next to the Arch, the Metropolitan Building is the most impressive structure in the St. Louis skyline.

We rode up the elevator to the forty-first floor. As expected, the offices of Michaels, Raper, Conway, and Phillips were plush. We stepped off the elevator into a lobby that had money written all over it. Although the furniture and artwork meant absolutely nothing to me, I was sure it cost a fortune. The lobby conveyed the impression that the firm was a major player in the legal world. They were in the "big leagues". I wondered how many physician mistakes it took to pay for this elegance.

We were ushered into Regina's office immediately. Regina Phillips, all smiles, stood up to greet us as though we were long lost friends. Regina, now in her early sixties, looked much younger than her age. The tightness around her face indicated that she was no stranger to plastic surgery.

Her office was every bit as nice as the firm's front lobby. We were led to the leather chairs in front of her massive, mahogany desk. I couldn't help but notice the plaques and photographs hanging on her walls. It looked like a shrine. She had numerous photos of herself smiling next to celebrities and politicians. In the photos, I noticed Bill and Hillary Clinton, Al and Tipper Gore, and Johnny Cochran. There was even a picture of her shaking hands with Mark McGwire. She had no fewer than ten plaques to showcase her numerous civic contributions.

To prevent anyone from obtaining the mistaken impression that she was too focused on her career, she had on display numerous family photos. Her enormous desk and walls were adorned with pictures of her husband, children, and grandchildren. Somehow, I found it difficult to imagine her at the soccer fields watching her grandchildren.

Still smiling, she began the conversation. "Hi, I'm Regina Phillips. It's so nice to meet both of you. Please have a seat."

No sooner had we sat down, when Nancy came back into the office to offer us coffee and rolls.

Still annoyed at the rude manner in which I was treated when I called earlier, I saw a chance to get even. "Sure, we'd both like to have some coffee and rolls," I replied. "In fact if it's not too much trouble, could you make mine a cappuccino?"

Just as I was really enjoying myself, I suddenly felt a sharp pain in my arm as Lisa pinched me. I looked over, saw her icy stare, and knew I'd better back off.

"On second thought, regular coffee will be just fine. It's so soon after lunch that I think we will pass on the rolls."

Nancy looked relieved as she began pouring the coffee.

Eager to get down to business, Regina pulled out a notepad. "So, tell me exactly what happened to you at St. Vincent's Hospital."

Lisa responded right to the point. She quickly informed Regina there was no case. We were here because we believed she was a target of the serial killer. We made up the case, so that we would have an opportunity to warn her.

Regina's smile suddenly turned into a scowl. She began trembling. At first I couldn't tell if she was upset because she was a murder target or because she had just lost a potential million-dollar settlement. My guess was the money. I was right.

She stood up and shook her finger at me. "You're the nut who called earlier, aren't you?"

"Look, lady. We're just trying to help you."

"Get out now, before I call security."

"Fine. Lisa, let's go. We've done our duty. We've warned her. Now I'll be able to sleep at night."

I had had enough of Regina Phillips. At this point, I couldn't care less what happened to her. As I started to open the door to leave the office, Lisa stopped me. She turned to Regina.

"Ms. Phillips, I know this sounds strange, and I know you have no idea who we are, but we have real evidence suggesting your life is in danger. We have gone to a lot of trouble to warn you. The least you could do is to hear us out."

Regina motioned for us to sit, and I reluctantly walked back to the chair. We then walked her through the information we had gathered. She never said a word or changed her expression. When we finished, she told us it seemed farfetched that the boy involved in Patricia Wells accident was the serial killer. Still unsure about us, she demanded to see the evidence.

We decided to meet later that night at her house. We agreed to bring the newspaper clippings and photos obtained from Ricky's apartment, as well as the evidence we had linking Ricky to Patricia Wells and Lora Smith's murders.

Part 3:
Justice For All

Chapter 34

Those who worked for him and were close to him knew something was wrong. Compared to most politicians, the speech was decent. But for Jim Bryant, the speech was nowhere near the high standards he had established for himself. Something was wrong. The fire was missing. His heart was not in it.

The majority of those in the crowd didn't seem to notice, however. They did not realize he was off his game. They could not tell his mind was preoccupied. They had paid five thousand dollars a plate to dine with the leading candidate for president of the United States. As long as their names made it on the attendance roster, they didn't care. Most were corporate CEOs, who were here to try to buy a political favor.

The crowd also did not notice the two, armed bodyguards in attendance. One sat directly behind the senator, and the other stood a few feet to the right of the podium. Both bodyguards wore suits, so everyone assumed they were new additions to the senator's campaign staff.

Jim Bryant was nervous. In fact, he was more nervous than he had been at any time in his life. Not only was his candidacy in jeopardy, his life was at risk. Ever since he had learned that Ricky Henry was after him, he hadn't been able to sleep or eat. He saw Ricky's face around every corner, behind every door.

As he rattled off his canned jargon about reducing crime, ending welfare, improving family values, passing campaign reform legislation, he was really thinking about Ricky. Roy Weston had to come through. If Roy didn't take care of Ricky, he would have to find another hired assassin very quickly. He had no idea how he would go about finding someone. He had always relied on Roy.

He finished his lackluster speech and went through the motions of shaking hands and slapping backs. He then left the banquet hall, flanked by Roy's two henchmen.

He reached into his pocket and pulled out a Pepcid and two Tylenols. He hoped the Pepcid would help sooth his nervous stomach. The Tylenol would numb the pounding he felt in his head.

He had already made the decision not to go home tonight. It was too risky. He had decided that until Ricky was killed, he would stay with Natalie. Taylor was told he had late meetings scheduled each night this week, so he would be sleeping at the office. This was plausible, since he had actually stayed at the office many times before. His office had a fold out couch and a private bathroom with shower.

Jim had not warned Taylor about Ricky. In a way, he hoped Ricky would come to his house. Maybe, once Ricky realized the senator wasn't home, he would go ahead and kill Taylor. That way, Jim would be rid of her without the political fallout of a divorce.

Jim had his chauffeur drive around the block a few times until he was sure no one had followed him to Natalie's house. He then ordered the bodyguards to follow him into the house and check each room just to make sure Ricky wasn't around. He then positioned one of the bodyguards in front and another in back of the house.

Once inside, Jim headed straight for the liquor cabinet and the bourbon. He was frustrated with himself. Until now, he had always been able to see the positive in any situation. He was one of those who believed the glass is half full, not half empty. This time, however, it was difficult to find anything positive to hang his hopes on. As the second shot of bourbon began to be absorbed into his bloodstream, he began to feel a little better. It was amazing that the liquor always seemed to provide him with a different perspective. He began to think positive. Maybe Roy had found Ricky by now, and his problem had already been solved.

He was startled as he heard the doorknob turn. He looked up and was pleased to see Natalie walking toward him. She was stark naked. He smiled. Things were definitely looking up.

It was five o'clock in the afternoon, and Ricky was restless. He still had three hours to go, and he hated waiting. As he looked out his hotel window, he could see the city streets becoming busy. Rush hour had started.

The euphoria he had felt earlier in the day had faded. It had been great while it lasted, though. He had followed Regina to the restaurant and had even managed to sit at the table next to her. He had a whole hour to stare at her, and relish what he would be able to do with her tonight. Once she had glanced over at him and he had smiled at her, but she quickly looked away.

"She thinks she is too good to even acknowledge me. She doesn't know it, but she will have to acknowledge me soon enough," he thought.

He was very familiar with her schedule now. It was a Wednesday night, so she would be attending the monthly board meeting of the local American Red Cross Chapter. The meeting would end by eight, and she would be home by eight thirty. He would be there waiting for her.

Her husband, as usual, was out of town on business. Ricky was hoping he would be home. He had originally planned to kill Regina's husband in front of her to increase her suffering. Now, he would have to find an alternate means to make her suffer. That wouldn't be a problem, though. He had always been good at improvising.

He lifted the knife from the top of the dresser. The sunlight peering through the window reflected off the blade, making it glisten. Rubbing his fingers gently along the edge of the blade, Ricky muttered to himself, "Revenge is sweet."

It was difficult for him to take his mind off Regina, but he knew he had travel plans he needed to make. He picked up the five-inch thick St. Louis area yellow pages and looked up the phone number for American Airlines. Using the phone next to his bed, he called the airline and booked a one-way flight from St. Louis to Washington for seven a.m. the next morning. He was looking forward to his first trip to the nation's capital.

It was dusk as Roy drove his SUV onto the Tenth street ramp leading to the interstate. The green minivan was two cars in front of him. Roy had been following them since the near disaster at the St. Louis police station earlier in the day.

Before he had entered the ramp, Roy crossed Clark Street. Several blocks to his right was the police station. He chuckled as he glanced in that direction. Several hours had passed since the shooting, but the scene was still in total chaos. Hundreds of people were milling around. He could see several vans from the local TV stations, accompanied by camera crews and reporters.

I'll bet the reporters are loving this, he thought. *They won't have to worry about digging up another story for the next few nights. They should send me a Christmas present.*

By tracing the license plate of the minivan, Roy had learned that the owner was Rob Gipson. He quickly discovered that Rob had grown up in Sikeston and had lived next to Ricky as a kid. In fact, he lived next to him at the time of Dr. Lora Smith's murder. *That had to be the connection*, Roy thought. Somehow, Rob figured out that Ricky was responsible for murdering Lora Smith. That, and the physical description of the serial killer provided by Melissa Grogan, led him to suspect Ricky of being the serial killer.

Roy was also fairly certain the Lisa in Rob's van was Lisa Rogers, the wife of Darrell Rogers. It only made sense that if Rob thought Ricky was Lora Smith's real killer then he and Lisa would have a common interest in proving it.

What worried Roy was whether or not they had confided in anyone else. If others knew that Ricky was the killer, and that Senator Bryant had an indirect role in the murders, then he may not be able to protect the senator. At this point, he had to assume they had kept the information to themselves.

What was interesting was the fact that Rob and Lisa had also tied Ricky to Patricia Wells murder twenty-six years ago. That took some pretty nifty detective work, especially for an accountant and a social worker.

The whole situation was becoming very interesting. He knew that Rob and Lisa had visited Regina earlier in the day. He had followed them into the lobby of the Metropolitan building, and observed them enter the elevator. He knew they were there to see Regina because he watched them locate her name on the building's directory in the lobby. He suspected they were now leading him to Regina's house in the Central West End.

It was becoming darker by the minute, and he almost missed seeing the minivan take the Kingshighway exit. Now, he was certain they were heading to Regina's house. He followed them north on Kingshighway, passing between Forest Park on the left and the large Barnes Hospital complex on the right.

The minivan turned right on Lindell. As he drove along the commercial district of the Central West End, Roy spotted two guys wearing tight leather pants and holding hands while strolling along the numerous shops and restaurants. "Queers" he muttered. He had no tolerance for those who preferred an alternative lifestyle. If this assignment weren't so important, he would have stopped and blown the queers away.

There was plenty of time for that later. Now, he had to take care of these two before they had a chance to go to the police. Roy smiled as he thought of his luck. *I must be living right to be this lucky*, he thought.

If Rob and Lisa were correct and Regina was, in fact, Ricky's next target, he could simply hide out at Regina's and wait for Ricky. If everything went according to plan, he could kill Rob, Lisa, and Ricky without ever leaving her house.

Roy saw them pull in front of a large three-story, brick house. He knew most of the houses in the Central West End were built before the turn of the century. He also knew the majority of the houses were priced in excess of one million dollars. *Regina must be a pretty good lawyer to afford this,* he thought.

He watched Rob park the minivan and saw them walk up the steps to the front door. He then drove his car to a nearby restaurant. He parked, slid the pistol under the back of his shirt and briskly walked toward the house. Within minutes he was standing outside her front door, hidden behind a large oak tree.

Chapter 35

The house was every bit as impressive as I expected. I knew from the Central West End address that the house would be large. The houses in this neighborhood were considered mansions by St. Louis standards. Like all the majestic homes around it, the house and lawn were in immaculate condition. Back in St. Louis' heyday in the late nineteenth and early twentieth centuries, this was where the movers and shakers lived.

Lisa and I rang the doorbell at fifteen minutes after eight. An elderly woman, wearing an apron, answered the door. "Please come in," she said with no emotion. "Mrs. Phillips will see you in the parlor."

I gave Lisa a quizzical look. I didn't realize people still used the term "parlor". As I looked around the interior of the house, I was amazed at its opulence. Once again, I began to feel sorry for the poor doctors who had paid for it all. We were led into the parlor and asked to sit in two very uncomfortable chairs. A few minutes later, we heard Regina's voice. She was telling the woman who had greeted us that she could go home for the night.

We heard the front door shut, and a few seconds later Regina appeared in the parlor. She sat on a chair immediately in front of us. Without so much as a greeting, she rudely jumped right to the point. "Okay, let's see this 'so called' evidence you say you have."

There are some people whom you initially dislike when you first meet them, but ultimately you begin to warm up to them and end up liking them. Not Regina. The longer I was around her, the more I disliked her.

Angrily, I grabbed my folder of evidence and removed the three photos of Regina. "These came from Ricky's apartment," I said as I showed her the photos of herself. "These newspaper clippings also came from his apartment. As you can see, the articles all involve you and Patricia Wells."

I continued. "I lived next door to Ricky when I was twelve years old. I know for a fact that he blamed you and Patricia Wells for the misfortunes he experienced in his life. He killed Patricia Wells and now he's coming for you. Let's not play games here. We know you helped cover up for your friend, Patricia Wells, the night she killed Tom Henry."

I had Regina's undivided attention now. She turned flush and began to speak. I raised my hand in the air to stop her. "Let me finish. Lisa and I also have evidence here that strongly suggests that Ricky murdered a Sikeston doctor, who lived a few blocks from his house. It is our opinion that Ricky takes the anger he harbors toward you and Patricia Wells out on other successful, professional women. I don't know if you remember, but Ricky has two hideous scars from the accident in 1968. These scars were identified by one of the St. Louis victims."

I was now pointing to Lisa. "This poor woman's husband was wrongly convicted and executed for one of Ricky's murders. So, we have a vested interest in finding the truth here. You see, Mrs. Phillips, at this point I do not care if you believe us or not. We have done our duty. We have warned you. Now, we will be leaving. Good luck to you."

I gathered our evidence and indicated to Lisa that I was ready to leave. She started to object, but she could tell that I was in no mood to compromise. I had had enough of Regina Phillips. Besides, despite being the saint she is, I believe Lisa also had her fill of Mrs. Phillips.

Regina never said a word as we began to make our exit. Apparently, she was somewhat humbled by our revelation. We were about three steps from the parlor door, when we heard a door open from the opposite end of the room. We turned and saw a man appear in the doorway. For the first time in my life, I was facing the barrel of a gun. For a second, I could not catch my breath.

"Stop right there, you two. You're not going anywhere." The man then pointed the gun at Regina, and motioned for her to join us.

Regina appeared defiant as she stood up and stomped over to us. She sneered at the man, as though this was just some minor inconvenience. She acted as though having a gun pointed at her head was an every day occurrence. For all I knew, and based on what I had seen of her so far, maybe it was.

The man was now standing in front of the parlor door that led into the kitchen. He was approximately fifteen feet away from us.

I wanted to ask Regina if she believed us now, but I refrained. I was so scared I'm not even sure I could have gotten the words out if I had wanted to.

Regina looked at me and whispered. "Is that Ricky?'

He must have heard her. "No, lady. I'm not Ricky. My name's Roy Weston." He then turned to Lisa and me. "I must admit. I am very impressed that you were able to piece all this together. Now, I have to ask you a question. Who have you told?"

By this point, I was pretty sure I had it figured out. Roy Weston worked for Senator Bryant, and he was probably responsible for the shooting at the police station. He was also, more than likely, the one who killed the detective, Eric Lowe. I knew we were going to be killed anyway, so I figured I might as well learn the truth before I go to meet my maker. I chose to ignore his question. "Do you work for Senator Bryant?" I asked in a shaky voice.

"You didn't answer my question, partner. It's none of your business who I work for. I suggest you tell me right now whether or not you told anyone what you know about Ricky or the Senator." Just for emphasis, he pulled the hammer back on the pistol and pointed it directly at my head.

Lisa quickly spoke up. She reasoned that our only hope was to convince him that others were also aware of what we knew. Then maybe he wouldn't find the need to kill us. "Yes, we've already gone to the police," she said.

He smiled. "You're lying. You forget that I was there with you when you tried to go to the police. That poor police officer; what a shame. He happened to be at the wrong place at the wrong time. Kind of like you are now. I just want you to know that if there were any other way, I would let you go. It pains me to have to kill two beautiful women."

Again, he raised the pistol. This was it; the end of my life. I was going to die at age thirty-seven, in an attorney's house in the Central West End of St. Louis, leaving behind a wife and three children. I heard Lisa mutter the beginning verses to Psalms 23. I closed my eyes, just wanting to get it over with.

I expected to hear a shot, but instead I heard a gasp. For a second, I wondered if I was already dead. I knew I was still alive when I realized I could open my eyes. I saw the gun fall out of Roy's hand, and then I watched him fall to his knees. Blood was pouring from his neck.

Behind him stood a thin man, dressed in black. As soon as I saw the scar, I knew it was Ricky. He had apparently been hiding in the kitchen, on the other side of the door.

As he fell from his knees to the floor, Roy turned his head and briefly caught a glimpse of the only man ever to have beaten him. He tried to speak, but due to his sliced carotid artery, the only sound that would come out was a gurgle. He was drowning in his own blood.

I put my arm around Lisa as I stared at the infamous serial killer; my former neighbor. Ricky bent down over Roy and picked up the gun. Still holding the knife, he started to walk towards Regina. Never saying a word, he looked over at me, and our eyes briefly met. I saw a flicker of recognition in his eyes. He then stared at me for a long moment as if he didn't know what to do. Instead of continuing toward Regina, he turned and walked slowly out of the parlor, toward the front door. I have no idea why, but I followed him. Before opening the door, he looked back at me. I thought I saw a slight grin form at the sides of his mouth. It was the same grin I saw twenty-five years ago when we played catch in my back yard.

As the door closed behind him, I walked over to Lisa and sank to the floor. I was dazed. When I finally regained some form of consciousness, I said a short prayer thanking the Lord for another chance at life. My first thoughts were of Stacy and the kids, and of how close I had come to never seeing them again on this earth.

I made a vow right there on the spot. I would be a better person. No more fishing on Sunday mornings. No sir, I would be sitting in the church pew every Sunday morning from now on. No more cursing; never again would I swap R-rated jokes at the office coffee pot. Never again would I take a second glance at another woman besides Stacy. From now on, only pure thoughts would enter this mind. I had never been so grateful in my life. I knew that only by the grace of God was I still on this earth.

I looked over at Lisa and saw that her head was still bowed. As expected, she too was saying a prayer. I realized she was probably the reason the Lord had spared us. God probably needed her to stay on this earth to complete her good deeds.

Regina was sitting on the floor, with a blank expression on her face. She was staring straight ahead at the door in which Ricky exited. I noticed that her right hand was trembling.

For what seemed like an eternity, the three of us sat quietly, reflecting in our own private way what we had just witnessed. I guess we were too shocked to speak or move. We sat a foot apart from each other, and Roy Weston's body lie no more than five feet in front of us. A large puddle of blood had formed around his body, and his blood was trickling along the hardwood floor towards us.

I was the first to make a move. I stood up but my legs were so wobbly I had to grab the wall to keep from falling. Regina followed. She made it to her feet and immediately walked over to the telephone, that was sitting on a coffee table. Without saying a word, she began to dial 911.

Suddenly, I had a thought. "Hold on Regina. Don't call the police just yet. Let's see if old Roy here has something on him that will link him with Senator Bryant."

I have no idea why I called her by her first name. I guess appropriate formalities can be disregarded once you've been through a life and death experience with someone.

"What's Senator Bryant have to do with this?" she replied.

We had not explained that part of our theory to her yet. I did my best to explain, as succinctly as possible, Jim Bryant's indirect involvement in these murders. Unlike before, this time she believed us without hesitation. She expressed astonishment that Jim Bryant would knowingly allow an innocent person to die for political gain. My intuition, however, told me she probably would have done the same thing if faced with a similar set of circumstances.

Regina and I walked over to the body. Lisa remained seated with her head bowed. Roy's clothes were now soaked in his own blood. Somehow, I managed to pull his wallet out of his back pocket. Regina helped Lisa to her feet, and the three of us left the parlor and walked into the kitchen. We then emptied the contents of the wallet onto the kitchen counter.

The contents were what you typically expect to find in a wallet: drivers license, credit cards, insurance cards, etc. There were also several business cards, none of which appeared to be linked to the Senator. There was a folded index card with three numbers written on it. There were no names or references written next to the numbers.

"Let's find out who these numbers belong to," I said.

"Hold on a minute," said Regina. "Let me grab a tape recorder. If Jim Bryant is on the other end of one of these numbers, I want to get it on tape."

Apparently, the initial shock of almost being murdered by two different people had already worn off. Regina was once again thinking like an attorney, and she saw this as an opportunity. She would be known as the attorney who had survived a serial killer and brought down a corrupt presidential candidate. She became ecstatic as she thought of the exposure she would have. She would appear on *60 Minutes* and *Dateline*. Her story would become a best seller. She would become a national celebrity.

While Regina was dreaming of fame and fortune, I was beginning to fume. As I thought of all the harm caused by Jim Bryant, I became furious. All these deaths could have been prevented. I had never hated anyone so much in my entire life as I did him at that particular moment. I wanted to bring the bastard down.

Once we were satisfied the recorder was ready to go, I turned on the phone speaker and dialed the first number. It was for a local Dominos Pizza.

The second was a cell phone number. The call was answered on the first ring.

"Yeah. Is that you, Roy?" asked the voice on the other end.

"Hello, Senator Bryant"

Realizing I was not Roy Weston, the senator became nervous. "Who the hell is this and how did you get me private number?"

"Let's just say I'm an acquaintance of Roy's."

"Where's Roy?" demanded the senator.

"Well, if I were to venture a guess, I'd say he probably didn't make it past the pearly gates. I'm looking at Roy right now, and I really don't believe he will be of much help to you in the future." I replied.

The senator was now near panic. "Is that you, Ricky?"

"No Senator. I'm not Ricky, although I wouldn't be surprised if Ricky isn't looking for you. You see, he knows you hired Roy to kill him. I, along with my two friends here, know all about your dirty little secrets. We know you allowed Darrell Rogers to be executed, despite having knowledge that Ricky was responsible for the crime. We also know you hired Roy Weston to kill Eric Lowe, the detective who was bribing you. In a few minutes the police will know and, by tomorrow, I suspect the whole world will know. I suspect you will have a visit from the police tonight; unless of course, Ricky gets to you first."

"Who are you? I'm sure we can come to some understanding. How much do you want?"

"We want to see you suffer in a prison cell just like Darrell Rogers did. This time your money won't be able to help you, Senator."

Before he could respond, I hung up the phone. We played back the tape to make sure we had a clear recording. Regina then completed her call to the police.

Chapter 36

Four hours had passed since we called the police. It was now one O'clock in the morning, and we were still at the downtown police station trying to explain our story. When the officers first arrived on the scene, we had not appreciated the difficulty we would encounter in convincing them of what had occurred. We had naively assumed that with a dead body, the taped conversation with the senator, and the evidence gathered from Ricky's apartment, the police would immediately believe us. We expected them to be thrilled and to proceed with the arrest of Ricky and the senator. We were badly mistaken.

When the police first arrived at Regina's house, they were immediately very suspicious. They did not believe our account of events. After all, our story did sound ridiculous. When we first began explaining what had transpired, the initial response was raised eyebrows and smirks. By the time we finished, we were all three in handcuffs, being read our rights. Before we were led outside to the squad cars, we did manage to convince them to allow us to bring the folder of evidence with us to the police station.

After having had time to think about it, I can't say that I fault the police. Our story just didn't make sense. It's just not plausible to believe that three people's lives were saved by an infamous serial killer. We were asking the police to believe that the man lying on the floor in a pool of blood had come to the house to murder all three of us. At precisely the same time, the St. Louis serial killer, who had eluded the police for years, showed up at the same house to murder Regina for something she had done to him over thirty years ago. But instead of murdering her, he decided to slice the other killer's throat, steal his gun, and simply walk off, allowing all three of us to live. He allowed us to live in spite of the fact that we could now identify him. It sounded too strange to be true.

We had to enter the police station through the back door because the front door was still damaged from Roy's bullets earlier in the day. We were then led to a conference room on the east side of the building. Among those sitting across the table from us were St. Louis Police Chief, Bob Recker, and the Special Agent in Charge of the FBI's St. Louis office, Don Davis. There was also several other St. Louis homicide detectives and FBI agents in the room.

I was seated directly across from Chief Recker. His piercing eyes were fixed on me like I was some sort of criminal. He was a hulk of a man; at least six feet three, with wide shoulders and a protruding belly. He looked like an ex-weight lifter. I remembered from an article in the St. Louis Post Dispatch that he played right tackle for the Missouri Tigers in the 1970's. Like many ex-football players, his muscle had turned to fat. To me, he appeared very intimidating.

Special Agent Davis had the opposite appearance. He was a small, wiry man, who appeared to be in his mid-thirties. He wore wire-rimmed glasses that made him look intelligent. Whereas Chief Recker gave the impression he solved his cases with brute force and intimidation, Special Agent Davis made you think he solved his cases through research and reasoning.

While Lisa and I remained fairly calm, Regina was furious. Back at her house she had been belligerent when the officers failed to believe our story. Her arrogance and rudeness were probably the main reason we were hauled off so quickly to the station. Apparently, the officers weren't all that impressed with the fact that she was an attorney.

Regina was now seated at the conference table, fuming. She reminded me of a coiled rattlesnake about to strike. She stood up, pointed her finger at Chief Recker, and let him know that she personally knew the mayor and several councilmen. She would see to it that he lost his job over this. The chief didn't appear to be too worried.

Lisa, the epitome of reason, realized that Regina's antics were doing us no favors. She grabbed Regina's arm and jerked her back in her seat. Just as Regina was about to spew out more of her venom, Lisa told her to shut up. Regina was so shocked at this uncharacteristic display, that she stopped talking.

Since I originally pieced everything together, Lisa felt I should be the one to explain it to the police. As I began recounting the events, it sounded so strange that I wasn't even sure I believed it. I knew one thing for sure. If we couldn't convince the police soon, we would be spending the night in jail. I wasn't looking forward to bunking with some two hundred fifty pound murderer named Bubba. As I talked, the detectives and agents constantly interrupted me, asking questions. After about ten minutes of this, I realized I was having no luck whatsoever. I was also becoming angry. Finally, I had enough and had a few choice words to say to the police chief. Lisa then grabbed my arm, leaned over, and whispered to me that she would like to take a shot at it. I was grateful.

Lisa was terrific. She began by telling them she knew our story sounded far-fetched. She pleaded with them to hear her out. She started from the very beginning and walked them through the entire chronology of events: the car accident in 1968 that killed Ricky's father; Regina's involvement in the cover up of Patricia Wells crime; the murder of Patricia Wells; the murder of Dr. Lora Smith; the involvement of Jim Bryant in the prosecution of Darrell Rogers for the murder of Dr. Lora Smith; the subsequent St. Louis murders; the realization by Jim Bryant that Ricky (not Darrell Rogers) was responsible for killing Lora Smith; and the hiring of Roy Weston by Jim Bryant to cover-up the truth.

She then explained how she and I figured it all out. What turned the tide was when she explained in detail how Roy Weston attempted to kill us at the police station earlier in the day. Based on the details she gave, they knew she had to have been there. They knew then we were either telling the truth, or we were the ones responsible for the shooting.

When she pulled out the photograph of Ricky, I knew we had finally convinced them. Chief Recker looked at the scars, and immediately recalled Melissa Grogan's description of her assailant. "Well I'll be! They are telling the truth. This Ricky fella is our man."

The mood in the room changed immediately. I could tell the officers were becoming excited as they realized they now knew the identity of the killer. The pressure from the public to solve the crimes had become intolerable. They were relieved. The nightmare may finally be over.

Chief Recker was grinning ear to ear. He stood up, shook my hand, and pounded my back as though I had just sacked the quarterback. All of a sudden, we were transformed from suspected murderers to heroes.

Just as I began basking in my newfound glory, another detective entered the room. He handed a report of some sort to Chief Recker.

The chief reviewed the report and sat back down in his seat. "Boys, it also appears they are telling the truth about our good senator. These telephone records show numerous calls back and forth between Roy Weston and Senator Bryant. We also have information here that links our dear friend, Roy, to organized crime. Apparently, he was a big time mob hit man for the Balducci family in New York. The Feds could never obtain enough evidence to arrest him. I think its time we wake up a judge and obtain an arrest warrant for the senator."

"Hold on a second, Chief" said Agent Davis. "You're talking about a United States senator. We have to be one hundred percent certain of his involvement before we have him arrested. The only hard proof we have is the taped conversation, which may or may not be his voice, and the telephone records. Can you imagine the fallout that will occur if we're wrong?"

"We're not wrong, Davis. I knew there was something phony about him. All that family values junk he spouts off is just for show. I never did like that weasel."

I had to admit that the chief and I agreed on that point.

"Our decision to arrest him has nothing to do with whether or not you like him Chief," said Agent Davis. "If we issue a warrant tonight, you know somehow it will be leaked to the media by morning. It will be the top story on the morning news shows. We are simply not ready at this point to handle that. This is a political hot potato. I need to involve the FBI director on this one."

I looked at my watch and noticed it was now almost three o' clock. I had been through enough and saw this as a good opportunity for us to leave. "Well, since you finally believe us, I think we will be going home now. It's been a long day."

Agent Davis spoke up. "You will be key witnesses for both of these cases. In Senator Bryant's case, we still do not know exactly who is involved. It's possible that Roy is not independent and continues to work for organized crime. If that's the case, you are still in serious danger. We need to keep you in protective custody until we know for sure whom we are dealing with."

Two hours later I was lying in a bed at the Holiday Inn at Westport Plaza. Despite being exhausted, I couldn't sleep. I kept thinking about Carla and of how this would impact her. Her life would be changed forever.

I knew I had to contact her the first thing in the morning. I did not want her to hear this for the first time on the news. As a result of my recent FBI connections, I learned that she now lived in Savannah, Georgia. I also had her telephone number. I was dreading the phone call.

Dawn was beginning to break as Ricky looked out the window, while seated at the airport snack bar. A DC9 was taxing into the airport concourse. He nibbled on a muffin and sipped a cup of strong, black coffee. His flight would begin boarding in about forty minutes. He was anxious to get on the plane.

Ricky thought about Regina Phillips, and why he let her live. He had been surprised to see Robbie Gipson. Even though it had been twenty-five years since he had seen him, he recognized him right away. He never forgot a face. Normally, he would not have hesitated to kill anyone interfering with his plans, but then he remembered how good Robbie and his family had been to Carla. They had taken care of her after he was arrested and his mother was in the hospital. He owed them. Despite his hatred of Regina Phillips, he just could not bring himself to harm Robbie Gipson.

He knew now that Robbie had been there to warn Regina. He had no idea how Robbie knew he was planning to kill Regina. It didn't matter though. There would be time to deal with her when he arrived back from Washington. The wait would make the experience that much more enjoyable.

Ricky's thoughts were interrupted when a man, seated at the next table, reached up and adjusted the sound on the overhead television. The bottom of the screen indicated there was a breaking news story. The reporter was standing in front of city hall, announcing that the St. Louis police had identified a suspect in the serial killings. The reporter went on to say that Police Chief Recker would be holding a news conference in one hour. Ricky looked up just in time to see his picture on the screen.

He quickly rose up from his seat and tore up his plane ticket. With his identity now made public, he would not be able to fly. He then walked briskly down the concourse and through the terminal. No one seemed to pay any attention to him as he made it safely outside the terminal.

Once outside, he was relieved. He knew with his distinctive scar, he would be easy to spot. He must keep a low profile. Instead of taking the airport shuttle, he chose to walk through the long tunnel connecting the terminal with the intermediate term parking lot.

As he started his SUV, he reached under the seat and found Roy's gun. By now, the police would know his license number and would be on the lookout for his vehicle. He may need the gun if the police spotted him and tried to pull him over. They would never capture him alive.

He knew it was risky remaining in St. Louis. His picture would soon be plastered on the front page of the newspaper. He would also be the lead story on each of the local news channels. Leaving St. Louis wasn't an option, however, until he finished his business. This time, he was determined not to let anyone get in his way.

Chapter 37

May 20, 2003

The sunlight peering through the bedroom window momentarily woke Jim Bryant. He opened his eyes and looked over expecting to see Natalie next to him in the bed. She was not there. He tried to get out of bed, but the wave of nausea and the pounding in his head made him lie back down. He fell back asleep.

Ten minutes later he was aroused by a burning sensation in his chest. He stood up and had to grab the side of the bed to keep from falling down. He staggered to the toilet, barely making it before he threw up.

His headache was unbearable. He reached into Natalie's medicine cabinet and grabbed a handful of Tylenol and quickly gulped them down with water from the bathroom sink.

At first, he didn't remember anything from the night before. He was used to hangovers, but never one like this. He stumbled into Natalie's living room and sat down in her recliner. He tried to remember. What had he done the night before to make him feel so lousy?

As his mind began to clear a little, another wave of nausea swept over him. This time, as he knelt over the toilet, he remembered. The dry heaves he was experiencing now had nothing to do with the alcohol, but was the direct result of the phone call he received last night. It was all coming back to him.

He walked back into the bedroom and climbed back into the bed. He wished he were dead. It was all over now. He would never be President. His career would end in shame and humiliation. Instead of greatness, he would be remembered as corrupt. All the good things he had accomplished would be forgotten.

He saw his suitcase next to the bedroom door and wished he had followed through with his plan to leave the country. His worst fears were realized when he had answered the phone last night. Not only had Roy failed to kill Ricky, someone else had discovered the truth. His first thought last night, as he hung up the phone, was self-preservation. He had intended to flee the country. Then he realized that he would rather be dead than to live out the remainder of his life as a failure.

His next thought was to end his life. He had taken the pistol Natalie kept in her dresser drawer. He placed the gun to his head and tried to pull the trigger, but he just couldn't do it. He was a coward, and he hated himself for it. He needed some help. After four of five shots of bourbon, he was ready to try again. This time he would have pulled the trigger, but Natalie came in the room.

He remembered how appalled Natalie was to find him with the gun pointed to his head. She took the gun from his hands and pleaded with him to tell her what was wrong. He drank more bourbon, then told her the whole story. Her reaction was anger. She said she no longer knew him. He recalled her saying something to the effect that their whole relationship had been a lie, and that she was a fool. With tears in her eyes, she left the house. He hadn't cared.

As he closed his eyes, he remembered what he did next last night. He had opened her medicine cabinet and found a prescription for hydrocodone. There were seven tablets remaining of the painkiller. This was his way out. He reasoned that an overdose had to be easier than shooting himself.

He estimated the seven pills and the fifth of bourbon would be more than enough to do the trick. He washed down the pills with more bourbon. He then remembered sitting down in the recliner to wait out the last hour of his life.

Within thirty minutes, the pills started taking effect. At first he felt euphoric; so good in fact that he regretted taking the pills. Then he began having trouble catching his breath. It was becoming harder and harder to breath. The last thing he remembered was lying down in the bed, feeling very dizzy. He had thought for sure he was dying.

Then he woke up this morning to the worst hangover he had ever experienced. As he stared out the bedroom window, he cursed himself. He didn't even have enough guts to kill himself.

He found the remote and flipped to CNN. As he expected, the story was already out. CNN was showing a taped press conference of St. Louis Police Chief Bob Recker, informing the public that they had identified a subject in the serial murders. A picture of Ricky Henry was then shown. He was described by the CNN news desk reporter as the man who had terrorized the city of St. Louis the past ten years.

Following the conclusion of the press conference, the reporter then informed the audience that there was a breaking news story. "Sources close to CNN have just confirmed that Senator (and presidential candidate) Jim Bryant is wanted for questioning in the Ricky Henry investigation. At this point, we do not know the senator's exact involvement. Attempts to contact Senator Bryant have been unsuccessful. Stay tuned for further details."

Jim's head was beginning to clear a little, and the Tylenol was numbing the pain in his head. He began to focus. Maybe he had overreacted last night. As he sat in the recliner, he tried desperately to think of a way out of this. He soon realized it was hopeless. There was no way out. For the first time in his life, he couldn't count on his family's money to bail him out of trouble. No amount of money or influence could undo what had already been done.

The anonymous caller from last night had obviously already met with the police. The caller's story would be easy to confirm. The police would be able to link him to Roy Weston through phone records and wire transfers from his bank account to Roy's.

Even if the police could not prove he had hired Roy Weston to murder Eric Lowe, they would still be able to prove that Eric Lowe had blackmailed him. They would discover the five million dollar disbursement from his accounts and the subsequent deposit in Eric Lowe's account. They would also find that numerous phone calls were made to Roy, immediately following the payoff and just prior to the murder.

The final nail in the coffin that would tie everything together was Ricky Henry. Investigators would learn, just as Eric Lowe had discovered, that Ricky was the real killer of Dr. Lora Smith. They would interview Mrs. Hammond's son and would find out that Eric Lowe was aware that Ricky was the killer and used this information to blackmail him.

The pieces of the puzzle would all fit together. Jim hired Roy Weston to murder Eric Lowe to prevent further blackmail attempts and to ensure that no one ever learned the truth that Ricky killed Dr. Lora Smith. Ten years later, Jim hired Roy Weston again. This time it was to make sure Ricky was never arrested for the serial killings. When one of his victims gave a physical description, Jim became nervous and instructed Roy to kill both the witness and Ricky. In summary, Jim Bryant was responsible for three murders and for concealing evidence that would have prevented at least ten additional murders.

Jim knew that in the unlikely event the police would not prove for sure he was responsible; the circumstantial evidence would be enough to bury him. Even if he weren't convicted, he would be ruined. In the eyes of the public, he would be guilty.

The worst part would be his father's reaction. His father would be devastated. All the successes and positive accomplishments he had achieved during his life were done to win his father's approval. He would never be able to handle his father's rejection.

Jim knew he had to do something. He had no intention of sticking around for the humiliation and disgrace that he knew was inevitable. The gun. Where did Natalie hide it? Although the details from the previous night were fuzzy, he didn't remember her taking it with her when she left.

He desperately searched the bedroom drawers. Then he remembered the safe, where she kept her jewelry, stock certificates, and other valuables (most of which he had paid for). She must have placed the gun in the safe. He knew she had written the combination in her telephone book. Within minutes, he had the safe open, and sure enough, the gun was there.

With the gun in his hand, he walked back to the recliner in the living room. Before he checked out, he wanted to reflect one last time on his life. He knew he had some time before he would be located. The police nor anyone else knew where he was at the current moment. He and Natalie had been so discreet it was unlikely anyone would find him here. It was also unlikely that Natalie would tell anyone about the affair or that he was at her house. She would be too embarrassed.

He thought about leaving behind a note, saying how sorry he was for what he had done. Maybe he should apologize to the family of Darrell Rogers. What about the families of Ricky's victims? He surely owed them an apology also, since he could have prevented their murders. The more he thought about the suicide note the worse he felt. What good would the note do, anyway? Besides, there was a slight chance that with him dead, the investigation would not be as intensive. He saw no benefits to admitting his guilt in writing.

He was sorry. Not for Darrell Rogers or the murder victims and their families, but for himself. For all his regrets, however, he knew he would do it all over again if he thought he could get by with it. He wished he could have been more like his mother and younger brother. They always did the right thing. They weren't ambitious; they were content with their lives just the way they were.

He, on the other hand, was power hungry, and was never content with the status quo. He had to be the best, no matter the cost. He was born that way; raised that way. His father had demanded that from his first born. This turned out to be his downfall.

He looked at himself in the mirror. He saw the face of a man who had come within an eyelash of being the president of the most powerful country in the world. He realized that the gamble was worth it. With any luck at all, he would have made it.

Despite his strong public positions on morality, he was not a religious person. He attended services each Sunday at the First United Presbyterian Church. It was all for show, however. He knew Americans wanted to see their leaders in church each Sunday, so he obliged. He believed in a God, but he never really believed all that nonsense about needing a personal relationship with him. That was for the weak. He wasn't even sure he believed in heaven or hell. For the first time in his life, however, he wished he believed.

He decided not to prolong the inevitable. The longer he waited the harder it would be. With shaking hands, he grasped the gun. Placing the barrel of the gun in his mouth, he quickly pulled the trigger.

Chapter 38

After a fitful four hours of sleep, I finally climbed out of bed at eight o' clock. I managed to make it to the sink and washed my face. The mirror confirmed the fact that I was exhausted. My eyes were bloodshot and had dark circles under them. It was obvious this ordeal had taken a physical toll on my body.

Even though I had been exhausted when I arrived at the hotel last night, I had trouble sleeping. My body was physically tired, but my mind was in overdrive. It wasn't fear that kept me awake. I wasn't concerned for my own safety. I didn't really believe I could be a target of the mob, which is what the FBI feared. Even if they were correct, after everything I had been through, I wouldn't have been nervous. My nerves were suddenly made of steel. After taking on Roy Weston and Ricky Henry, I figured the mob would be a piece of cake.

The real reason I was unable to sleep was a feeling of guilt that I could not shake. I began reflecting on everything that had occurred and realized I could have prevented it. If only I would have suspected Ricky sooner. If I had been more observant, all those women would still be alive. I, as much as anyone, had been aware of Ricky's potential for violence.

When I did finally doze off, I had a horrible nightmare. I dreamed I was at my own funeral. I saw Stacy and the kids standing in front of my casket, crying. I woke up from the dream in a cold sweat. After the dream, I was only able to doze off a few minutes at a time. The dream made me realize once again, how lucky I was to still be alive. Never before, had I realized how much I loved Stacy and the kids, and of how good my life was.

Now as I brushed my teeth, all I wanted was for this nightmare to be over. I wanted to be with my family. I longed to get back to my routine; the safety and monotony of my job; the little league baseball games; the choir concerts. I wanted to hug my kids.

I was grateful the hotel furnished the room with an in-room coffee maker. Within minutes, my room was filled with the wonderful aroma of brewing coffee. I mixed a small package of Coffee Mate in my coffee cup and walked over to the standard desk and chair that is found in every hotel room.

On the desk I found the piece of paper with Carla's telephone number. I decided to wait a few minutes before I called her because I wanted to prepare myself for the call. I wasn't sure of the proper way to tell someone that her brother is a mass murderer. I was too nervous to eat, so I thought the best thing to do would be to drink a couple cups of coffee. At least I would be alert when I called her.

I found the remote lying on the desk, and I flipped the television on. I was surprised to find that every local station was reporting on the case. Word had already leaked to the press.

I listened to the reporter describe the major break in the case. The police had identified a subject. I was very surprised when she gave the name of the suspect. I knew I needed to call Carla before she saw it on the news.

Reluctantly, I picked up the phone to call her. My stomach was in knots as I began dialing. Just before the first ring, I noticed the television station had switched to a news conference. I hung up the phone when I saw that Chief Recker was the person speaking. He was behind a large podium in front of the city hall building. Beside him stood Special Agent Davis. There was a large crowd of reporters standing in front of the podium.

Chief Recker was clearly enjoying his moment in the spotlight. This was his ten minutes of fame and he was prepared to take advantage of it. The press conference would, no doubt, be viewed on the national news later in the day. This fact did not go unnoticed by the chief.

Begrudgingly, he introduced FBI Special Agent Davis. He left no room for doubt, however, that he was the one in charge. As he spoke, it was clear he was not bashful about taking credit for the break in the case. Humility was not one of the chief's strong suits.

"Ladies and gentleman, I am pleased to report to you that we have identified a suspect in the eleven unsolved murders. Due to the due diligence and the excellent investigative work of my detectives and myself, we will be making an arrest in the near future. The suspect's name is Ricky Henry. Although I am not at liberty to discuss the specific evidence linking him to the murders, I can tell you he matches the physical description given by Ms. Grogan. We also have fingerprints that place him in the residence of at least two of the victim's."

A reporter in the front row broke in. "What made you first suspect Ricky Henry?"

"Um, I cannot divulge that at this time. I can tell you it was the result of excellent work by my department," the chief responded.

You can't divulge it because you had nothing to do with it, I thought. *It was handed to you on a silver platter. I guess that fact just slipped his mind.*

"What role did the FBI play in the investigation," asked another reporter.

"Well, they did provide some ancillary assistance to us," he explained. He then gritted his teeth and tried in a futile attempt to smile at Agent Davis "I do appreciate the help provided by the FBI, however, I want to reiterate that it was the St. Louis Police Department that diligently worked days and nights to solve this crime. I am pleased to report that the citizens of the great city of St. Louis will soon be able to live without fear."

"What is your response to the rumor that two private citizens are responsible for solving these crimes? Is there any truth to this?" asked a female reporter.

The chief appeared stunned by this question. Instead of answering the question, he indicated that he needed to end the press conference. After all, he had a mass murderer to arrest. In a flash, the chief was gone and the interview was over.

I turned off the television and shook my head in amazement. *What an ego?* I thought.

After leaving the airport, Ricky felt it would be best if he left town, temporarily. He drove out into the hill country, approximately twenty-five miles west of St. Louis. He decided he would spend the rest of the day in the woods.

Nature and the outdoors always helped him collect his thoughts. Anytime he had a problem, he would head outdoors; preferably to a place far from human contact. This is what he remembered his dad doing when he had a problem to solve.

Usually when he was alone in the woods, he would connect with his dad. He would feel his presence. This is when he would reflect on those wonderful times they spent together so many years ago. He would relive the peaceful walks through the woods; the stories they shared around a campfire; snuggling up next to him in the tent. For a while, he was once again a seven-year old boy.

Ricky walked along the rocky banks of the Meramec River. This was one of his favorite spots. The air was clean and crisp, and the rushing current usually had a soothing effect on him. The water was cold and clear, and despite the heat and humidity, the air was cool and refreshing. As he walked along the riverbed, he would look for deer, squirrels, turkey, and other wildlife.

Usually the river and woods helped him relax. Not this time. No matter how much he tried, he could not suppress the rage that was building inside him. When it became this strong he had to release it or he would go crazy. Killing was the only way to release this inner rage. When he was like this, his mind became obsessed with Regina Phillips and all the other women who had treated him like dirt.

Approximately fifty yards ahead of him he saw a fallen oak tree, with its uprooted trunk extending to the water's edge. This would be a good place to sit and rest. As he surveyed the beauty around him, he decided he may as well set up camp here. Maybe if he really focused, he could put Regina out of his mind for a few hours.

Hr unhooked his backpack and removed his gear. He always kept his pop-up tent, sleeping bag, flashlight, kitchen utensils, matches, and backpack in the back of the SUV. As a result, he was always prepared to camp.

Every police officer, FBI agent, and highway patrolman were now searching for him. He knew that. He was safe here though. In fact, he could hide out indefinitely if he wanted. He considered himself a survivalist. He'd had plenty of practice. His stepfather had taught him to survive under the harshest of circumstances.

Once when he was only nine years old, he ran away from home after one of Frank's beatings. He vowed he would never return. Despite below freezing temperatures, he managed to hide in the woods around Tyler, Kentucky for three days and three nights before Frank finally found him. As punishment for this transgression, Frank locked him in the outdoor storage shed for three whole days. No light, no food. This was more than his mother could stand. While Frank was at work, she ignored his orders and let Ricky out of the shed. When Frank found out, he sent her to the hospital with a broken jaw. The emergency room doctor was told that she slipped and fell on the ice.

On one hand it would be fun to hide out and make the authorities sweat. Think of all the attention he would receive. It would be enjoyable to once again make them look like idiots; especially that arrogant chief of police. At the press conference, he promised an arrest in the near future. Ricky scowled as he thought of the smirk on the chief's face.

"Not too long ago he wasn't smirking," he thought. The police had been no match for him. He had taunted them and made them look like fools. "The chief of police is too smug and arrogant to realize he has no chance. I will only be caught if I allow them to catch me," Ricky said to himself.

As he stared at the river, he realized he could wait no longer. If he didn't have relief soon he would explode, or worse yet, have to face the nightmares and voices. He could no longer afford to be patient. The urges, which had been growing stronger as the day progressed, were now irresistible. The job needed to be completed.

The police would no doubt be looking for his vehicle, so it would be a challenge. He lived for challenges, though. It would be him versus Chief Recker and the entire St. Louis Police force. The prize would be Regina Phillips. It would happen tomorrow.

The next day: May 21, 2003 – 9:00 a.m.

By the next morning, the city of St. Louis was a media circus. The suicide of the leading Presidential candidate had set off a media frenzy not seen in this country since the assassination of President Kennedy in 1963. This time, instead of Dallas, the spotlight was on St. Louis.

The details of Senator Bryant's connection to the St. Louis murders remained sketchy. Unconfirmed reports surfaced that the senator was responsible for several murders for hire, and was somehow involved with the suspect in the St. Louis serial killings. Although no one in the media knew for sure why the senator had taken his own life, they knew the answer would be found in St. Louis. So, reporters flocked to the city by the hundreds.

The city of St. Louis was founded in 1764; by a Frenchman named Pierre Laclede. During the city's two hundred forty- year existence, only the 1904 World's Fair brought the city more attention.

Lisa and I had to wade through thousands of people inside the airport terminal. Reporters from around the world were arriving in St. Louis. Due to the heightened security measures enacted after the nine-eleven terrorist attacks, we could not meet Carla at the gate as she disembarked from the plane. Instead, we were forced to wait for her at the X-ray check-in point, outside the concourse.

As we approached the entrance to the concourse, I studied the arrival monitors that listed the status of incoming flights. I was relieved to see that Carla's flight was on time. She would be exiting the concourse any minute. As I looked at the mass of humanity approaching in front of me, I realized I might not even recognize her. It had been twenty-four years since I had last seen her.

I had spoken to Carla by phone the previous day. Making that telephone call was one of the most difficult things I had ever done in my life. As expected, she did not take the news very well. When I first told her about Ricky, she didn't believe me. Even after telling her that I saw Ricky kill a man right in front of me, she was in denial. It took a good ten minutes before she finally accepted the truth. She insisted on being here for Ricky when he was arrested, so she tried to catch a flight last night. All flights from Savannah and Atlanta were booked, so she was forced to wait until this morning.

I tried to discourage Lisa from coming with me to the airport. I felt it might be difficult for her to see Carla. Lisa assured me, however, that she held no resentment towards Carla for what Ricky had done to her husband. Instead of anger, she had only empathy for her.

When Carla finally exited the concourse, I recognized her immediately. She was even more attractive as a grown woman than I could have imagined. Her features were striking. She could easily have passed for a model. Needless to say, she had aged very well.

I felt awkward and nervous as I approached her. She immediately put me at ease, though, when she embraced me. As she stepped back, I noticed the same warm smile I remembered from years ago. Her eyes were red, which indicated that she had been crying. I saw her glance around at the chaos in the airport, and I knew it had to be extremely difficult for her, knowing that her brother was responsible. I was very grateful that no one at the airport recognized her as Ricky's sister.

Chief Recker had given me strict instructions to bring Carla down to the station as soon as I picked her up. Since Carla was closer to

Ricky than anyone else, he thought she may be able to provide some clues to Ricky's whereabouts.

On our way downtown, Carla filled me in on her life. She told me her mother had died a few years ago of lung cancer. After Frank's death, her mother had managed to straighten out her life. She gave up the gin and tonics and was able to find gainful employment as a secretary. She and Carla ended up settling down in Eastern Tennessee, near her mother's sister. Carla and her mother remained close until her death.

Frank's life insurance money enabled Carla to afford to go to college. She married a successful antiques dealer after college and moved to Savannah, Georgia. My heart ached for her as she told me about her husband's untimely death. I guess some people are just meant to suffer through more tragedy in their lives than others. Carla told me she had finally gotten over his death, and she was now very content with her life.

The meeting with Chief Recker went better than I expected. Carla's attractiveness seemed to melt away his tough guy façade. He was actually cordial to her. Unfortunately, though, Carla was unable to shed light on Ricky's location.

The chief was clearly frustrated that they had been unable to locate Ricky. They had placed an APB out to every precinct within three hundred miles of St. Louis. So far, nothing.

Chief Recker thought there was a good chance Ricky may return to Regina Phillip's house in the Central West End. He stationed several undercover officers in and around her house. Regina, meanwhile, was under protective custody in a separate location; no doubt irritating the officers responsible for her safety.

Just as we were about to leave the station, a short, stocky detective burst into the chief's office.

"Doug, what are you doing? Can't you see I'm busy?" hollered the chief.

"Chief, one of our officers just spotted Ricky's vehicle. He was on North Kingshighway. It looks like he's heading toward Regina's house."

The chief's face lit up. "Okay, let's go. Dispatch all available units. Get a move on!" He was clearly excited. He could already see himself on the cover of *Time* magazine.

We hurriedly followed the chief as he stormed through the station toward the outside parking lot. It was difficult keeping up with him as he made his way through the busy, congested work area. The aisle that served as the hallway between the desks and cubicles was very narrow. There were several detectives huddled in clusters in the aisle, presumably discussing the cases assigned to them.

The chief failed to see the need to slow down, even when his fellow officers happened to be in his pathway. As he barreled down the aisle, detectives began scattering to avoid a collision. A younger looking detective, however, had his back to the chief and never saw him coming. The detective had a stack of papers in one hand and a cup of coffee in the other. Without breaking stride, the chief plowed past him, bumping his shoulder, sending the papers flying and causing the scalding coffee to splash in his face. The detective let out a piercing scream that could be heard throughout the building. The chief never turned around to inspect the damage he had inflicted. Instead, he growled and muttered a few curse words. He was on a mission and nothing was going to stop him.

He scoffed when I asked if we could ride along with him. I didn't think it was too much to ask, considering we had solved the biggest case of his life for him. Obviously, he didn't feel he owed us anything.

We weren't deterred, however. The three of us climbed in my minivan, and soon we were in hot pursuit right behind the chief's squad car.

We followed a caravan of cars, with whirling red and blue lights, through the downtown streets to the exit ramp. Once on the Interstate I stomped on the accelerator, testing the limits of my 1995, well used minivan. I glanced at the speedometer and realized it was the first time I had ever gone ninety miles an hour on Interstate 40; although I had witnessed many other drivers do so during rush hour. I was determined to stay right on the chief's bumper.

We were driving west on Interstate 40, and by now were losing ground to the faster squad cars. Just as we approached the Kingshighway exit, we saw the caravan of sirens in front of us use the median to make a u-turn. They were now suddenly heading east on the interstate. They screamed past us in the opposite lanes in hot pursuit of a black Jeep Cherokee, which I assumed was owned by Ricky.

I slammed on my brakes, turned the wheel to my left and drove through the median. We were soon right back in the hunt. The black Cherokee in the lead turned off onto the Market Street exit. Heading east on Market, it made a right turn onto Jefferson Avenue. There were now at least seven sirens following. In addition, there were now squad cars approaching from the opposite lane on Jefferson. They were closing in on Ricky.

Ricky was forced to make a sharp left turn onto Park Street. After running through several stop signs, he approached historic Lafayette Park. He must have thought he would have a better chance on foot. He slammed on his brakes and jumped from his vehicle. Before the officers could get out of their cars, he was sprinting through the park.

I parked the minivan and Lisa, Carla, and I climbed out. In front of us was quite a remarkable scene. There were now dozens of officers sprinting through the park, chasing the infamous serial killer. Running as swiftly as a deer, Ricky emerged from the opposite end of the park. He ran up the stairs to one of the houses on Lafayette Street and yanked on the front door. It opened and he was quickly inside.

The large homes in the Layfayette Square district are of Victorian architecture, built in the latter half of the nineteenth century. St. Louisans refer to them as "painted ladies". Ricky was now inside one of these "painted ladies".

We took off running after the officers. I was completely out of breath when we arrived with the other officers in front of the house. I realized just how out of shape I was when I noticed that neither Lisa nor Carla seemed affected by the run. I made a mental note to begin an exercise regimen when this nightmare was over.

I felt a little better when I looked and saw the chief pulling up the rear. He arrived a good two minutes after us. He was wheezing and coughing worse than I was, and it appeared as though he could go into cardiac arrest any second. I guess the ex football star hadn't stayed in tiptop condition.

The chief took a few seconds to replenish his body with needed oxygen. His men stood silently, awaiting their orders. As the color slowly returned to his face, he surveyed the scene and pondered his next move. Not knowing if anyone besides Ricky was in the house, he remained cautious. He did not want to risk an innocent death.

I looked around and couldn't believe what I had gotten myself into. Here I was, a person who most would describe as a stereotypical accountant and family man, huddled among at least twenty officers, attempting to capture the most infamous murderer in St. Louis' history. Never in my wildest dreams could I have imagined being part of something like this.

It was now late morning, and the early summer sun was bearing down on us. The combination of the long run, heat, and my nervousness caused sweat to pour out from my body. My shirt was soaked.

Carla approached the chief and pleaded with him to allow her the opportunity to talk to Ricky. She felt she might be able to convince Ricky to turn himself in. The chief agreed, but told her she would have to do it from the car.

One of the officers handed Carla the radio microphone. She cleared her throat and began to speak. Her voice was loud and clear, and could be heard throughout the neighborhood.

"Ricky, it's me. Don't be afraid. Please trust me. I'm here to help you, just like you used to help me. I won't let anyone hurt you. You need to come out and surrender to the police."

Carla's voice began choking, and tears welled up in her eyes as she continued. "Ricky, you have to come out now. Please do this for me. I love you, and I want to see you. I still need you."

Ricky looked out the curtain and could see the officers gather in front of the house. It was not supposed to end this way. He had made a vow to his father to punish those responsible for the injustice done to him. Now, he realized he may not be able to complete the job. His father would be disappointed.

He was angry at himself for being so careless. He had allowed his emotions to control his actions. Patience had always been one of his better qualities, but with his identity now known, he knew his window of opportunity was slipping away. As a result, the urge to kill Regina had grown stronger and stronger. This time, he had been unable to resist. As a result, he had foolishly driven to her house. He knew the police would be expecting him. He should have ditched his vehicle and approached the house on foot. He had beaten them so many times that he had become overconfident.

Quickly, he combed the first floor of the house, looking for a way out. He started to open the back door, but realized there were several officers waiting in the back yard. His only other hope was to take a hostage.

Just as he started up the stairs to the second floor, he heard a clank that sounded like two coat hangers hitting each other. He walked toward the area, where he thought he heard the noise, and saw a closet. As he approached the closet, he heard a muffled sob. He opened the closet door and saw an elderly Hispanic lady in a maid's uniform. He had no desire to harm her.

"Come on out of there, maam," Ricky commanded in a soft tone.

The housekeeper, shaking in fear, obeyed without saying a word.

"Is there anyone in the house besides you?" Ricky asked.

Still sobbing, she shook her head no.

"Don't you worry, now. I'm not going to hurt you. Go on upstairs where you'll be safe"

Relieved, the housekeeper quickly ran up the stairs. Ricky walked back over to the front window. He had two options available to him. He could die right here, right now, or he could surrender.

He looked out at the officers, with their rifles pointed toward him. A rush of anger swept over him. The police. What had the police ever done for him. Their job was supposed to be to protect innocent citizens, especially children. Where were they when he a kid? Not once did they ever try to help him. All those times when Frank beat him, they did nothing. Even when his third grade teacher filed a report with the police after he showed up at school with a broken arm and multiple bruises, the police simply accepted Frank's lies and left the house. After they left, Frank became enraged and beat him again.

No. He would not surrender. He would die here. First though, he would take out as many of them as he could. Grabbing the pistol, he set his sights on the Chief of Police. Just before he fired, he heard a voice on a loudspeaker. The voice sounded familiar.

It was Carla. His sweet, innocent sister. The only person he had in the world.. What was she doing here? He listened to her beg for him to turn himself in. She said she loved him, and she needed him. Years ago, he had made a vow to protect her. Now she needed him, and he could not let her down.

A tear slid down his cheek. For a moment, he forgot his surroundings. Everything went blank. All he could think about was Carla. He wanted to get to her; to hold her. He set the gun down and started toward the front door.

As I knelt behind one of the squad cars, I stared at the front of the house. Carla had just finished pleading with Ricky to give up and turn himself in. She now had her head on my shoulder saying a prayer for Ricky.

The curtains in the front window began to move, and we could see Ricky peering from behind them. The chief gave a signal, and the officers raised their rifles. The curtain then closed. Everyone was tense. The chief pulled out a handkerchief and wiped the sweat from his forehead. A few moments later, the front door slowly began to open. At least twenty rifles were aimed at the door. The officers waited for a signal from the chief. A sick feeling suddenly permeated throughout my body.

Ricky emerged from behind the front door and took a step. He was now in clear sight. I looked at his hands and was relieved that he wasn't holding a gun. He was turning himself in.

"He's surrendering Chief. Tell your men not to shoot! " I pleaded.

"Hold your fire!" shouted the Chief.

It was too late. A single shot rang out, and Ricky staggered. He stumbled for a few steps, and then regained his balance and slowly walked down the porch steps, through the small yard, to the edge of the street. Never taking his eyes off Carla, he made his way toward her. I could see a red stain forming around his chest. He then fell to his knees in the middle of the street.

Carla started running to Ricky. The chief grabbed her by her arm, but she broke free. She reached him, and I could see a smile on Ricky's face as she embraced him. The officers moved into the street and formed a circle around them.

Ricky kissed Carla's cheek and then fell to the ground. He whispered something to Carla that I could not understand. Then he closed his eyes. Carla began crying. One of the officers knelt beside him. "There's no pulse, Chief. He's dead."

Unlike the officers standing over him, I did not have a sense of joy. As they shook each other's hands in congratulations, I felt for Carla. I knew she did not see Ricky as a killer. She saw him as her older brother. The person, who for so many years, had protected her from her stepfather. I knew she was hurting inside.

As I looked at Ricky's body, I had mixed emotions. A part of me wanted to hate him for what he had done. Like the rest of the city, I needed to view him as a monster. He was responsible for taking more innocent lives than I could fathom.

As much as I wanted not to, however, I couldn't help but feel a little sorry for him. For a fleeting second, I did not see the face of a mass murderer. Instead, I saw the face of a scared, seven-year-old boy who had just lost his father.

Chapter 39

There were only five people in attendance at Ricky Henry's funeral: Carla, my mother, my father, the minister, and myself. I was glad Mom and Dad decided to attend. They felt it was important for Carla. The funeral home could not find anyone willing to conduct the service, so I asked the senior pastor of my church. He readily agreed.

In an attempt to prevent the media from being present, the funeral notice was not published. It was a short service. The Methodist minister read a few passages from the Bible and discussed the fact that God loves everyone; despite the magnitude of their sins. No flowers graced the casket. Other than the minister, no one spoke.

Immediately following the service, Carla and I followed my parents back to Sikeston. We had decided it would be best for Carla to fly back home out of Memphis, instead of St. Louis. She had no desire to deal with the reporters, who would undoubtedly be looking for her at the St. Louis airport. Our plans were for her to spend the night at my parent's house, and then I would drive her to the Memphis airport the next morning. If everything went as planned, she would avoid the reporters.

Since Ricky's death, the media had been relentless. They had been dogging us, demanding to interview the serial killer's closest living relative. Carla had refused all interviews.

Carla wasn't the only person the reporters were seeking. Word had leaked out that Lisa and I were responsible for providing the tip that led the police to Ricky. Like Carla, both Lisa and I had refused to talk to reporters. Regina Phillips, on the other hand, had been making herself readily available to them. This morning, she had been a guest on the *Today Show*.

Regina's recollection of events was a little different than mine. According to her version, she was an innocent victim. Just like all the other victims, she had been selected by Ricky simply because she was a successful (and attractive) professional. She never mentioned that revenge might have been a motive. She also conveniently omitted her role in the cover up of Patricia Well's blood alcohol content during the investigation into Ricky's father's death thirty-five years ago. To hear her tell it, she heroically defended Ricky's attack, and as a result, the people of St. Louis no longer had to live in fear. The reporters loved her. I had even heard a rumor that she was negotiating a movie deal with Fox for the rights to her story.

Even though Lisa and I didn't particularly care for Regina Phillips, we decided it would do no good to make public her mistake from thirty-five years ago. Covering up Patricia Well's lab results was certainly a crime. The fact that Regina was now exploiting the situation for profit was despicable. In our way of thinking, the fact that she barely escaped death at the hands of Ricky was punishment enough. Enough people had been harmed by this ordeal. We just wanted it all to end.

While Regina was turning out to be quite a media darling, Chief Recker wasn't faring as well. Once the reports surfaced that two civilians, not the St. Louis police, actually solved the case, the media turned on him. The subsequent reports in the *St. Louis Post Dispatch* were not very flattering of the manner in which the investigation was handled. The Chief was now making himself scarce.

I wasn't worried about what was reported on TV or written in the newspaper. I was tired of Regina, Chief Recker, and the whole mess. I just wanted to be left alone. I wanted my simple, plain, boring life back.

While I felt sorry for Carla, I was very happy for Lisa. She finally received the vindication for her husband that she had fought for all these years. Although the outcome couldn't bring Darrell back to life, it did set the record straight and restore his reputation. True to her character, Lisa did not seek restitution from the State of Missouri for the wrongful death of her husband.

While the St. Louis news focused on Ricky, the national news attention was on the events surrounding Senator Bryant's suicide. The FBI was beginning to piece together his involvement with Roy Weston and the murders of Eric Lowe and Melissa Grogan. When asked for a response, his office staff refused to comment.

As I pulled into my parent's driveway, I could hear my kids playing in the back yard. It was the most pleasant sound I had ever heard in my life. I immediately sprinted to the backyard, where all three ran up to me. I hugged them, vowing never again to take the blessings in my life for granted. I realized then that a person never fully appreciates what they have in life until they come close to losing it.

After visiting with my parents for a couple of hours, Carla decided she wanted to drive around Sikeston. She hadn't been back to town since she and her mother moved away back in 1979. Although the time she lived in Sikeston was full of tragedy, she claimed she did have fond memories of the people and the town. Stacy, Carla, and I took off in the minivan for the grand tour.

Much had changed since Carla left town twenty-four years ago. Sikeston, like so many small towns in America, had lost much of its unique character over the years. Gone were most of the small café's, drug stores, hardware stores, and dime stores. These were replaced by fast food franchises and big, national discount and department stores. Sikeston now had every fast food chain under the sun, along with several of the upscale chain restaurants. Many feel this is progress. Many believe the large franchises provide better selection and better service. I am not so sure.

Many of the stores that were once part of Sikeston's vibrant downtown closed many years earlier. In its place were chain stores in strip malls on the outskirts of town. The individual businesses that used to make Sikeston unique, and gave it it's own identity, are gone. The three of us talked about how unfortunate it is that small towns are all beginning to look alike.

Sikeston's wealthy neighborhoods had become even more prosperous and ostentatious; its poorer areas even more run down. Like most of America, its middle class was slowly eroding. Unlike many towns, however, Sikeston managed to retain much of its charm. It remains a very clean, safe town; with nice sports facilities, parks, and recreational areas. In many ways it has improved. There are many new neighborhoods, a new golf course, and a new performing arts center. For better or worse, I still considered it my hometown.

Carla became excited as we drove by Kirby's restaurant. She was surprised that it was still open. For old times sakes, we stopped in and ate a hamburger. Just like we had done twenty-four years ago, we ordered a hamburger topped with fried onions. It was still the best hamburger around. The only difference is that I now required two or three Rolaids to be able to handle the fried onions.

Mom had prepared a big dinner, and was a little put out with us when she learned we had eaten a hamburger. Never one to disappoint my mother, I still ate a full plateful of her delicious chicken and dumplings. I even found room to finish it off with a large piece of homemade cherry pie.

After dinner, we were all feeling miserably full, so we decided to take a walk. As we walked the old neighborhood, I noticed how little things had changed since I had been a kid. Many of the same neighbors were still there, only much older.

Mrs. Winters, my parent's former next door neighbor whose dog had been killed by Ricky, had passed away ten years ago. A middle-aged couple, Floyd and Dorene, now lived there. Stacy and I had become good friends with them, and we usually got together whenever we would visit my parents. Floyd was quite a character. He was the kind of person everyone loved to be near because he had the uncanny ability to make everyone laugh. He was an electrician by day, an Elvis impersonator by night. Twice a year he made a pilgrimage down to Memphis: each January to celebrate Elvis' birth; each August to mourn his death. Stacy and I went to Memphis last August to hear him perform on Beale Street during Elvis Presley weekend. We were surprised to find that he was quite good. It was humorous to see middle-aged women hang all over him as he shook his overweight hips in his much too tight and revealing white costume. He loved the attention. In addition to performing in Memphis, he would occasionally perform at local nightclubs on certain weekends during the year.

As we arrived back at the house, we saw Floyd walking out his back door toward his car. Judging from the outfit he was wearing, it was obvious he was performing tonight.

"What in the world is that?" asked Carla in amazement.

"Oh, that's just Elvis," Stacy laughed. "The fat, not the thin, Elvis."

" Hey, Floyd, come on over here. I want you to meet someone," I yelled.

Carla looked stunned as Floyd strutted towards her. He had on his white, rhinestone jumpsuit. He was at least forty pounds too heavy for the costume. He looked like the Pillsbury Doughboy with long hair and sideburns.

Floyd looked Carla up and down and grinned. "Hey baby. You sure look good," he said using his best Elvis impersonation. Without saying another word, he walked away singing his rendition of *Burning Love*.

Carla burst out laughing. "Welcome back to the neighborhood, Carla" I said. Stacy and I were both glad to see Carla smiling.

Around ten o'clock, Stacy and the kids turned in for the night. I still had too much on my mind to sleep, so I walked out to the back porch and sat in my favorite porch swing. A few minutes later, Carla came out and sat beside me. For a long while, we said nothing. We simply stared out at the back of the house that Carla used to call home.

Carla finally broke the silence. "You know. I still remember the real Ricky; the little boy that lived back in Kentucky with a real dad, mom, and little sister. He was sweet and loving. Dad used to call him "slugger", and Mom would call him her angel. He would spend hours playing with me and reading to me. I will never forget him."

She continued. "It's hard to believe so much could go wrong. I want an honest answer, Robbie. Whose fault do you think it is? Do you believe Ricky is solely to blame?"

"I don't know, Carla. I've been wondering that myself. I know there are a lot of kids who are abused and have a horrible childhood, but don't turn out to be killers. Who knows though; in Ricky's case maybe he had some underlying psychological quirk that manifested itself when he was abused. Anyway, I am positive Ricky would not have turned out this way if your dad hadn't been killed or if Frank hadn't abused him. I think Patricia Wells, Frank Kroetz, and the rest of society shares in the guilt. Every child deserves a chance to grow up in a safe, loving environment. Ricky never had that chance."

She looked down at her feet as the swing moved slowly back and forth. "Thanks, Robbie."

"For what?"

"For everything."

About the Author

Brad Bloemer is a certified public accountant and holds a Masters degree in healthcare administration. He has been employed as a hospital chief financial officer the past eleven years.

He lives with his wife and three children in Murray, Kentucky and Sikeston, Missouri. He is currently writing his second novel.

Printed in the United States.
35506LVS00004B/46-102